Asylum for Men and Dogs

A novel

Zdravka Evtimova

Fomite
Burlington, VT

ISBN-13: 978-1-953236-78-4
Library of Congress Control Number: 2022942778
Fomite
58 Peru Street
Burlington, VT 05401

9/30/2023

"It was pleasant to sit in the cool of the evening with their feet on the great stone and… see the herons flying upstream, their color matching the sky so closely they might have been eyes of wind."

—Annie Proulx, *Them Old Cowboy Songs*

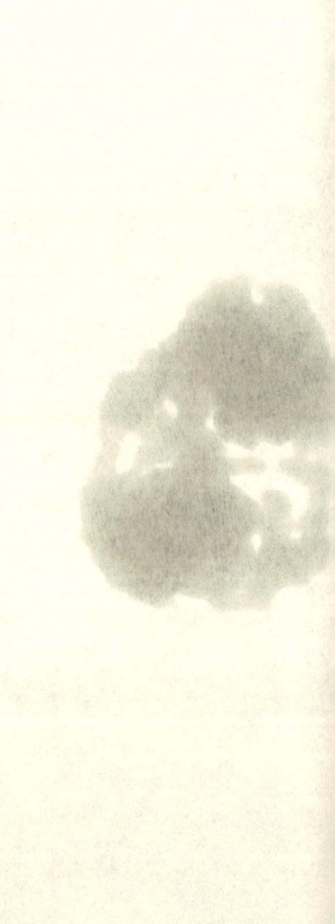

I HID IN THE PANTRY, but I still could hear them shout. My father was yelling at my mother. He used such words that if I started shooting my mouth off the way he did, dad would cut off my ears on the spot. In the convenience store, I'd heard ugly things, too, and I knew this was the way people spoke. When I asked dad what those words meant, he slapped me across the face. I got accustomed to keeping mum because I found out quickly that everything men said was filth. If you didn't want to get a smack on the bottom, you hid in the pantry. Its only window was small, but you could see the letters printed in your ABC reader.

I didn't know all letters; however, the pictures in the book left clues for me. "H", for example, jutted out next to a picture of a horse, and it meant this letter was a horse. Every time I saw an "H", I loaded heavy bags on its back. Mother sent me to shop for vegetables at Pishman market because everything was much cheaper there. She had taught me, "Sweep in front of the woman's stall," I swept in front of it and the woman gave me two tomatoes more than I had paid for.

I brought the woman water from the mineral spring, and she gave me a cucumber, then I hauled the bags, heavy as submarines, thinking about "H", the horse's letter. The horse carried the bags for me all the way home. I slowly learned the letter "G", grass. My dad ordered me, "Go dig the potatoes," I went to the field. After a while, my hands hurt like open wounds, I thought about the letter made of green grass and sat down to get some rest on it.

I taught myself to be happy when mom and dad quarreled. The secret was to hide in the pantry with my alphabet book. Many horses lived in this book, and grass grew there, too, so I was curious what exactly this fairytale was about. It was clear that the horses chomped on the grass, but I wanted more than that. It felt good when nobody paid any attention to me. Dad quickly fell asleep if there was no brandy in his bottle. One evening he was snoring, and I learned to change the TV channels. I hated to watch how men kicked a ball. I knew the ball hurt if you hit it hard because it had skin like you and me. So, I ran away from this channel and watched an old woman blabber on about happiness. She couldn't tell happiness from a haystack if you ask me.

If you wanted to pass unnoticed, you had to be plain. If you were as pretty as my mom, every guy looked at you. If you were ugly like my mom's boyfriend, everybody glowered at you; therefore, it was wisest to occupy the middle ground. You'd better be neither pretty nor plain, neither tall nor short. The best thing was to be an old woman, but I wasn't a crone, I was a child, neither tall nor short. I surely was a pretty child for people called me "Cutie!" I hated it and went to Arisana, the hairstylist. I swept the floor of her barbershop, brought her a bottle of water from the mineral spring, and asked her very politely, "Arisana, thank you, please, shave my head."

"Why should I do that?" she asked.

"It's very hot," I lied to her. "Lice eggs hatch quickly in your hair in summer, and lice bite like tigers."

Arisana shaved my hair to the bone, and I became neither short, nor tall, neither pretty nor plain. I put on my black T-shirt I'd bought for 50 cents, swept Fedo's Second Hand Shop, and brought Fedo water to drink. His wife was ill and fat, so I folded the second-hand clothes for her. They all smelled of an old drawer. Fedo's wife said Europe smelled exactly like that, so I had to regularly air the room. The old dear lump of lard! She gave me a black T-shirt and black short pants for free. The pants were too tight, and the T-shirt was wide as a desert around my ribs. Fedo's wife gave me a pair of sandals, very much worn, huge, and nearly endless. No one cared to look and check if I padded back home or shuffled my feet someplace else.

I was a free child. The street was my heaven. If I sat down to get some rest, folks tossed small change at me, the money landed by my old sandals, and I got rich quick. The minute I came back home, I immediately got dolled up. My green dress dad bought me last year looked good enough; dad was keen on making it clear his daughter wasn't a beggar.

One day, mom kissed my cheek and said, "Goodbye, Annie!"

"Why are you kissing me?" I asked, scared. "Are you going to die?"

"Yes, I'll die," she said and laughed.

"When folks die on TV, they don't laugh. They sob," I corrected her.

"I will die," was mom's final word. "Look at these…" she produced a bar of chocolate as long as the floor, a new dress, almost brand new from Fedo's store, a pair of new second-hand sandals, and a five-lev bill. "Goodbye, my girl."

The TV said dead folks went to the sky, but apart from the moon and some stars I hadn't seen any man or woman there. The sky was far from our house, and the airplane had to slog its way up to the clouds for a week before it took mom there. Even worse, if mom and Kosso, her boyfriend, had spent the money on booze, they couldn't buy any tickets and they'd have to go to heaven on foot. Mom would get tired, Kosso would get drunk or a kidney crisis would hit him, so the couple would fall behind schedule.

"How will I know you've reached heaven?" I asked her before she'd turned her back on me. She said, "Every time it starts to rain, you take a bucket and collect the rainwater. I want you to know that I send you raindrops. Wash your face with the water from the bucket, and you won't be sad anymore."

"Goodbye, mom," I said. "Don't hold Kosso in your arms when he's drunk. He's heavy. You'll have kidney problems, and I'll be sorry for you. You and your raindrops will be in pain."

Mom put her suitcase on the ground, took a step toward me, and kissed my forehead, tears big as lentils springing into her eyes.

"Don't be afraid. You won't be in pain when you die," I lied to her.

Mom wasn't a chicken-hearted woman. She took her suitcase, gave me another five-lev bill, and started for heaven. She got into Kosso's jalopy, a rusty Opel Cadet, and I've never met her since.

My father's girlfriend took mom's place in our living room. The girl-friend was a huge and very healthy woman. Her name was Darina. Neither dad nor she said anything for days. They lay down on the floor and did exactly what the TV taught them to do. Nobody bothered me, so I didn't mind love, on the contrary, I thought well of it every time I could grab my ABC book. I struggled to read. Reading was hard because I couldn't grasp it was possible to arrange pictures in place of letters to make a word. Darina kept mum, and I couldn't ask her a question. I found out a way, though. I swept the kitchen, removed love from the floor, and immediately brought Darina a bottle of mineral water. She drank from it. Our neighbor's donkey swallowed hard as her, guzzling and slurping for an hour until the beast saw the bottom of the bucket. Darina swilled mineral water, gargled with it, and didn't stop gulping until she saw the bottom of the bottle.

"Which letter is this one?" I asked as I showed her my ABC book, in which a truck was painted.

"T," she said.

I brought her more water. She drank like our neighbor's donkey, I showed her another picture, and she rumbled, "P". I remembered the letters, and ran around the backyard like a chicken with its head pecked for a long time, mumbling "T, T, T", "P, P, P." Our neighbor's boy, Shush-omir, peeked over the wall which separated our backyards, and asked, "Are you going nuts, or are you hungry?"

I was scared I might forget the letters I'd learned, so I kept on repeating them in my mind "T...T...T" and "P...P...P", looking at the truck and the pig in my book. Shushomir padded across their garden, but after a while, I saw him again. He climbed onto the wall, and the wall was as high as the top of the cherry tree.

My dad and Shushomir's dad hated each other's guts; they had fought over mom for love, over a boar in the woods, over a lamb, a haystack, or a glass of brandy. If the two men met by chance, they brawled, cursed, and punched each other in the face. My dad was huge. He was even taller than tough Darina, and Shushomir's dad was bigger than both of them. Shushomir's mom, on the other hand, was undersized, and her eyes were blue like homemade flea spray, so I wasn't afraid of her. She watched me carefully, and she had not tried to beat me up so far.

There was a way: If you didn't want to get beaten up, you either hid in the pantry or swept the path to the woman's front door and brought her a bottle of mineral water directly from the mineral spring. I swept the area in front of Shushomir's house and left a bottle of mineral water at the threshold. Once, the boy kicked it, but his mom spanked his bottom. Since that day, the woman had stopped hating me, and on Wednesday, like on a weepy TV show, she gave me a bag of food. Unfortunately, I tripped over a stone and after I fell on the ground, a dog snatched the bag under my nose.

Now Shushomir sat on the wall, which was six feet high. He could easily climb trees and walls for he was as thin as a worm, but I was thin like a thinner worm and I could climb to the top of anything more quickly than him. In addition, I could distinguish between sorrels, dock leaves, and sheep's sorrel, and I'd often noticed Shushomir's cat grazing on yellow grass when she was sick. So, when I was feeling very sad, I grazed on the same grass. On certain days, I suspected I had turned into a cat, so I rushed to tough Darina's mirror — she didn't let me finger her things, but she didn't scream at me because she couldn't speak. I was very happy she was mute; however, it turned out I had hallooed before I was out of the woods.

"Kid!" she roared. "Don't touch my mirror!"

The truth was she didn't roar. Her voice had our neighbor's braying donkey in it, so if I wanted to use something she'd bought for herself, I had to first sweep the kitchen floor and bring her a jug of water. She drank for an hour and a half and finally said, "Do as you please."

I snatched Darina's mirror and looked at myself in it. All right, I wasn't a cat, I was a girl, my head shaved to the bone, a black T-shirt, wide as a parachute, touching my ankles, and black short pants under it. It was a wonder I could squeeze into those damned pants. The mayor's wife's baby could comfortably wear them. I thought I wouldn't bring my pigs to the wrong market if I swept Fedo's second-hand store floor one more time. Fedo's fat wife was so kind you'd imagine she lived in a TV series, and I hoped she'd give me a bigger pair of pants.

"Hey! Catch!" yelled Shushomir from the top of the wall. He threw a bag to me; it smelled so good that my nose felt like tearing itself loose from my face to fly to the bag. I even thought it had, but I was wrong. Not my nose, it was my stomach that had taken to its heels. Now, I had no belly and no guts, and a hole was surely gaping in my midriff. I was scared stiff.

"Catch!" Shushomir yelled again as he threw a pair of pants at me. They were blue, with zippers, like the jeans I saw on TV yesterday. For a moment, I forgot I had no stomach and stared at the pockets as if I'd never seen a pocket in my life. I was sure our TV knew nothing about happiness. It had never said a word about how enormously de-lighted you were with a pair of new pants. You were ready to extract your heart out of your chest and put it in the smallest pants pocket, then your heart, which normally didn't trust anything, would see for itself what a gorgeous piece of clothing Shushomir had tossed to me. Even if my heart did have eyes, it was an unfortunate prisoner amidst the ribs and couldn't see a thing unless you took it out in the daylight.

Suddenly my neck caught fire and I said to myself, "It snapped in two, my scraggy neck. This is the end." My dad kicked the bag which smelled so good. I thought again my neck would fall apart, and it would've been better if it had because after the third whack I collapsed in a heap on the ground. It served me right for being so dumb. I should have dropped down onto the grass after the first blow.

"I'll kill you!" Shushomir yelled.

"No, I'll kill you," my dad yelled back.

"Big and stupid as a brush!" Shushomir had vanished from the top of the wall and was shouting from their backyard. I was on the other side of the barricade, and knew one way out: I grabbed the broom and started sweeping the ground in front of dad's feet. Then I brought him water to drink, but the bottle of water didn't do the trick.

"Give me a knife!" he roared. He was hollering, but I didn't believe he'd chop off my head. He couldn't kill a chicken, and mom called our neighbor to do it. Now, it was Darina who cut poultry necks. She was bigger than the house, and the knife looked like a needle in her hand. My father slashed the gorgeous pants with the knife. I could count only to six, but he cut them into more than six pieces. He thrust the pieces into the bag, which smelled good, shoved a stone into it, then stone, pieces of cloth, rich smell, and bag flew over the wall, landing with a huge thud in Shusomir's backyard.

"Idiot!" Shushomir's mom shouted.

My dad didn't shout back. He didn't have a soft spot for loose talk. He and Darina started their love affair on the grass, but I knew everything there was to know about love and wasn't interested. I kept on asking myself why that bag smelled so good. What was in it? I thought and thought and cried for the gorgeous pants which had shown me what happiness was. Now I had no stomach and could never find happiness; there was a hole where my belly used to be, and I was very hungry. I ran to the field and started grazing on the thick dark-green grass Shush-omir's cat gobbled when she was sick. Now, it was a sure thing I'd become a cat. I touched the back of my neck where dad had slapped me, and it seemed cat hair had already grown there.

"Hey, kid!" Darina's voice exploded so powerfully as if I had shattered to smithereens all windowpanes in the house. I dropped the only vase mom had left me before she went and died in her big suitcase. I lost my grip on the thing, it fell on the floor, jangling like two hammers hitting each other. The vase broke into four pieces. It was the only thing mom had given me, so I sat down and sobbed like a worm over the shards. At a certain point, my father's big woman panted more terrifyingly than Gasho the dog as she threw toilet paper into my lap.

"Wipe your nose!" I suspected she'd clout me around the ear, and her hands were almost as big as dad's, mind you. She didn't. "Stop whining!" the huge girl said, and instead of smacking me, she shoved a coin into my hand. "Go buy yourself a sweet cake."

I didn't buy a sweet cake. I knew only one rescue operation, I swept the floor for Darina with a tiny broom. My mother had bought the thing before she got into the decrepit Opel minivan, which took her to her death. I snatched the broom, dashed across the street, and swept the area in front of Dima's bakery shop, making the whole square sparkle, then I brought Dima three bottles of mineral water.

"Drink, aunt Dima," I said to her. "Drink as much as you please, and your kidneys will be as good as new." Then I whimpered like Gasho, our dog, when he was hungry, "Give me a dime, aunt Dima, please. I want to buy a pot of superglue to put a broken vase back together."

She gave me a dime, then gave me two more dimes, and thinking about or remembering something, gave me three pennies more.

"You are wonderful, aunt Dima," I told her honestly and stood on tiptoe to kiss her cheek. "I will sweep the area in front of your shop as long as my mom's broom is whole and strong."

I'd noticed I was in luck every time I used my mom's broom. Death surely thought it was Ok for mom to help me from her Opel minivan.

After half an hour, I swept Kinna's Beauty shop until its floor shone, and I brought the woman a bottle of mineral water. She chucked me a dime and screeched, "Damned pest!"

Then I swept the square in front of the small convenience store, the street next to the beer shop and the meatball eatery, and I scrubbed the floor of the Fruits and Veggies Store at the end of the main street. After I counted the money I'd earned, it became clear I had to sweep five hundred times the square if I wanted to buy a tube of glue that could make a shattered vase good again. On my way home, I clasped the coins in my hand, brooding. I had to sweep stores and scrub floors for two hundred years before I earned enough for the tiniest tube of glue. What the hell.

"Why are you crawling as if a horse had just kicked you in the head?" somebody asked. Shushomir! "Are you sick?"

"My dad doesn't allow me to talk to you," I told him. "I want to, but I mustn't. He'll beat me up."

"Ok. I'll do the talking, and you'll give me a sign if you don't understand me," Shushomir suggested.

I simply couldn't believe what a clever kid he was.

"You don't feel sick," Shushomir said and I nodded. "Are you hungry?"

I nodded again then I spoke despite the ban on talking to him, "I'm not that hungry."

"There's something else. It makes you wobble along the street as if a dog has bitten you, eh?"

I nodded again.

"What is it?"

I nodded my head three or four times.

"You're confusing me," he said. "Did somebody give you a thrashing? I'll clout him one."

Then, running the risk of being locked in Gasho the dog's kennel for the night, I shouted, "I broke my mom's vase and I don't have money to buy glue for it. The only thing mom left me was this vase."

"Poor kid," Shushomir sighed. At times, he was quite kindhearted. "Wait, I've got some glue that can make a shattered vase as strong as new. You won't be talking to me while we're gluing your mom's vase back together. Your dad won't throw you out to sleep in Gasho's kennel."

I was amazed by Shushomir's intelligence. I rocketed to the sky like a hawk — you could often see those filthy pests under the clouds in Radomir; if you tried to lie to your mom, the nasty bird would swoop down on you to peck at your lying brain. I collected the shards of the broken vase, and Shushomir brought the glue bottle. We were scared and went neither to his nor to our backyard. If we had, my father would have skinned me like a goat, although he was a chicken-hearted man. The sight of blood made him sick, so my mother paid our ailing neighbor to gut goats for us. Now it was the big woman, the ogress, as Shushomir had dubbed her, who chopped off the animals' heads.

We hid behind the newspaper kiosk, and I was very careful not to talk to Shushomir. If I did, dad would hang me; there would be no blood smeared down my blouse and he wouldn't take fright. We glued the shards together, the vase became more marvelous than before, and I could keep the only thing mom had given me. Then something went very wrong. Shushomir and I super-glued our fingers together.

"What will we do now?" the boy gasped. "They'll sure cut off our arms."

I was scared stiff if I'd have to live on without my right arm. How could I sweep the floor or carry bottles of mineral water? They'd better cut off my head. I started whimpering without meaning to. To be honest, I hated a whimpering kid's guts. Sniveling was proof you were stupid as a brush and couldn't think of a way out.

"They won't have to cut off our arms," Shushomir ventured, trying to get me to calm down. "They'll only cut off a couple of fingers. Let's go check what my mom thinks about it."

Although Shushomir's mother was a fat woman, she sang beautifully. Every time she saw me, broom in hand, in the street, she gave me something to eat — a pear, a sliced quince, and yesterday she put a bar of chocolate in my pocket. She didn't say a word, though, so I suspected she might have used poison to kill me, rip me open and steal my organs, planning to sell them. I didn't know what an organ was; it was surely something made of gold. Oh, come off it. I had no gold at all, but the woman didn't know it. So, I carefully rinsed everything Shushomir's mother gave me. I washed the chocolate with dish wash soap, but the thing was very lovely nonetheless.

"What have you done, silly children?" For a moment, Shushomir's mother was too stunned to add another word.

I knew a crazy guy in Radomir, Crackpot Racho by name, and I immediately suspected I'd become as loony as he was. Vera, Shushomir's mother — my dad said she was a stupid turtle — produced a bottle that stank to high heaven. I'd rather she cut off my arm, but the woman didn't cut it. She spread some smelly liquid on our skins and unstuck our fingers.

"Please, merci, thank you, Aunt Vera!" I said. I watched lots of movies on the TV and I saw that men and women said all the time "please", "merci" and "thank you". I wasted no time jabbering away about gratitude. I grabbed the broom and started sweeping the kitchen floor. Even before I offered Shushomir's mom mineral water, she said, "You don't have to clean this room, girl. Have a seat. Here," and she ladled out two huge bowls of soup, one for me and the other for Shushomir. I drank three bowls and Aunt Vera pointed out, "Oh, my! You are starving, Annie." She was wrong, of course.

"She's starving because no one can cook at her place," Shushomir explained. "Look at her. She is as thin as a safety pin."

"I can cook," I said and it was true; I baked potatoes in embers, roasted peppers, and chestnuts on an open fire. In the autumn, I picked walnuts, a big sack of them, sat near a stone and — bang-bang, crash-crash — I gorged and gorged myself on walnuts and swelled up like a balloon. Parallel to walnuts, I guzzled platefuls of sorrels, young nettles, bread, and when the sour cherries were ripe enough I didn't stop chewing for days on end.

"This is for you," Shushomir's mother said as she put a lump of cheese, a piece of ham, and a loaf of bread in a plastic bag. I jumped and started sweeping the floor again. Before my mother died in that big Opel combo van, she had explained to me, "There is no such thing as a free lunch, Anna. If you eat something without paying for it, they'll cut your throat." Well, a plastic bag of food is not a free lunch, I said happily to myself.

"Please, merci, thank you, Aunt Vera!" I cried out feeling like a million bucks. I wanted to kiss her, but perhaps I smelled of the nasty glue or my clothes stank of manure, so I only bowed down low to her the way a knight did in a movie I'd seen.

✳ ✳ ✳

So far so good. Well, not so good... My father's big new wife nabbed me, her hand heavy as a ton of bricks on my shoulder.

"Listen!" she began. Her voice was as long and fat as the distance from the kitchen stove to the hilltop. I froze in my tracks. My father's voice was big too; maybe this was the reason they didn't talk to each other and took a shortcut to love the way it happened in all movies. Their love had no end or a shore to it, so I thought love was nuts all over the place. If love didn't happen, I snatched the broom and swept hard in front of Darina, hoping cleanliness would soothe her. Oh, wasn't she dangerous! Even if I had ten feet, I could fit them all in one of her clumpy shoes, and there would be enough room left to put up a donkey for the night inside.

This day, I couldn't explain — even if my life depended on it — why I had tucked Shushomir's plastic bag under my shirt. The ogress didn't say anything. She lifted me with one arm — the mountain of a woman she was — and shook me. The plastic bag fell on the floor.

"Are you hungry?" she asked. And I suspected she'd thrash me within an inch of my life here and now.

"No," I told her the truth, praying that she wouldn't throw the plastic bag back into Shushomir's backyard. "Please don't dump the bag on the ground."

"Take a seat."

I took a seat and didn't dare to budge. She ladled out a huge dish of foul gruel — green, reddish, and brown all at once.

"Eat!"

I was scared to disobey her, so I ate and ate and ate, and tears rolled down my cheeks.

"You think it has a disgusting smell?" the mountain asked me.

"Yes," I muttered as a potato chunk stuck to my throat the way the nasty glue had dried on my fingers.

"Are you crying for your mom? Don't press this vase against your chest. You'll break your ribs."

I tried hard to swallow the potato and, making efforts to ignore how ugly it tasted, I thought of Gasho the dog. If the poor beast had been here, he'd have gobbled down this poisonous lunch.

"I don't have children," the big woman said. "I'll never have little ones. Do you want to be my child? Here, take this bar of chocolate."

She did give a bi-i-i-g bar!

"I want to be your child," I agreed on the spot.

"Ok," she gave me a dubious once-over. "If I see you begging for money, I'll break your neck!"

"Ok."

"If I see you smoking, I'll break your neck."

"Ok."

"If I catch you in a lie, I'll break your neck."

"Ok."`

"If I see your clothes are dirty, I'll break your neck."

Before I could say "Ok", she stood up and the house shook. The woman went out of the room, and I availed myself of the opportunity to bite into the chocolate bar. It was as magnificent as the universe. I knew what the universe was. I had seen it on TV. They said it had no end. The chocolate bar was the same; there was no end to its loveliness. The mountain brought me a floral dress, and the second I caught a glimpse of it, my blood ran cold. I'd feel conspicuous in it, like a freak left in the middle of the town square. Dogs, snakes, and men would stare at me.

"It is very gorgeous," I said and it was God's truth. "This gown is not for me. I'll get soup and dirt on it, and you'll immediately break my neck."

She didn't say anything as she shook me in the air, taking off my black T-shirt and my black pants. Then she made me put on the new gown.

"My God!" On the TV, they spoke like that to a guy nailed to two crossed boards, a stressed and overworked man I liked and pitied so much. When I was feeling jaded, I told him, "I am stressed and over-worked just like you, God. Please look at my gorgeous dress!"

"Look at you, Anna! You're beautiful!" the mountain said. "You shaved your head, but it's Ok. Go for a walk in this dress. Tomorrow I'll buy you two more expensive ones. I've already ordered them. Now, you are my daughter. If somebody beats you, tell me. I'll break his neck," she looked at me her dangerous green eyes blazing. I was scared stiff of guys with green eyes. The car my mother chose to die in was green as well. Darina's voice, endless as a highway, thundered, "If you smoke pot, I'll break your neck." She bent, kissed my shaved skull, and said, "How are you doing, my little girl?"

* * *

You wouldn't understand what it meant to me.

He drove on, maybe a mile or even two until the child was out of sight then he stopped the car. Looking at him, you thought of an old grave… He had thick hairs on his arms and legs. Why hadn't I noticed this before? A day ago, I told my daughter I would die, and the child whispered, "Mom, did you pack death in your carry-on bag?"

"Yes, I did," I said. "Death sleeps in every carry-on bag a woman has."

Kosso had agreed with me we should go to London. I spoke English fluently, the words seemed to fly in the air and every one of them was a path to a clean place. I'd work as a washerwoman for several households, a caregiver of an elderly woman, I'd been a nanny and a shop-girl.

I had to run away from the pit my daughter's father had chucked me. I abandoned my child, a small, skinny tyke, a black T-shirt, and black pants. My heart, my liver, and my lungs exploded inside me. I thought it was impossible to take my leave of her. She asked, "Mom, can death take me too in your bag? I'd better die. I don't know the Bulgarian alphabet, so no one will miss me. You'll find a new place to live. I'll ask death to let me visit you from time to time. I'll put on a clean T-shirt. I'll clean Fedo's second-hand store, and he'll give me a new pair of pants, I'm sure."

I'd rather the child didn't learn the alphabet. The books would fling her into the mud that was choking me. My blood was in her veins.

…The man with the thick hair stopped his car again and again. We made love. In the beginning, it was fun, but after he turned off the engine again, I wished I was dead. It was a silly thing to chase after freedom if your mind was a prisoner of lies.

He stopped the car, stuffed chocolate chip cookies in his mouth, bit into a chunk of bacon, chewed on a beefsteak, then love happened quickly. The back seat of the car was sticky.

"Stop it," I said.

"Fifty miles from here we'll be at it again."

"No," I said.

"Yes!"

He snatched my carry-on bag and hurled it across the road, a narrow mountain lane with potholes that resembled bad teeth. The bottomless sky stared at me, the forest dangerously silent.

"Eh?" he snarled.

"No," I said.

He pulled me by the hair as he rummaged in my bag for money. If you were a woman who had lived in Radomir for years, you learned your lesson. You didn't put your money in your bag, you shoved it under your dirty linen. The man kicked me out of his car, started the engine, and drove off. I remained alone on top of Balkan Mountain or was it Sredna Gora Mountain? Within a minute, the rumbling engine gave me the creeps.

He was coming back. Had he made up his mind to run over me? I grabbed my bag and threw it, saw it slip down the sheer slope, and jumped to catch it.

The hill was sand and pebbles as I rolled like a tattered mattress, the man flinging stones at me. I was in luck he found no discarded garbage to dump on me.

I had 100 levs, a carry-on bag, and the month of June endless in front of me.

"I'll find you. I'll chop your head off and I'll shove it into…"

If I explained what he'd said, no one would read this story to the end.

Quietly as a snake — my Chinese zodiac sign was Snake — I sneaked through thorns, thicket, rocks, and when it became impossible to breathe, I lay down on the ground. A tangle of briers clawed at my face as the man screamed in the distance. A Snake remembered all her wounds and would have her revenge. I would not forget what you did to me. I'd remember your name. I'd pay you back, Kosso, you can take my word for it!

* * *

The masseuse was an old, quiet woman, her light, luminous skin as discrete as an old song, "Just a minute more. Please be patient, Madam."

"Concentrate on my legs," the client said, her voice a blade able to cut everything it pleased; however, the massage therapist was accustomed to taking care of wounds inflicted by sharp instruments. She added, "Your skin glows, Madam."

"Don't give me that. I pay you and I don't care what you think."

"Yes, Madam. I wanted to say you looked great."

"I know. What do I pay you for? To look like shit? Now tell me. What do you think of Mr. Percha? Don't beat about the bush."

"Your husband looks sick to me, Madam."

"Cut the crap. Has he asked you out 'for a walk'?" The client did not grumble when the masseuse patted her sparklingly white skin. "Did he pay you for his massage?"

"He did, Madam."

"How much?"

Wasting no time, the therapist answered, her delicate hands generating waves of peace through her client's legs that looked powerful as columns of a Roman temple, their ankles and calves thick and strong.

"Five hundred."

"Give me back four hundred," the lady ordered. "My husband is not all there. He doesn't know what he's doing."

The masseuse had left in advance eight fifty-lev bills on the chest of drawers near the massage table.

"I see you've calculated correctly the cost of your services," the powerful ankles said. The lady's cell phone rang. "Fresh orange ginger juice," she ordered as she listened to what the phone reported to her. "Beat him up," the woman issued another order to her telephone. The masseuse concentrated on her client's heels first. "Did you think about Elizabeth?" asked the lady with the sturdy feet, her question a trigger of a gun.

"I did, Madam," the masseuse answered.

The trigger said, "Look me in the eyes." The massage expert obeyed. "Bring me the ax!"

The masseuse did not seem taken aback. She scurried to the wall, opened the redwood chest of drawers, a masterpiece her client had purchased from Brazil, then produced a most ordinary ax; the truth was the thing was not at all ordinary. It glittered dangerously and was big.

"Pick it up!" the ankles instructed. "Now the ax is your mirror. If the word gets out…"

"It will serve its purpose," the masseuse finished the sentence.

"I'd hate to see you getting beaten to a pulp, though. Nobody else can cut my hair the way you do. You won't be able to do it if they break your thumbs. What would you say about my daughter Elizabeth, eh? Can you recommend a good nanny for her?"

The masseuse stared at the shining axe. On it, the reflection of her face was a yellowish blotch, a wound, its indistinct outlines a hint at stabs or knives.

"I'd recommend my daughter, Madam."

"You've never told me you have one."

In the street, the month of July experimented with its scorching heat, alternating it with a stiff wind, a spatter of rain, after which the sun came back again unstable as Aquarius, Mrs. Percha's Zodiac sign.

"Tell me about your daughter."

"She was four years old, or perhaps five," the masseuse spoke slowly, in a meticulously correct Bulgarian, her dainty fingers slaloming down Madam's cheekbones. Madam's cheeks were big and wide; Madam's face looked heavier than her two ankles put together.

"Don't waste my time," Madam said.

"She was five years old. Her father, an accountant, made good money but was a fool. I was a fool too. I believed I was born to make the world an honest place, a noble one, etc. I am Lena, my daughter's name is Anna. I told her 'I will die tomorrow, child.' I packed my luggage, sold the TV set, the fridge, the table, the beds. My husband, the accountant, was on a business trip to Greece, and I took the kid to my mother-in-law. My mother-in-law hated my guts, and I, on my part, was not in love with her. She was surprised when she saw me with the girl. The old saucepan was shrewd enough to guess what was happening.

"You're dumping the kid off. Are you trying to run away from the town?"

"I have to see a doctor," I lied to her. "It might be the worst."

"Second-rate women don't die of cancer," she said; however, she accepted the child. Before I closed the door, she added, "Chemotherapy is an expensive pleasure. I won't give you a cent."

Years passed, I graduated in Bulgarian literature from the University of Sofia. You know that, Madam, and…"

"With your Bulgarian literature, you'd have bitten the dust!" Madam commented.

"Yes, you are right," the masseuse said, her head bowed. "I was good at painting from an early age. At six, I cut little girls' hair for thirty cents. At nine, I invented short perm hairstyles for a buck or cut boys' hair with scissors for 85 cents. I came to believe the art of makeup had turned into a calling for me and paid loads of money to attend cosmetic courses. The presence that some intellectuals describe as God — or shall I call it solitude — had thrown a gift my way. A man's skin tells me what hurts him. It's the smell that speaks to me. At times I suspected a dog lived in my nose."

"What does my body odor tell you?"

"You are nervous, Madam. Last week you were on edge."

"What about my husband? Can you smell death in his skin?"

"Yes, I can. His death is soft and friendly. Death will stay with him, and for a long time he will smolder like the eyes of that fish," the masseuse pointed at the eel swimming in the aquarium.

"I'll have none of this. When did the idea of death pop into your muddled head?"

"I am afraid my head is not muddled, Madam. My mother could catch the smell of death. I can catch it, too."

"Tell me more!" the woman with the thick ankles said. She rose from her chair and jabbed a finger at the masseuse, which was a sign that the massaging efforts had to be abandoned on the spot. If Madam stuck out a thumb, the massage expert's fee would plunge sharply. "Come on. Talk to me about death."

"My mother believed that every man carried death in his hand as if it was his car key or his toothbrush. If you eat fat or guzzle vodka etc., you…"

"If you use 'etc.' one more time, I'll kick you out of my house," the ankles grumbled.

"Yes, Madam. I understand. Death gets sick and tired of staying with the same man and leaves. At this point, the man breathes his last. This was what my mother thought."

"Your mother was an oddball," the woman said as she raised her index finger. The older woman went on giving Madam her back massage adding gentle touches as if she was caressing a newborn baby. "I want to know more about your daughter. You told her you were dying, snatched your suitcase, and arrived in the capital."

22

"Yes, Madam. I was in love with a bigwig in the art world, the idiot I was. Bigwigs marry influential women, not down-and-out ragdolls like me. I lived in his villa for a couple of months, pretending I was rich until a lady arrived. She looked years older than I was, and had a refined way of sniffing. A man with big muscles accompanied her. He beat me black and blue. It was only natural he desecrated my honor and my spirit."

"What! Your honor? Don't make me laugh. He raped you, eh?"

"That's putting it mildly, Madam," the masseuse said. "I hate to remember this summer. Let me add that he is the man I live with now. Today, he's quietly and slowly paying off his debts."

"Paying off his debts. How?"

"At that time, his skin had a distinct scent that made me think he would soon come back to me. I sensed I was in his thoughts and his blood. Death waited for him in the scars and bruises his fists had left in my chest. It turned out that I was right all along, Madam. The following evening, he crept into the shovel shed where he'd dumped me. He took me to his house. His mother was old. The minute she clapped eyes on my face, she called down a curse on me. Well, God must have misunderstood her. After a week, she was run over by a truck. Madam, it is hard for me to describe how perfectly her son took care of me. I believe he stole an old car to take me to a doctor. He stole other things as well; I'm not sure if it was a motorcycle or gold neck chains."

"Do you think an idiot can rob me blind at knifepoint? Let him try. I'll gouge out his kidney then I'll roast it. The wretch will eat it in front of me. You can take my word for it."

"I believe you," said the masseuse and started to carefully wash off Madam's make up.

"Go on," the strong woman ordered as she produced a two-hundred lev bill, then folded it up and thrust it into the masseuse's trouser pocket.

"Okay. Stop whatever you're doing. I want chocolate milk! Wait. Tell me the story to the end."

"Yes, Madam. The doctor who examined me said I'd have no children. 'Will she survive?' asked the man that had beaten me to a pulp. 'Probably not,' the doctor answered, and the man started to cry. Perhaps he whimpered about his deceased mother, hiccupping and blubbering all over the place. It hurt so much. I asked Death, "Let my bones be. Let me meet my Maker like everybody else.'

I couldn't stand it anymore. Every day, the man gave me lemon juice with honey, rubbed my arms to ease the pain, and kneaded my sore muscles. After five months, I learned to walk again although the doctor thought this was impossible. The bully taught me to perform deep tissue massage, to fix a splint on a broken leg, and to prepare herbal extract powder. He didn't know I could distinguish between the smell of fear and the odor of death. His smell was of a man who wanted me. I held him chained to my skin he had ruined, and I rendered him as useless as a piece of driftwood.

"Does my husband smell of desire? Can I chain him to my…let me use the appropriate term… to my genitals?" Madam asked, a wry smile slaloming down her face.

"Madam, would you like me to speak to you gently, or you'd prefer to know the truth?"

"Don't mince words. I can handle anything," the big face hesitated. A worried look flitted across the woman's face, her blue eyes aglow with determination.

"His skin is scared, Madam."

"Tell me something I don't know."

"It is still early to think about it, Madam."

"Stop muttering. Speak up or, to put it plainly, you'll have to talk to Ivan."

"If Ivan smashes my fingers, how will I give you a massage tomorrow?"

"Around here, masseuses are a dime a dozen," the powerful woman pointed out, her voice a frozen puddle.

"His skin smells of loneliness, Madam," the massage therapist said. "I am not sure I can recommend a way to overcome this. Maybe you could help him calm down and take the place of loneliness in his heart. I know loneliness lasts long. On the other hand, nature abhors a vacuum."

"He is a worm. I don't care if he finds another woman. I want to know if the thug who left you incapacitated is still alive."

"Death has different ways of talking to one. The sublime entity some people call God, and I call chance, sent this man searing pain. He loves me. I call 'drudgery' what other women perceive to be 'love', and I won't be anybody's slave, Madam."

"You're wrong," the woman's wide ambitious face lit up. "If wishes were horses, beggars would ride."

"Yes, Madam," agreed the massage therapist, her eyes focusing on her employer's toes. Madam immediately beckoned to her to come on and apply the fond de teint where it belonged.

"So, you recommend that your daughter should take care of my daughter?" the strong voice said. "How come this daughter of yours found you? You told her you were dying."

"I was foolish enough to send her money when my granddaughter was born. At that time, my partner didn't feel very well, but he was not ill. I can speak about several types of massage which can help you get back on your feet if your massage therapist wants to do them. The man stole a ring or a necklace, I cannot remember exactly what, Madam. He gave me one thousand levs and I made my granddaughter a gift of it. This was a step in the wrong direction. My informer, an old woman I'd hired, told me my son-in-law spent the money on booze.

My daughter — I thought she was a housewife of limited intelligence not to say downright stupid — turned out to be a woman having an acute sense of smell. She caught my mole spying on her."

"That's a load of hogwash!" Madam said. "Are you pulling my leg?"

"No, Madam," said the masseuse. "After a couple of days, my daughter showed up in the room where I lived with the man who had ruined my life. 'You are my mother,' she said. 'I'm glad you hadn't passed away the way you said you would. Perhaps you survived because I'd hoped against hope you'd live. I was curious how you looked. You look good.' I half expected she'd beg for money. She didn't. I gave her a fiver, though. Madam, I believe you must earn your bread through the sweat of your brow. The bucks you give a girl are a knife that will cut her throat. A woman who grabs at the money she hasn't worked hard for is not my daughter. She stayed four minutes in my room, didn't say 'good-bye', and didn't give me her phone number. She vanished, and that was all. Maybe you know what snakes do. In the spring, they hide under a stone, in the summer you find the stone and no snake under it."

"I don't care about reptiles. Did your daughter try to get in touch with you again?"

"Yes. She dropped in on me when I wasn't expecting her. 'I don't have a place to stay for the night, mother. I can't go back to my husband. He lives with another woman. She will kill me.' 'Will she?' I asked her. I despise cowards, Madam. If my daughter, pretty though she is, has turned into a pot of jelly given to fits of hysteria, I'll forget I gave birth to her. I've been living alone for years, so daughter or no daughter makes no difference. Heat or frost are all the same to me. I have a roof over my head and Euros in my bank account. I appreciate your advice, Madam. I only invest in financial institutions in Germany. If I don't understand the business, I don't touch it."

"Stop blabbering!" Madam ordered as she slurped her chocolate. Firm and abundant flesh coated her massive bones; her drink was loaded with calories, so Madam and her masseuse had to dance the Argentinian tango. Madam was convinced that traditional Argentinian dances reduced cellulite on the buttocks and thighs. The masseuse, almost sixty, didn't have a trace of cellulite, the old bag she was. "Tell me more about your daughter. Is she good enough for my little girl?"

"I asked what had happened, and my daughter gave me a straight answer, 'I was with a man who had lots of money and a position of influence. Every twenty miles, he stopped the car and insisted on intimacy with me.'"

"Why don't you speak like a normal woman? I am fed up with your prissiness. He screwed her every ten miles. This sounds both interesting and inspiring."

"My daughter said 'No'. He threw her out of his car, dumped her bag on her, and drove off. She was rolling downhill towards the thicket when the monsieur came back and started hurling stones at her."

"I find it amusing," Madam whispered, a smile flickering across her face. A second later, Madam declared, "Listen to me! I'll hire your daughter to take care of my child on one condition: I insist that she puts me in touch with the twenty-mile guy. I want to buy him a cup of coffee," Madam chuckled. "He hurled stones at her head, didn't he? I wish a stone had split her skull. She doesn't deserve any better."

✳ ✳ ✳

I grabbed the broom Darina had bought. It was a brand new thing, and it was easy to sweep the floor around her big feet. She hit the ceiling for no reason at all. I could tell she got angry: two red notches like heating wire lit up on her forehead. She'll clout me one, I thought to myself.

"I told you to quit it!" Darina snapped. It felt as if the Mayor's donkey and Misho the beggar's jenny-ass brayed together in unison. I wished Darina had clouted me one.

"Mom made me sweep the floor if I wanted something. There's no such thing as a free baked potato,' she told me, but I don't know what a free potato is. If I don't use the broom or forget to bring you mineral water, you'll hit me over the head, Darina."

"You're my daughter now, aren't you?" the huge one asked quietly, and this time it was only Misho, the beggar's jenny-ass that brayed. "What do you want?"

"Teach me one letter of the Bulgarian alphabet," I said. "There's no such thing as a free baked potato," I repeated. "What must I do for you so that you teach me?"

"Call me 'mom'!" the big woman thundered.

"Mom," I told her and I couldn't believe my eyes: the heating wire died and stopped heating her forehead. Her mouth dropped open as if it was a catfish biting a hook, her lips quivering or pouting — I couldn't say what. Was she going to beat me black and blue or only kick me? The woman raised her hand. Something must have gone wrong: her fingers sank into my hair and tried to comb it.

"You are a beautiful child," she said. "If somebody beats you, I'll bust his head open."

She had no time to teach me any letter of the Bulgarian alphabet.

Two burglars entered our backyard "without prior notice" as a lawyer said on the TV the other day. I knew one of the thieves very well, Racho the shepherd. Many times had I swept the floor in front of him in the pub, and more often than not he gave a dime. I didn't care about the second bandit. I swept the floor in front of him, too, and I brought him mineral water, but he kicked my ankles, so I learned to avoid him. Grab the broom quick, I said to myself. The big woman, like the ogress in the fairytale about the cannibal and his wife, rapped me on the knuckles. I bit my tongue and dropped the broom on the ground.

There was a huge heap of roof tiles in our backyard, and the two thieves started hauling them one by one out to the street. I remembered the day my mother bought these roof tiles. Every evening, when the earth turned into a child-eating monster, she took a walk and I stayed at home. Mom wanted to build a magic parlor for herself. I didn't know what a parlor meant, maybe it was a bigger heap of roof tiles. Mom said she could smell death and I believed her; she had packed her death in a suitcase. If they stuffed you in a locked box, you'd stink to high heaven, I was sure of that. Death had nobody to play with, it was all alone, and I could feel it get up on tiptoes to look for a guy. At first, I didn't know what it meant. On the following day, people said this guy died near the place where I had caught the smell of death.

Mom wanted a magic parlor, and it was a fact. I knew what "magic" meant, I'd seen it on TV many times. They turned the princess into a frog and a frog into a princess. Mom would positively turn a couple of frogs into ladies, so I could sweep the floor for them and make extra money. I could even bring some bottles of mineral water just in case. I loved frogs. This was the reason I collected them and made efforts to convert them into princesses.

"Darina," I said. "Two men are stealing roof tiles from my mom's magic parlor."

"Don't tell me your mom did magic," Darina rumbled as she tapped me on the back of the head, very lightly this time. "Look at the idiots. They are stealing the roof tiles. They are!"

She rushed forward, and her brown dress, long and wide like a blanket, flapped in the wind.

"Leave these roof tiles!" she shouted, the two donkeys, the jack and the jenny, kicking in her huge voice.

The two crooks flinched away from her.

"Oh, buffalo Darina, how are you doing?" asked Racho the shepherd, the first thief I liked better than the other.

My giant mom said nothing as she stepped towards the burglars. She was taller than them both. The worse one winked an eye at Racho the shepherd, then within a second, the two thugs charged into Darina at full speed. I could hear something snapping and splitting — crack, crack! Crack! Was it her head or her bones? I couldn't say. I rarely swept the floor in the pub, and every time the drunks started breaking bones or splitting heads open, I made myself scarce. That was why I had trouble orienting myself to skirmishes or tussles.

"Arrh! Rrr!" the big woman roared. A peal of thunder crashed overhead, and two clouds dropped dead from the sky. A swallow nest collapsed on the ground and dry mud fell from the eaves. The two guys exchanged glances and the air was filled with the smell of death. Roasted almonds — that was what death smelled of. Darina grabbed two roof tiles. I couldn't believe how quickly she did it. Racho, the guy I knew well, relaxed into a supine position. I didn't know what "supine" meant, I'd heard this word spoken on TV, but it surely meant that his mouth was full of blood. The other guy relaxed into a supine position, too.

"Bring me a strong rope," my new mom shouted to me.

* * *

The first thing Darina taught me was to find out where she kept her coils of rope. They were at the bottom of the closet where she stored her dresses, two of them altogether, absolutely the same, big and brown, next to three knives that lay between an ax and a saw. This was all you could find in Darina's closet. The first time she tied my dad to a chair with a piece of rope, she kicked me out of the room.

"Get out, Annie," she said and I obeyed her, but I left the door open a crack because I wanted to see what she'd do. She took off his belt and started hitting him with it.

"I haven't come to your house to wash a drunkard's socks! I want to love you. I'll give you a glass of brandy later. Or I'll beat you until you sober up."

"Darina, darling, I'm sober now!" he said trying hard to lie to her. Dad was older, taller, and much leaner than the woman, and he couldn't put her off the scent.

"Let me see!" she said. I couldn't say what she was looking at. The ogress hit him with the belt and marched out of the room. He sat tied to the chair, his head drooping. After an hour, the woman would check up on him, and if she thundered, "Give me some rope!" my dad started to cry. I couldn't explain why he didn't dare to knock at the front door of his own house for a week, even a fortnight. Finally, he learned his lesson. Dad came back home sober as a fish, with no bottle of brandy, vodka, or cognac in his hip pocket. The meaning sank in: the dumb movie about their love would start again. I sat down on the gnarled bench in the garden hoping against hope I could turn a frog into a princess or perhaps put on a black T-shirt, so no one would notice me when I loitered in front of the news stand.

It turned out it was stupid of me to get a haircut. I failed to become invisible. Everybody stared at my skull because it shone like a bottle of brandy. As a result, I made myself a paper hat and crammed it down my head, trying to hide both my eyes and my ears.

* * *

"Rope!" Darina roared and I shook in my pants. The wheels of two very heavy trucks hissed in her voice. I ran to the closet and dragged two more coils of rope to her. Meanwhile, the thug I didn't like — he'd kicked me twice — stirred and groaned. Darina pushed him hard the way he'd pushed me, or even harder, for the guy rolled onto his stomach and prepared to die. Darina wasn't scared at all; me neither because I couldn't smell burnt almonds, which meant that death was heading someplace else. On the other hand, I wasn't afraid of death. It was lonely like me. Every time death escaped from my mother's suitcase, it visited the pub and swept the floor in front of the drinking men.

Darina tied the nasty guy and he began screaming to high heaven. Racho stirred too.

"Don't beat uncle Racho!" I pleaded. "He is a good man!"

However, Darina kicked him, too. He didn't even roll onto his stomach because his head banged against the roof-tile he had planned to steal. I ran to the spigot, filled up a bucket of water, and poured it on his neck.

"Don't you be afraid, Uncle Racho," I told him. "You don't smell like death. Here, drink this!" I said as I poured some water from the bucket into his mouth. Darina gave me a gentle push; the water, the bucket and I went tumbling down the cement landing as she began tying the good thief up. Desperately, Racho held the tie-string of his pants. After my big mom was done, she snatched the nasty guy's belt and gave the two burglars a thrashing.

"If I catch you trying to steal something from my backyard," she began, two heavy trucks and two butcher knives clanking in her voice, "I'll cut off your balls. You!" she rumbled as she turned to me. "If you give these idiots anything, I'll lock you in the cellar. You'll stay there three days and three nights, and you won't have anything to eat for a week."

She hit good Racho's back twice and kicked the thug's ass seven times. The woman carefully aimed, her knuckles crashed against the mean thief's forehead and her fingers got the rope knot loose. Then she grabbed the thief's shirt collar and dragged the man away from our backyard. I saw her chuck him out in the street. After a while, she took a step to Racho.

"Don't beat him. You'll crack your knuckles!" I screamed. I was sure Racho was a drunk who had a heart of gold. The other day, he bought me ice cream, 'Come here, child, eat this before brandy fuddles my head.' This was the reason why I repeated, "Don't break his bones, Darina, please."

The second she raised a hand to hit me, a thought crossed my mind and I whispered, "Please, mom, don't beat him up."

She dropped her arm back to her side, then suddenly grabbed Racho by the throat and thundered, "You'd have puked blood for a week if this girl hadn't stopped me." Then she untied the rope, clutched at his neck, and lifted him into the air. "Beat it. Now!"

It was the first time that I had seen a grown man bow down to a woman, his buttocks bending and twisting like a thorn in a storm.

"Thank you and merci, please, Madam, thank you, please, and merci very much!" Racho lisped through spittle and blood as he wiped his mouth with his sleeve. Within a second, the poor soul bolted like a rabbit to his hole, unfortunately, tripped over the vicious guy who'd kicked me in the pub. By mere chance, Racho didn't go sprawling on the pavement by his friend's side. "Merci, thank you, Madam! Thank you, merci very much!"

"Come here," Darina ordered me. "Now, I'll teach you a very important letter of the Bulgarian alphabet."

She took my hand. Her fingers were stained with dry blood, but the blood didn't faze me. An open wound wasn't my mom's cup of tea. My mother wouldn't smash a cockroach, she couldn't kill chickens, so she asked a neighbor to help her. This man was old and smelled of roasted almonds. He said he was waiting for death to toss him into a black suitcase. The man killed chickens for mom, and mom gave him her herbal remedy for hay fever.

"Bring me a bottle of brandy. One of the idiots bit by hand," Darina said. "I want to clean the bite mark." I brought her a bottle and she held up her left hand. "Pour brandy into the gash."

After a minute, Darina, in blood and brandy, wrote a letter of the Bulgarian alphabet on the sidewalk, B.

"This is B, the brandy's letter," she said.

"It's my dad's letter, too," I said. "He drinks brandy all the time."

✳ ✳ ✳

Gritting her teeth, Darina shouldered my father and carried him to the table. In front of him, she put a big chicken dish, a bag of tomatoes, five slices of brown bread, and didn't let him drink a drop of brandy before he gobbled all the food.

"I can't eat anymore," my father complained, but the big woman shook a bottle of brandy in front of him, and he sniffed at it like a puppy.

I hate guys who kicked or beat dogs. After a puppy died, the air smelled of roasted almonds the way it did if a child breathed his last. My dad chewed and chewed, hating every crumb, tears in his eyes. I didn't know why Darina thought he had to stop drinking. Maybe because they said on the TV that brandy killed you. It was evident she didn't want him to meet his maker just yet. The woman snatched the bottle away from his mouth.

"Just one more sip, Dari! Please!"

Then these two started the love nonsense again. I read and read and read my ABC book until Darina left my father meek and weak as a lamb. One day, I drank a sip of brandy to see how it felt. I choked and kicked and I found out the TV wasn't lying. The bottle did kill you. However, my dad didn't scare easily; Darina did the same kissing affair to him the movie stars did to their guys in the movies, and dad pulled himself together. Now I knew: brandy killed you and love brought you back to life.

"Do you want some more?" Darina asked him, but dad didn't dare to say a word and fell asleep as peacefully as our grownup chickens.

I could easily lull to sleep those sweet beaks. I thrust the chicken's head under its wing as I sang, "Sleep, rooster, sleep!" My father slept as if Darina had thrust his head under a pullet's wing. At times, dad snored so thunderously that I woke up and thought, "I'm dead. The mommy bear has eaten me and now I am in her stomach." However, I always found out I was in my bed, the carpet nailed to the wall tickling my nose. A girl in funny shoes and a dress as wide as our City Hall looked at me from the faded carpet. "You won't be lonely," my mother explained to me. "I'll die soon, and you'll talk to this girl who lives on the carpet." So far so good, but this kid had not learned to speak, and I talked to Gasho the dog, to the nettles and the grass, on which our cat was grazing when she was sick.

* * *

Sometimes I crept to the clump of elderberry bushes where the fence between Shushomir's backyard and ours had fallen apart. I put on my oldest clothes, i.e. my father's coat as blue as bacon gone bad, and I slunk past the stones into Shushomir's empty dog kennel. I didn't dare to call out the boy's name because a week ago my dad gave me a thrashing with a bunch of nettles.

"If I catch you again jumping over the fence...." Bang! The nasty bunch seared my arms and legs, and blisters as big as molehills appeared right away. "If I catch you talking to Shushomir again!" Bang! The nettles gnawed at my arms.

That evening I threw up my dinner and puked all over the floor. My face turned red like a bucket of red paint. Mom still hadn't met her maker in her suitcase, so she poured water on my head, then put me in a washtub full of hot water and herbs. It seemed both herbs and water were red as if someone had butchered a cow in the washtub. My father kept mum, his tail between his legs. I loved mutts; Gasho the dog was my bosom buddy and Shushomir was my best friend. Mom said to my father, "I'm leaving you."

At that time, I didn't know what "I'm leaving you" meant. When I saw mom packing clothes in her suitcase, I was quick to grasp that she wanted to get to the bus stop. I was wrong again. She was preparing to die. Mom had stuffed her pants and skirts and blouses into her suitcase, so how could she accommodate death in it, too? Or perhaps mom's clothes were death's? That was hardly possible for they didn't smell like burnt almonds.

"Don't go," my father pleaded. "The child can't live without you."

Mom didn't say anything. She wasn't given to jabbering away about her problems, on the contrary, I often saw her reading books, all of them on magic. Her tomes remained in our house, and I was burning to learn the Bulgarian alphabet as quickly as possible. I constantly dreamed of being able to do magic at children's parties. One way or another, nobody had stolen the roof tiles, so I made up my mind to build a magic parlor where I'd be able to turn pebbles into chocolates. I so much wanted to be a box full of candy bars! All kids would run to me, and I'd always have someone to play with. Now, I was as lonely as an empty kennel.

My mom's old blouse was itchy on my shoulders as I sneaked into Shushomir's backyard through briars and elderberry bushes. At a certain point, I sniffed at the wind, guessing what his mother had cooked for dinner. The woman was short and plump, had much grease in her, and I was sure that was the reason she cooked so well. I stood on tiptoe, breathing in the magnificent aroma and thinking of the meal she had fixed. Mom didn't cook at all. She read her magic books and gave me sausages to eat to keep mum.

Dad shouldn't notice I'd planned to go over to Shushomir's place; he'd grab a bunch of nettles if he did, so I croaked like a lonely frog. On TV, all lonely frogs turned into princesses.

Shushomir's mom came out of their house with a bowl in hand. My nose was as good as a cook; it immediately recognized the wonderful soup that still simmered in the bowl.

"This is for the little frog," Shushomir's mom said after she brought the meal to the elderberry bushes. I could see a spoon and a chunk of bread in her hands, and I croaked loudly and happily until I believed I'd become a village pond full of frogs. "Dearest frog, have some cake" the woman added as she left the bowl and the spoon on the ground. I found a big paper-wrapped sponge cake. I ate, and ate, and ate. In the end, I couldn't even croak anymore to thank her. Old habits did die hard. Every time dad started a fire in the old stove, I collected charcoals and put them in my pocket. Now, I took out a piece of charcoal and I drew a heart on the wrapping paper of the sponge cake. A heart meant that you wanted to say, "Thank you, Aunt Vera. I feel like kissing you on the cheek. The soup was so delicious!" On the days when I had lost the piece of charcoal, I crept deeper into Aunt Vera's backyard and waved at her. She pretended she hadn't noticed me, but waved back at me, and it felt like I'd kissed her on the cheek.

Shushomir would show up a minute later. He'd also pretend he hadn't noticed me, but he'd wave his hand slowly and beautifully in my direction. I'd hope he'd slip behind the church; I wouldn't talk to him because I knew for a fact my dad hated his dad's guts. I'd just walk past Shushomior and I'd wave at him. He'd wave at me too.

On Mondays, I didn't sneak through the elderberry bushes because mom read a fairytale to me, and this was the best thing in the world. Her voice was more delicious than Aunt Vera's soup, tastier than a piece of fruitcake.

* * *

"Mom, can I come with you?" I asked her back then, and she said, "No, you can't. I am going to die."

"Can I die with you?" I asked.

"Don't go," dad said as he rose from his chair. "The house is sad without you."

On the following day, why was I blathering about days if I didn't know if it was a day, or the night had fallen when my mom read fairytales to me? She was a day and a night, she was grass and a house. Stinging nettles and a path through the nettles was mom. On that day, she took her suitcase. To be honest, I couldn't say if a day or a year had passed when the rusty Opel cadet, Kosso's jalopy, ground to a halt in front of our house. Mom, death and her suitcase got into the car. I was scared. My father stank to high heaven of roasted almonds, and I forgot all other offensive odors under the sun.

This lasted until Darina came back to me from some unknown place.

"Eat," she grumbled as she ladled soup into a bowl and shoved it in front of my mouth. "You'll stay in this kitchen until you drink the last drop of this soup. A poisoned cat, that's what you look like, Annie."

Day in, day out, I sat behind a bowl of soup, my friend Gasho the dog squatted on his haunches, thinking perhaps that the ogress would make him drink soup, too. At a certain point, the huge woman left me alone. Slowly, although I am not a bad kid — mom used to say that only bad kids whimpered — I turned on the waterworks. My tears dropped into the soup and I couldn't swallow a drop of it even if the future of Gasho the dog depended on it.

After an age or two, Darina let me go, and although I hadn't put on my dad's shabby blue coat, I slunk past the elder bushes, croaking sadly like a frog that would never turn into a princess. Vera, Shushomir's mother, showed up, a clean, steaming bowl in hand, but I didn't feel like eating as I crept through the hole in the fence overgrown with nettles. All their leaves teemed with slugs and lizards that bared their huge teeth at me. Aunt Vera came up to me, took my hand, and led me to the faucet to wash my face.

"You're such a pretty little girl," she said.

After my face was clean, Shushomir suggested, "Let's play marbles."

His dad didn't kick me out, although he detested my dad's guts the way the dogs from the upper end of the village hated the mongrels from its lower end.

We played for hours. Shushomir beat the pants off me and, at the very end of the game, he let me win by a head. I didn't win all the same, and the poor boy gave me his cap to cheer me up. Day in, day out, he gave me a cap, always an old one, and shortly after our tournament was over, I had all his caps in a shoebox. One Sunday dad chucked this box into the river.

Within an hour, my skin turned red-purple like the pail of purple paint, and since mom had already died, no one knew how to make weed and root extract to ease my itch. Darina took me in her arms and paced up and down as she shouted at dad; then she put me to bed, grabbed dad by the collar, and mouthed a few words. After an hour or perhaps a year, I couldn't tell if a year or a minute had passed, dad gave me two boxes full of caps, all different colors, all sparking and so beautiful that I gasped for breath.

Big Darina didn't let me drift off. She put the caps on my chest and I had to sleep in her arms. I was quite angry, but she started rocking me and sang "Go to sleep, go to sleep, little baby…" Knives clattered in her voice again, but this time all their blades were blunt and none would hurt me. When I woke in the morning, I found out the woman still held me in her arms as she slept, snoring like a volcano. I thought her snoring sounded better than her song.

✳ ✳ ✳

"No more hiding and no more running away from anybody big and strong!" Darina rumbled. "If you run away from somebody, I'll break your head." She didn't break my head, she kissed me on the forehead instead, then asked, "Why haven't you put on the red T-shirt your dad bought you for one lev from Fedo's second-hand shop?" The thing was classy, a brand-new second-hand T-shirt. Her second question was why I had donned that black rag and the black shorts. These looked like a shabby piece of lace on my ass. "I want nobody to notice me, Darina," I said. "If they notice me, they'll beat me up."

"Show me who beats you!" she said as she removed my black T-shirt and black shorts. After that, the big woman lit the stove and burned my clothes in it. I watched them flare up through the hole of the hotplate. It felt as if my brain was burning, and my belly rumbled. Darina flung the red one-lev T-shirt across the room. I had no other pair of shorts, and she gave me old blue jeans, so tight that an ant couldn't put them on. The smell of burnt almonds hit me.

"I'm dying," I told her. The woman got scared. She dragged me out of the damned trouser legs, pitched the jeans into the fire, then helped me put on my panties under the black T-shirt. It was endless, this T-shirt, and it could easily keep me, the sky, and the house clothed. I liked it.

"Let's go!" Darina said as she grabbed my hand, then she marched out of the room as energetically as if she was a horse and a bulldozer rolled into one. All the time an idea was racing through my mind, "She'll wrench my shoulder." I made efforts not to whine because every time I did, dad rapped me over the knuckles. I did groan once when Darina was about to twist my arm. The worst thing was the huge one stopped in her tracks and stared at me. "You're cooked, Anna," I thought, but I was not. She clasped me to her and carried me in her arms as if I was a baby who'd pissed in her pants.

Darina took me to the readymade garments shop — not the shabby second-hand store, far from it! It was the most expensive store I'd seen in my life. You could buy a lawn sprinkler, pairs and pairs of garden shears, frying pans, knives, socks, and pants, and lo and behold! The big one and I stopped in front of two girls' dresses, so expensive I couldn't even read the labels that showed the prices.

"Put this one on!" the huge woman said. It was not a dress. It was a star trimmed with lace and gold, with silver and gemstones. I put it on and the dress sparkled on my chest, neither too wide nor too tight, my dream frock!

"How much is it?"

"Thirty-five levs."

I heard this and I truly was about to kick the bucket. She'd never buy me this dress. Thirty-five levs… I calculated. A cigarette pack and three days' brandy for dad cost thirty-five levs.

"I'll buy it," Darina said.

I didn't dare to budge. She grabbed me under the armpits and lifted me to the ceiling as if I was a zucchini casserole. After a while, she removed my shabby trainers and let me walk barefoot on the floor. In a flash, big Darina returned a pair of sandals in hand — a treasure, gold buckles with gemstones on them, and red tiny heels so beautiful my eyes hurt. Darina helped me put on the sandals that were neither wide nor tight on my feet, my perfect fit.

"How much?"

"Forty-five levs."

One hundred boxes of cigarettes and many bottles of brandy.

"I'll buy the sandals too," Darina said, her voice a palace of gold with gemstones on the windowsills. "Look at you!" she added as she pulled me to the mirror. I looked hard and long and I had trouble recognizing my face. A girl, her head shaved and flat like a cockroach, her dress more expensive than a million cartons of cigarettes plus ten bottles of brandy! The kid's feet sang with joy unable to believe they had a new pair of sandals. I was scared to breathe. You never knew with gold buckles. You could bust them if you coughed or gulped for air, and you could make your terrific frock filthy.

"I am afraid to walk, Darina."

"You are pretty. Look at you!" boomed her voice as tough as old boots. "Let's go home."

We immediately set off for our old house, she taking huge strides like the wind, I quickening my pace, a happy wolf pup in her wake.

"You'll no longer hide your face from people!"

"Ok," I agreed. "Can I put on the red T-shirt? I'll leave the dress on my bed and I'll look at it from a distance."

"No way! You'll put on this dress now…" Darina started.

"Or I'll break your head?" I finished, looking at her. This was the first time I'd seen her smile; a face as big as a house, a clean and beautiful one. I was sure I saw chicken soup simmering on the stove, and the kid I caught a glimpse of in the kitchen was happy, gold and silver sandals sparkling on her feet.

"You're very pretty when you smile like this, Darina," I said.

She flashed me a new smile as broad as an expressway. If guys beamed like this, it meant they didn't think evil thoughts, but, for all I knew, Darina never thought evil thoughts. Her thoughts were usually big and sweet.

After we came back home, she took to cutting fresh green beans and I thought hard: what should I do to show her how much I loved the new dress and the sandals? I knew only one thing, of course. I grabbed the broom and started sweeping the floor in front of her. She smiled another expressway at me, and I brought her a glass of water — a whole saucepan of water did I bring to the big woman.

"Drink, Darina," I blurted out. "It feels good when you smile."

"Come here. Let me teach you how to cook green beans."

The poor darling, she cooked worse than a flea. The brown sauce didn't even begin to thicken, she had not peeled the potatoes properly, and failed to cut the meat into pieces because it was still frozen. The big sweetheart dumped the chunk complete with ice and frost into the stewpan. The green beans had a hard time boiling on the naked flames. Darina had used my old shoes and my shabby trousers to keep the fire burning, but I didn't mind. Suddenly somebody knocked on the door.

Why should dad knock like this? He's drunk. That's for sure, a thought cut me like a shaving blade. Now, I'll have to bring Darina enough rope to tie dad with. She'll sure thrash him with his own belt. She'll be raging mad just like our dog Gasho when a stray cat sneaks out of our backyard.

It turned out dad wasn't knocking on the door.

It was aunt Katerina, our neighbor, an old woman bent to the ground like the grass we called "green telephone". Its mean leaves crept all over the place, and dad ordered me to weed all strawberry beds. Even if you looked for nastier grass with a magnifying glass in hand, you wouldn't find worse ones under the sun.

"Darina…" aunt Katerina began, unable to stop.

The old woman was whimpering like a babe in arms. Why? I couldn't smell roasted almonds, and it meant she wouldn't be pushing the daisies one of these days. "Darina, Filan stole my two turkeys! He showed up at my door exactly like the two crooks who wanted to loot your roof tiles. He came into my kitchen, ate my cheese sandwich, and ordered me about like he was my boss. 'What do you want, Filan?' I asked him. He kept mum and he broke into my henhouse. There, he caught my two turkey hens. 'Hey! Hey!' I hollered as loud as I could. 'Leave my birds alone!' but he…" the old woman burst into big tears that fell on the rug I had just swept, getting it wet. Her old tears went on rolling down her cheeks and I thought to myself, 'Tears are salty. We could use salt to kill bacteria and disinfect Darina's green beans.' "I have no more turkey hens, Darina. I am diabetic. I must eat meat. I told Filan, 'Please! Please!' 'Shut up, or I'll break your neck,' he growled. Help me, Darina! Make him give my turkey hens back to me!"

Darina said nothing. She took Aunt Katerina by the hand and asked her to sit on the sofa. I didn't like it. The old woman's dress was gray and dirty, and it was me who slept on the sofa.

"Wait here," Darina said. She spoke so quietly I thought that instead of words, a snake was winding its way through her throat. She went out of the house, and I, a cockroach in her new dress and sandals, felt like a queen all dolled up for a party. This lasted half a minute, then, in panic, I rushed after Darina. If they beat her black and blue, I had to run to Doc Dragan; he'd sure give her an injection to bring her back to life. If huge Darina died, I had to run to priest Pepi the drunk to help him bury her. Our neighbors often sent me both to Doc Dragan and Pepi, the drinking priest, if a guy was about to meet his maker. I could hear the dying guy's steps that filled the street with the smell of roasted almonds.

Not far from the bakery, Darina caught up with Filan. I ran carefully, making best efforts not to ruin my new sandals. The minute I was near enough, I saw Darina's hands squeezing Filan's neck. The thief, coughing and spluttering, looked much flabbier and shorter than her, the turkey hens gobbling so powerfully as if they hadn't gobbled for a century and were trying hard to make up for their loss. Filan burped and spat, momentarily a knife blade flashed in his fingers, then both knife and fingers drooped like the soiled advertisement, tacked on the door of the Town Hall, offering farmland to rent. Darina tightened her grip on Filan's throat, and his face suddenly was a box of green powder made in Bulgaria to kill woodlice. After a while, Darina took out the belt from Filan's trousers — I could tell a genuine leather belt from a faux leather one.

If genuine leather hit a guy's back, the back cracked-cracked, hissing a lot at the very end of the belt. Filan's belt didn't hiss at all; it said only bang-bang-bang! The turkey thief attempted to run away, but Darina — even I didn't see what exactly she did, tripped him up? Or did she whack him? I stood there, staring at the man that wallowed in the mud, as fat as a bus that he was, the belt reciting the only poem faux leather knew — bang-bang-bang.

"I'll find you 10 levs!" Darina rumbled her voice a tangle of both genuine and faux leather belts. "You'll pay the penalty for causing problems for Aunt Katerina. I'll give her the money you'll pay me."

"I'm flat broke, Darina," the man tried hard to beat about the bush, all his words bald tires blowing out in his mouth.

"Then I'll break your thumb," the big one said as she bent down to tread on his hand. She was about to squash the thumb...

"No! No!" he hollered. "Wait! Take eight levs... Eight and twenty-four cents..."

Darina pocketed the money, took the shoes off his feet — a tattered pair of loafers just like mine used to be — the ones she had burned in the stove.

"If you pester somebody for money in this village one more time..."

"I won't pester anybody, Darina! I promise. I swear it!"

She threw the faux leather belt at his feet.

"Give the turkey hens to Katerina. She's waiting in my backyard. If you don't give the turkeys to her..." Darina's voice was a raging elephant, but it was the first time I'd said to myself, 'O, my Gosh, she has a beautiful voice!' I knew who Gosh was. He was my mother's God. He was painted on a piece of wood: a quiet man who helped the children and the poor. How could he help anybody? He was so thin! Thinner than me! This was the reason I loved him and I told him, "Don't you be afraid, God. I'll grow up. I'll be strong. I'll protect you from the bullies, the thieves, and from Filan."

I watched quietly when, lo and behold, Filan, a paunch of a man, stubble covering his cheeks just like my dad's, trudged through the mud, no shoes, no faux leather belt, his arms pressing the two turkey hens to his chest.

"Look at him, God. That's what you have to do when you become stronger. I'll help you. You can count on me, dear God."

I ran like a blizzard, the fool I was, forgetting I'd damage my silver and gold sandals. I grabbed Darina's hand and whispered, "Darina, please bend down."

The woman stared at me as if I had pissed in my pants, but did what I asked her. She smelled of burned brown sauce, and of the frozen meat she'd dropped in the saucepan with the green beans.

I kissed her cheek.

"Darina, teach me to fight!"

"I'll teach you to write the letter M first," she said. "This is the most important letter in your ABC book. It's your mom's letter."

* * *

I didn't recognize my mother, and she didn't recognize me. A small silver coin on display at a major museum, the woman was. She spoke quietly, a bespectacled lady who behaved like a university professor. I didn't feel anything for her. By the way, she looked fabulous in her Karen Walker jacket and Marc Jacobs blouse; the only thing we perhaps had in common was the easiness of movement. Her fluid silhouette gave you the impression her body was a pair of hunting foxes. Karen Walker's world would never be mine, but like a fisherman standing on riverbank hours on end, I waited on the brink of the fancy clothes universe Internet had let me peek into. I didn't even dream of slinky dresses or skirts, I was happy somebody had designed them. She exuded the same subtle pastel sadness I had felt since the day she told me she'd go away. She had had a narrow escape, transforming the capital city into a safe harbor where, despite her obstinacy, waves of solitude slowly wiped out her composure. Her steps were a stream of silence.

"She is one of my ten best clients who can well afford my services. Mrs. Percha is a lady of high repute in the power elite society. I dedicate seventy percent of my efforts and time to her. It is only natural I set out my financial conditions. Mrs. Percha is perspicacious enough to accept them and make no unsubstantiated claims. You look pretty," my mother said. "Your clothes are tasteless, and I can find the reason behind this:

the backwater provincial town. I'll pay for everything you need apparel-wise. It's a pity you are thinner than me."

"Thank you," I said to the woman who had run the risk of ruining her body in the course of an unwanted pregnancy.

"Your husband has kicked you out of his house," she conjectured.

"Yes."

"I am glad I do not know him. A mentally retarded provincial clown who drinks — the fact you are alive though not kicking impresses me. How's your daughter?"

My mother's house was elegant, a two-story affair among pine trees, and a manicured lawn at the front door. We were in her massage studio. She was Mrs. Percha's masseuse, make-up artist, and occupational therapist. She was already a wealthy woman. In the living room, an old man in a wheelchair stared silently at me.

"My husband, Mr. Stoyanov," my mother said.

"I told my daughter I'd go away to meet my maker," I said as a looked at the attractive middle-aged woman. "You told me the same thing when I was her age."

"Is she pretty?"

"Yes, she is," I said and gave her a photograph. A little girl, a black t-shirt, black shabby shorts, long tousled hair, a wolf cub. My mother looked at the photo and returned it to me. She did not comment.

"What time is it?" she asked, although she could easily check the gilded wall clock. I liked the decorative treatment of the walls, the wood paneling. I loved wood and I missed the cherry tree in my backyard I planted six years ago. I'd left behind the only young apple tree, my favorite. It was 5 pm, a hot afternoon in Sofia, Bulgaria.

"I have planned a surprise for you. The child you will take care of will arrive here in… in thirty seconds. If there is no spark and no harmonious contact could be established, you'll go back to your native village. If the little one likes you, her mother will hire you and you'll qualify for a cash bonus. I will not mince words. Mrs. Percha was intrigued by your story about the guy who kicked you out of his car on account of your refusal to satisfy his physiological needs. She is willing to pay you a pretty penny if you disclose the identity of the guy and his contact information. She is in favor of establishing closer cooperation with him."

I got up from my chair. It was not necessary to pull myself together, I could feel the air in the room like a thorn stuck in my foot, a corn on my toe. I couldn't stand the woman's Karen Walker jacket and Marc Jacobs blouse, the wall paneling, the expensive sofa, and the marble floor. I had no idea where I'd go. This place smelled of death, neither heroic nor instantaneous, disaster patiently carving into the flesh under the Karen Walker jacket. I walked to the door. A poem in a language I didn't speak was printed on it. I remembered the picture my mother had started painting and never finished: a rosewood door and a poem printed on it. The evening before she told me she was dying, she gave me the unfinished painting. I sold it and bought myself a second or maybe twenty-second hand bike.

"You are a drifter. You have no place to go," my mother said. "As far as I can see, and my ability to size up a situation is quite uncanny, your hubby has already found a new wife, a healthy and strong one, who doesn't hesitate to permanently offer him potato salad and physiological consolation."

Her insight into things frightened me. For years, I could not blot out a childhood memory — my mother managed to scare the pants off of all our neighbors. She read their thoughts, or perhaps her power of observation combined with vindictiveness led her to conclusions that made your skin crawl. She had no girlfriends and no boyfriends. I didn't have either.

"If you decide to go because you can smell death like me, I'll give you this," she shoved an envelope into my hand. "Six hundred levs. I'm not a generous soul, you know. If you work for Percha, you'll make much more than…" she hadn't finished the sentence when a man in an immaculate designer suit snuck quietly as a shadow of a kite into the ambient music of her voice. Behind him, an infantry armored vehicle of a girl burst into the room. She looked two or three years older than my daughter or perhaps was just bigger. My mother hid the envelope with the money in the pocket of her silk dressing-gown.

"You're the one, eh?" the girl growled, her hands balled into fists as she charged towards me at full-speed. The brat was after my stomach and if I hadn't jumped aside, her forehead would have landed somewhere near my belly button. The lassie wasn't fat, wasn't even heavyset, simply an iron strongbox of surplus energy. Like a claw-hammer, the little terror ran her head into an easy chair, overturned it, and fell prostrate on the floor. I couldn't say if it was pure coincidence or my mother's awe-inspiring ability to anticipate unpleasant events was at work: the muzzle of a gorgeous bear hide rug lay under the kid's face. The girl leaped to her feet, and the guy in the custom suit put in a great deal of futile effort to keep a curb on her temper.

"Hey-y-y," the girl purred, and before I had time to heave a sigh of relief, she pounced on my chest, seized me by the throat, and squeezed hard, her teeth sinking into my chin. It hurt so much I thought I'd pass out cold. I didn't know how it happened that I found myself staring at the bear's muzzle as the little claw-hammer kicked me. I rolled over onto my back. The grenade of a girl stepped on my chest, her pink trainer pressing hard. "Hey, wimp, if you can't knock me down, I won't hire you to take care of me. You understand, eh?"

Lying flat on the floor, I noticed there was no furniture in the room except for two easy chairs. The walls were covered by something thick and woolen like a quilt or a blanket. Perhaps mom knew or at least guessed what the girl mammoth was about to do, but she hadn't bothered to warn me. How typical of her, as they said on TV. When I was little, we went for a stroll, mom and me. She walked in front of me so light and soft I thought she was a bundle of moonbeams. We were in a field of grass. My shoes and feet got wet, but I thought that if this was dangerous, she'd tell me what to do. Mom didn't tell me anything, so I didn't pay attention and got stuck in a puddle of mud, all thick and sticky. Mom didn't sprint to drag me out. Relaxed and smiling she went on, not even looking at me, then stopped under a tree, just a stone's throw from me. I sank deeper into the muck.

"Mom! Mom!" I shouted, but she, comfortable and peaceful in the shadow, kept quiet, staring at me as I twisted in the mud in my best Sunday dress. Mom had always bought me expensive clothes and shoes. If she could buy a Marc Jacobs dress for me, she would have bought it, I was sure. Mom had taught me to iron my all blouses from an early age.

"What was that?" I shouted as I turned my head to the window.

"What?" the baby hippopotamus asked.

I snatched her pink trainer. After all, the little beast was a month or two older than my daughter, not more. I tugged at her leg hard as if I was pulling corn-thistle — this was prickly weed dad and I kept under control after mom declared she was going to die. He killed corn-thistles and a thousand thorns lodged under his skin every day. In the evening, he soaked his fingers in brandy, and at midnight he drank brandy and thorns together, then dad threw the tin mug on the floor, repeating "Your mother, your mother..." One day mom vanished into thin air; however, I'd already learned to very well weed a garden.

I pulled at the kid's pink trainer so hard she collapsed onto the floor like an empty trash can. Full of malicious joy, I hoped the little whale had twisted her ankle, but she had not. I got up quickly and stood straight as a bow-string, then ugly as it might well look to the gentleman in the designer suit, I pressed my foot down hard on the young miss's strong chest. I said, "You have to be polite if you want me to take care of you. Do I make myself clear, you little stain on the carpet?"

"Stain! Stain!" the child muttered beside herself with rapture. "Did you hear the dirty insult she threw at me? She's great!" the kid tried to bite my calf, but I pressed her back against the floor. Tough — not a kid, an armored door was she.

"Old Lena!" the girl shouted as she pointed her chin at my mother. "Call mom without delay. Tell her that I'll hire this woman here."

My mother's name was Lena, I was called Anna, and my daughter was Annie. I could not explain why all women in my family were quite strange. So, my mother who a minute ago behaved as if she were an executive director of a multinational corporation, suddenly turned into a gentle spinster, her manners a lake of sparkling refinement.

"Elizabeth! My darling!" I knew this tone of voice of hers well. She used it to lure cheeky youths into entering her backyard. Maybe a week before, their insolent lot had stolen all her ripe cherries and took her to the cleaners. 'My wonderful kids!' she said and gave them a bowl of red cherries she had sprayed with pesticide. The wonderful kids loved her, guzzled cherries from her bowl and had terrible diarrhea for days. "Elizabeth, think seriously, sugar. Make up your mind. Ask yourself if Anna will be able to take care of you, and if you'll be happy with her. Will your mommy be happy and pleased that you and I chose Anna? Think about mommy, my dearest Elizabeth."

On hearing the word "mommy" the young female alligator winced. Our dog reacted in the same way when a lout hit his back with a plank of wood. Now I knew: mommy was the tycoon and boss in this house.

"Please, please, my beautiful girl!" my mother said. "Let me introduce you to my daughter Anna. She can speak English, can't you, Big Anna?"

I was "Big Anna".

The man I ran away from called me Big Anna.

They called me Big Anna in the village where people thought I had a screw loose.

"Big Anna!" the little gladiator screamed as she pushed me in the stomach. "I'll hire you. You can kiss me now."

"I don't want to kiss you, Elizabeth," I said.

"It's not important what you want or don't want," the kid stared at me her knowing blue eyes glinting, and I was in danger of being trampled underfoot. "The important thing is what I want! My mother pays you, and you'll obey my orders."

I watched the child with interest, a cute girl; expensive Nike trainers, Levi's jeans for girls, a mango silk blouse and red silk socks. The kid ordered as she patted me on the cheek, "Kiss me. Don't waste time."

The white-haired gentleman in his immaculate custom-tailored suit, said as he stood aloof from the war dust, "You heard you were hired. Please kiss the young lady's hand and follow me. It's an honor and a privilege to take you to Mrs. Percha where you will have the opportunity to clarify the financial parameters of your remuneration."

"Oh, my princess," my mother said affectionately. "You are the prettiest girl in the world," I remembered the cherries she'd sprayed with pesticide.

"You are the prettiest old woman, Lena," the girl said. My mother kissed her then whispered in her ear, "Go say hello to Uncle Stoyanov."

"Come and say hello," somebody groaned in the adjoining room where Mr. Stoyanov, my mother's sick and old husband lived.

✳✳✳

"My name is Ivan," the man said.

The stocky girl kissed my mother's cheek. The woman looked so sweet, and my throat constricted as I listen to her declaring how magnificent, intelligent and irresistible the baby jackal was.

"Mrs. Percha hates it when women, wearing dirty pants like you, introduce themselves to her," Ivan told me. "Put on a skirt… that is, you will, if your legs look good," continued the man in the designer suit that bore a resemblance to a baronet from the Royal Court in England, then he gave me the once-over — I was a cow and he was a livestock trader from the neighboring village. "You're pretty. Delicate bones… that's no good. On the other hand, your show can be an overnight success… Everything has a price."

"I have no money," I said. Even a livestock trader didn't glower at cows like that in this part of the world. At times, the trader swore at the animals, but once in a blue moon, he talked to them peacefully.

"What was that envelope old Lena failed to put in your pocket? I surmise it was not full of newspaper clippings."

"Lena is not in the habit of giving anybody cash in an envelope," I remarked and he laughed.

"You two don't seem to be crazy about each other," the hero from the British Royal Court tried to get his hooks into me. "So far, old Lena has never mentioned she has a daughter," he declared. "Mrs. Percha's curiosity was aroused by your undesirable behavior, mine too, to say the least. You have probably heard there are particular methods of settling accounts that only a woman can successfully use. I am inclined to say this is the right direction of thinking…. for now."

The two of them, my mother and Elizabeth, entered the room again. Old Lena, an exquisite porcelain piece, breathing hard, carried the young muscular tapeworm in her arms, the parasite kissing her cheeks. Without the slightest warning, the child wrenched herself from my mother's grasp, rushed forward then creaked to a halt in front of me.

"Kiss me!" she ordered.

"No, I won't," I said.

"Are you crazy?" the girl asked. "I pay you. This means you have to obey my orders."

I happened to steal a glance at the old butler. I believed he went by this alias because, in all the movies I had seen, specimens of this type were either butlers or impoverished noblemen enamored of Her Majesty. Now, the butler's face was an endless smile, so warm that you experienced digestive symptoms such as gas and an upset stomach.

"My dearest little star!" exclaimed the nobleman who a minute ago dropped hints about female methods of settling disputes. "My magnificent princess! You and I will go to your mommy for advice, and your mommy will explain to that woman how she should treat a young beauty like you."

"I've already grown up enough to order a fishwife about," declared the girl. "If I can't fix a peasant, you must call me stupid. But I am not stupid."

"How many nannies have you fired since the beginning of the year?" my mother asked, and the butler, dissolving in a whiff of Givenchy cologne for men, set sail for her hand and ardently kissed it.

"Eight, my dear. Eight delectable chocolate soufflé cups were fired within three months," the baronet smiled as he winked at my mother. "You don't seem to be in raptures over your daughter, my dear Lena. A nanny for Elizabeth! The young woman is your flesh and blood, for God's sake. Why throw her to the dogs?"

"I'm not in raptures over anyone," my mother was beaming, but her voice was firm. I couldn't explain how she managed to produce sounds as soft as a baby's skin; on the other hand, mother was able to store rusty nails and razor blades in her words. Her sentences were a ruined building. A child had died there. I was this child. For a while, I forgot I had no home; I had nothing but a glimmer of hope that an envelope of greenbacks would land in my pocket. I knew mother promised you the moon, and a poem written on the sand of a crowded beach was all you got in the end. I walked out on the English butler and the refined woman, my mother, who was manna from heaven to the young alligator. I didn't look back, I didn't want to remember her beautiful face.

My thoughts often took me back to this afternoon, to my hope that died like a dog forgotten by his master. This old pretty woman had never told me, "I hope you'll do well on your math test."

I stood in front of the black Jeep Wrangler into which I'd climbed on my way to my mother's place. My mother was a cold-blooded and tight-fisted woman. She would give me no envelope of greenbacks. I recalled a childhood episode. I was running a fever.

"It's not a medical emergency," she said. "You don't need immediate medical attention."

"I'm dying," I whispered, the smell of roasted almonds a cloud in my chest, seizing me the way cobwebs caught insects, my swollen face yellow the color of an empty brandy bottle. I didn't die. I couldn't explain what brought down my temperature. The swelling went down of its own accord. My father sat by my side, sighing his willpower a bucket of mud. He was thin as a bad tooth and he cried but didn't dare to give me the antibiotics the doctor had prescribed. As a rule, the poor accountant obeyed my mother's orders; however, this time he pressed his cheek against my forehead, and we burned away together in the furnace of my high fever.

He loved her — the poor, vapid verb — he couldn't tie his shoelaces if mother was not around. It seemed her lungs brought oxygen to his body, and he accepted me as a part of her. After my mother told me she was going to die dad fell ill from drinking too much. At a certain point, he got lost somewhere. Did he meet his maker, or my grandma, his mother, asked him to come under her roof to help him slowly go out like a flame? Or did some silly soft-hearted woman take him in on his sickbed to clean his open wounds? I didn't know if he was still alive. Sometimes I remembered my father, that gentle, wonderful man. I thought of his tears that saved me from the smell of almonds. It felt peaceful as he held me in his arms.

"Wait!" the white-haired butler grabbed my shoulders.

He knew exactly when to get involved, when to withdraw or patch up a quarrel, and what the best way to ask for a raise was. I realized something important had taken place under my very nose. The young howitzer lay on the floor kicking wildly. The second she noticed I was looking at her, she let out a high-pitched scream not unlike a cat choking on a bone, one that had no intention of dying soon. Such a powerful roar at the girl's tender age… I was too stunned to speak.

"Don't let her go!" the girl bawled. "I haven't let her go. I'm the boss here. Bring her back to me! It's an order!"

The white-haired man made no bones about wanting to be promoted. In his opinion, he who hesitated was lost. He snatched me from the ground as if I was a box of snails that could smear their gunk on the beautiful floor. After a couple of seconds, he set me up straight in front of the sobbing girl's chin.

"Don't you weep, my dearest," my mother said so softly that the girl blubbered with double the force she'd used before.

The white-haired virtuoso with both brain and brawn reached into his pants pocket and produced a wad of banknotes — I appreciated this kind of activity — all were one-hundred lev bills. One thing was sure: I hated it when somebody, virtuoso or not, tried to shove the bundle of bills in my mouth. With no fidget or fluster, I stood up, said politely "Thank you" and started for the door. The girl, red in the face, bawled at the top of her voice, and I understood no word of the sentence she pronounced. This time, both my mother and the silk-haired butler caught up with me very quickly, and I could feel several inspiring hope wads of cash sink into my suit pockets.

"Talk to Mrs. Percha," my mother said coldly as if her tongue, esophagus, mouth, and all her internal organs were frozen a month ago.

I took a step to the girl prostrate with grief. The carpet was drenched with her tears, and a magnificent thing this carpet was. For as long as I could remember, I adored my mother's taste, impeccable, and accurate, verging on the supernatural. She could match colors, guys, and pockets to her plans. Each of her clients was her best friend and was always right.

"Stand up," I said to the child. "We will go and speak to your mom."

The young goddess forgot all about tears, sobs, and screams. She leaped to her feet, and before I could make out what she was up to, her fingers fished a wad of bills out of my pocket.

"Half the money is mine," the lass declared. "If I hadn't turned the waterworks, neither you nor I would have gotten a dime out of my mom."

She threw a one-hundred lev bill to my mother and said, "I love you, old Lena! Buy apple juice with my money."

After a short while, the lass rushed past my mother as if the woman breathed no more, then came up to the white-haired butler, kicked him in the ankle as hard as she could, and said, "Ivan, you didn't follow my instructions. You let this fishwife lead us a merry dance. She is an airhead from a backwater village."

It was a pleasure to watch as a smile spread over the butler's features. A caterpillar a lad had pierced with a safety pin: that was the story the expression on the domestic's face recounted.

"I will show you what fishwives can do," I told the young lass. "You, my dear, are nothing but a spoiled fool."

The girl opened her mouth. She let out a piercing scream, spat on my blouse, and quick as a bullet fired into a beast at point-blank range, charged towards me. I stepped aside, the young gladiator hurtled past like a Royal Marines helicopter and crashed into the wall. At this point, I'd like to put in a good word for my mother's considerable foresight: she had mounted thick acoustic foam to all the walls. Passing no comments, the white-haired patrician first pushed me, then tied my hands behind my back.

"Elizabeth, sweetheart," he said. "Show her what you're capable of. She can't run away."

My mother, the exquisite porcelain figurine, remained inert, as the little machine gun walloped me across the face. The butler's hands had clamped around my arms and I could hardly breathe. I could still speak, though.

"You are a coward. A worm hits a woman whose hands are tied."

The girl cane up to me smiling sweetly.

"I'd better be a worm and beat you up," she said. "Ivan, keep a tight hold on her! If she manages to wriggle free, I'll punish you after we get home."

"Dearest Elizabeth, you've been working too hard today," my mother remarked her voice tinged with commiseration that only a person massaging stars' rumps could master.

"If you hit me, I won't become your nanny," I said. "I know how to put a chicken to sleep and I can teach you to do it. I can teach you to climb a rope and ride a horse."

"Can you teach me to butcher a chicken and to set a horse's tail on fire?" unexpectedly, the girl raised her arms as she threw my mother a look of encouragement. "I want to eat almonds. Now! Give me almonds, old Lena. My mother says you must munch on raw almonds when you mthink hard." After a while, the energetic young hippo calf smiled. "I offered Maria, my ex-nanny, to let me kick her. I must be a sportsperson, mustn't I? I gave her one hundred levs every time I kicked her, and she was happy to put the money in her pocket. If you don't teach me to put a chicken to sleep, I will fire you. Be careful not to get my back up. You must be grateful for the money I and my mom pay you. My mom teaches me that money is the cure to all diseases."

My mother scuttled across the room, a bowl of almonds in hand, as the white-haired hero pressed my intelligent mug against the wall. The little one started munching away, slowly, working up a big appetite, letting grains of salt and dry skins of almonds fall on my chest.

"Ok," she said. "Ivan, let her go. I want her to teach me how to put a chicken to sleep. You come from a rural backwater," the kid turned to me. "Didn't it cross your mind I'd learned to ride even before I was born? My horse costs ten times as much as an airheaded nanny like you. Ok, I'll tell mom to hire you. However, I'll call you the Clodhopper."

The white-haired footman eased his grip, I yawned, stretched, and turned to the young lass. "Of course, you can call me 'the clodhopper'. Think — what will other educated people think about your mom after they hear you addressing me? Your mom doesn't have enough money. All she can afford is an uncivilized clodhopper hired to look after her only daughter. If a damn yokel takes care of you, you will soon grow up to be an uncouth country cousin."

The girl let out a scream, "More almonds! Now!"

I felt sorry for my mother's soft voice. It was a great pity she had an exquisite body. The young predatory pike ordered her around. The immaculate porcelain figurine accepted her predicament without shouting in anger, far from it! She brought almonds, and the pike after chewing and chomping on the nuts, at a certain point dropped the bowl on the floor. The thing didn't break; it was made of silver. Probably, my mother had hands-on relevant experience and training in this sphere.

"I'll call you Sassy," the child said.

"Sassy was a magnificently playful cat," remarked the white-haired champion who obviously had the brawn. "I used to love her a lot."

"Love her or kick her, I don't give a hoot," the kid declared. "Mom doesn't pay you to love pussycats, you fool. She gives you money to serve me. Let's go," the girl spoke and nodded at the same time. "I'll call her Craven."

My mother and the white-haired royalty sprang into action simultaneously.

"Dear Madam," the butler turned to me as he presented me with an old-fashioned fan, his face bright smiles all over the place. "Please follow me. Mrs. Percha is waiting for you. I have the distinct honor and privilege of driving you to her mansion."

I had a new dress! In the morning, Darina and I got dressed in haste: I donned my red T-shirt that was long as a bathrobe, and I tied it around my waist with a piece of packthread. Her dress was even longer than mine. Ten years ago, the thing must have been a curtain, a canopy or part of a parachute because it was coarse and yellowish-white. Darina had cut a hole in the cloth, so she could push her head through it; then she crammed her chest, stomach, ass and legs into the curtain, and tied it with a piece of string around her waist just like I did. We went to milk the goat, then we removed the weeds in the raspberry patches, I fed the chickens, and at half past ten when the sun was a chunk of rock about to collapse on your head, Darina said, "We're done. Now, we'll go sell what we've got to sell."

We loaded crates of strawberries and cherries we had picked in my father's garden; at the last moment we grabbed three lettuce bags so the lettuce inside remained crisp and crunchy, and I took five boxes of mulberries. We bathed in water heated up by the sun. Darina's lips glowed, red-lilac on account of the mulberries, and mine, almost black, glowed even more dangerously. Every time we went to the market, I put on my only gold-and-silver dress, Darina took a quick look at me and said, "What a pretty girl!

Then she, intent on not scaring our customers out of their wits, donned her new dress, light-green as a lizard.

"Annie, how do I look?" she'd ask me.

"Great!" I said honestly.

Although clothed in brand new outfits, we lugged empty crates and plastic bags to pack things in as we trudged up the hill under the baking sun. In the marketplace, we sat down in a conspicuous spot and started selling our fresh stuff. However, the best thing began even before we set out on our journey. Shushomir trailed along behind me, repeating, Change that dress, I tell you!" as he thrust a blue T-shirt into my hand, a garment faded as toothpaste. "Put this on, or some squirt will steal you from me when Darina isn't looking. Then I wouldn't see you anymore. You'd better hide somewhere."

I didn't hide, I sold mulberries, cherries, and strawberries instead. In the evening, Darina, Shushomir, and I had a good time — we chose The Big Mouth eatery. I knew Darina didn't have enough money. It was sad to watch as she counted nickels and dimes to pay for our grilled steaks, but they were so delicious I believed the cook had roasted them in gold frying pans. It went without saying that we ate more bread than steaks. At a certain point, I spotted a grease stain on my silver-and-gold dress, and simply couldn't stop whining; I shouldn't have gobbled the last piece of the steak, it did me in. What else could I do but whimper? I had one magnificent dress and it went to wrack and ruin! On the other hand, I had two magnificent friends, Darina and Shushomir. Wasn't that great!

….Then Darina kept mum for a long time, and I knew that a problem would crop up. She looked at me as she left her slice of bread on the table and said, "Your mom wants you to stay with her in Sofia."

"Hurray!" I shouted. "Hurray!"

Darina bowed her head. Shushomir stared at the ground as if he had trodden on a venomous snake.

"Don't go to Sofia," he blurted out. "This is yours. Take it."

He gave me a penknife, but I didn't want a penknife.

"I have nothing else," he said.

"Don't go to Sofia," Darina said, and the teddy bear in her voice, my favorite, stopped breathing. "Stay with me. I'll teach you to fight and I'll teach you to tie a knot in a rope."

"Stay with us and I will teach you all the letters of the alphabet," Shushomir said.

"You don't know all the letters. Then how will you teach me?" I asked.

…This evening, I couldn't say where my father was. Shushomir had told me they saw him in Pernik, and Shushomir's grandmother dropped a hint a day ago, "Your dad's probably looking for another woman. I believe he wants to kick out Darina. That's why you have to stay with your mom in Sofia."

"But my mom is dead," I told Shushomir's grandmother. "She died after the damson trees were out in blossom."

Shushomir's grandma turned to Darina, "Did he tell you to beat it, woman?"

Darina was very tall, taller than the clouds. She didn't bow her head. The clouds would break; she wouldn't.

"Yes. He said to me 'Go away!'" Darina said. "He's constantly telling me about his wife."

"Don't go to Sofia, Annie," Shushomir said as he turned to his mother, a short, stout woman. "Mom, can Annie live with us, with me, dad and you? She doesn't eat much. Every time Darina takes us to The Big Mouth eatery, she only nibbles at her slice of bread, and that's it. I'll give her half of what's on my plate. She'll sweep the leaves off the backyard and will bring mineral water for you."

"Annie's mom is alive. She's landed a great job and makes a ton of money."

"Annie, this is for you," mom Darina said as she passed me a plastic bag. "These are all your clothes — your panties, your red and blue T-shirts. You're wearing your new dress and your sandals."

"Mom Darina, why don't you come with me to Sofia?" I came up with a plan at last. "We'll sweep floors together and we'll bring mineral water to big wheels."

She didn't say a thing. There came a moment when the woman opened her mouth, but it was exactly then that an old geezer, tall and thin like a fork, Grampa Vlayko ran to us and started jabbering, "Lubo stole my weaned lamb, Darina. I was eating my breakfast when he entered my kitchen. "You have a lamb," he said. 'I like it and I'll take it.' And he went and marched into my sheep-pen as if it was his own. He grabbed my lamb. Help me, woman. Here, that's all I have." The old man produced an old black sock tied in a knot. His fingers trembled as he tried to loosen it, and the sock fell to the ground. As he bent down to retrieve it, the sky snapped the clouds like toothpicks and the paving stones in the street broke out in a sweat. Shushomir snatched the thing and gave it to the old man.

"That's the money, Darina. It's yours now."

In the beginning, Darina didn't reach for the thing, then she gripped the sock and thrust it into the old man's hand. He shook because probably a louse had bitten him.

"You said Lubo, did you?" five mongrels were growling in Darina's voice.

"Don't go! Don't beat Lubo black and blue," I asked her. "See me off to the train station instead." I hoped she'd kiss me on the forehead. She did that when I was running a fever. Then I could feel someone was roasting almonds for me, but I told death, "Leave me alone. I'm a scraggy child and I don't even know the Bulgarian alphabet. I know your name starts with the letter D, though, and the same is true for all donkeys. Let me be. I am Darina's only friend. I bring her water to drink, Ok?" After my big mom kissed my forehead, I stopped running a fever. Perhaps death saw how strong Darina was and knew how to fight. So, I remained safe and sound. Darina soaked towels in vinegar and put them on my forehead, on my feet, and hands.

"Don't beat Lubo up, Darina," I whispered, but she took no notice of me. If Mom Darina had made up her mind, you could whisper yourself hoarse and still get nowhere. She went to take her belt and her strong rope. But the rope she chose was short and Lubo was a big man; how could Darina tie him with it?

That was all our friendship was — a short piece of rope. If the rope was no good, friendship was no good! I believed I'd taught her to be my friend. She'd leave me in the lurch because I couldn't fight and didn't know the Bulgarian alphabet.

"I'll take you back home from Sofia!" her huge voice said, five hounds howling in it. They were good hounds, for sure. I could tell if a dog was good.

A black car as big as the village hall pulled out in front of me. A beefcake, all muscles, and biceps, bigger than Lubo the lamb thief got out of the luxury saloon. His hair was bone white.

"Are you Annie?" he asked.

"I'm not the Annie you're looking for," I said. "I won't go to Sofia without Mom Darina."

Shushomir's mother took the plastic bag from my hands. My red T-shirt, my panties and socks, everything I had in the world was in it.

✳ ✳ ✳

The tall woman had tied the hands of a big sunburnt guy behind his back. He lay on the ground, the dust mixing with a little puddle of his sweat. The woman had put on a huge dress belted loosely at the waist. She unbuckled her wide belt, took it off, then both buckle and belt crashed into the big guy's back. He tried to kick her, but the huge dress paid no mind to him as the belt bit into his back again. The woman said evenly and calmly as if she was about to have a snack of cheese just before bedtime, "This time, I won't break your arm. If you steal something from somebody in these parts, I'll break your left elbow. Within a quarter of an hour, give the lamb back to grandpa Vlayko. Give him ten levs and he will forget you've hauled him over the coals. I'll forget it, too, otherwise…"

Horribly and bloodily did the belt sink into the broad back. Tied to a young apple tree, the lamb bleated so hard you'd think it was intent on spitting its lungs out. The old Vlayko, a small dried mushroom, tottered to the creature, stroked its head and fished a crust of bread out of his pocket.

"Take a bite, boy, take a tiny bite," he said.

* * *

Two elderly women, wizened, dry as hoe handles, trudged down the track to the small square where the newsagent's shop jutted out, its window shuttered and boarded up. They came up to the old man and his lamb, after a while, another old geezer joined them, short-legged and stocky, a walking hip flask. His breath seemed to drill his chest like a gimlet, but he lumbered along slowly.

"Darina," started one of the rawboned women, the thinner one, a shabby kite of a grandma, two laths tied together in the middle. "Darina, he entered my kitchen and stole my spoons. He nicked my copper cauldron and my shovel, too. I saw him, long Vladi he was! I told the cop everything and he scratched his head. That was all the cop did. 'What!' he said. 'Do you reckon I'm the sun and I'm supposed to shine exclusively in your backyard, eh?'"

"Darina," began the other woman, thin and narrow like a cat. "It's long Vladi. He went and broke into my house. He sat down at my kitchen table, 'Give me something to eat!' he ordered. What could I give him? I had some bean soup, but long Vladi said, 'Slaughter a chicken and cook me chicken stew. Do it. Or I'll chop your head off with the pickax!' On the following day, I went and told the cop what happened, and the cop said, 'I've warned Vladi all right, but I'm not a street lamp. I can't glow exclusively in your house!' I slaughtered no rooster and no chicken for Vladi, and he, the mean lawbreaker he was, marched to my garden and lifted my garden hose, Darina. I trust you more than I used to trust my father, may he rest in peace! I can't water my tomatoes now, woman. The heat will bake my plants, every one of them! Help me, Darina. Please! He'll be the death of me, he's eating my liver and he's drinking my blood! No one dares touch him, I tell you. No one!"

The big woman stared at them, coughed, and looked them in the eyes, keeping mum. Suddenly, she grabbed a piece of rope, coiled it around her elbow, and buckled her broad leather belt. A minute later, she hurtled down the field, trampling through thistles and thorns towards a dingy house. The wall around the ramshackle building had collapsed, and what was supposed to be a backyard was buried under old truck tires, rusty pans, wires and old stoves, broken plastic buckets, and garden hoses.

I followed Darina on tiptoe. If she met her maker, I would at least close her eyes.

A guy in a dirty denim shirt, more of a patchy beard than a face on him, showed up in front of the house a cleaver in hand. His steps were all edge and hate as he charged at full speed towards my huge friend.

"I'll kill you!" roared the man and swiped at my friend.

I couldn't make out what Darina did — elderberry bushes and nettles were all over the place, sprouting leaves as thick as the lava of that volcano on the TV, a jungle of wild nettles surrounded me as if a crazy farmer had planted, watered and sprayed manure on the lousy plants.

The two women, two shovels that had learned to walk, didn't venture to stir or take a step forward, their eyes riveted on their socks. Perhaps the man in the dirty denim shirt had already bumped Darina off, and it was their turn now. First, the taller woman who looked a little stronger crossed herself, then the other one made the sign of the cross, her head bent low as if they had already hanged her.

"Good God, the live coals we've buried our heads under! The goon had butchered her."

They froze in their tracks, scared to look up, mute as the nettles at their feet.

The sun waited in the sky, an immobile leech, angry and hard. The leaves of the elderberry trees rustled their edges heavy with red bugs that smelled foul if you stepped on them. Even I knew that if one of those nasty red beetles bit you, you'd swell and develop a fat blister on your stomach. The pus in the blisters smelled of the red bugs or worse. It hurt a lot. It hurt so much you felt like cutting your belly off. Suddenly, hissing and whooshing sounds hit my ears; clearly, a belt cracked and sank into a guy's back. A voice as deep as a moat, cool and hard, said, "If you steal something one more time — it can be breadcrumbs — if you pilfer something from Aunt Dobra and Aunt Petrana, I'll break your left shoulder. Then I'll break your right shoulder, too."

Mom Darina spoke calmly as she was picking apples to make apple pie. A belt wheezed and twanged, then went crashing to the back as Darina's voice went on picking apples, "Give back the garden hose to Aunt Dobra! Immediately bring me Aunt Petrana's shovel. Now! If you one more time — I repeat, one more time — set foot in their backyards, I'll cut off as many pounds of flesh from your butt as many steps you've made." The belt grew tired, but the deep voice went on, "Within ten minutes! I want you to give back everything to the women — within ten minutes! Pay both Aunt Dobra and Aunt Petrana… How much? Let me see… you don't have a penny to bless yourself with. So… You'll weed their strawberry beds for them. Now. I'll be watching you!"

* * *

After the car started, I remembered one thing. Shushomir had sobbed.

"Annie!" he shrieked. "Annie!"

"Shushomir!" I shouted from inside the car, but the windshield was thick and long as that railway tunnel under the Balkan Mountain in Bulgaria. The glass ate my words and Shushomir couldn't hear me.

"Shushomir, I'm Okay. Nobody's baking almonds for me here. No one's going to die!"

The nasty glass of the rear window, black as a gallows, hit my nose, so instead of screaming I got to thinking: death is my friend. It tells me where it plans to go. Now it keeps mum; this means it's far from us. Don't you be afraid, Shushomir, I'll run away from them. I'll come back to you and Darina. You can count on that! Then I saw through the foul window the car wolf down the road the way fire gobbled old newspapers. I was just about to turn on the waterworks when I remembered what Darina had told me, "If you turn on the waterworks, I'll take your head off!" She'd take it off when pigs learn to fly, the sweet huge darling! She'd kiss me on the forehead, although I hadn't washed my hair for days. I knew what you had to do when you couldn't keep your eyes from brimming with tears.

"Look at Momchil the cat," mom used to say before she died in her deep suitcase. "Watch closely Momchil the cat, Anna! He grazes on the grass every time he's feeling sad and eats two or three leaves of grass, the dark green ones. You too, when you're feeling sad and your eyes get scared, chew on some dark green grass."

Darina had promised me, "I'll come and I'll bring you back home from Sofia, Annie."

I tried hard to roll down the car window. It wouldn't budge, its cold glass as dead as a slaughtered rooster. It didn't open, the foul window it was, but I heard what mom Darina roared the way I could hear a bell chime, "I'll come to take you back home, Annie, sweetie."

What will I do? I'll chew on that grass in Sofia; it grows everywhere, a common weed, its leaves rolled into a ball and bitter as an apricot kernel. I'll be waiting. Mom Darina, I haven't got a belt. I haven't got any piece of rope. Even if I have, I'm pretty scraggy and I can't beat anybody. Don't worry, Mom Darina, this dark green grass grows all over the place for cats and kids like me.

*** * ***

In the park of a beautiful residential district in Sofia, all quiet and clean, a girl, perhaps six years old or younger, crouched in the grass. This was an unusual picture in the best area of the capital city. Here children were not left alone in the playgrounds, so, what was this kid doing in the public open space? The grass did not look yellow or matted, and was not strewn with broken glass and garbage. The girl plucked blades of grass and sniffed at them. After a while, she put a tuft of grass in her mouth and slowly, intently as if the sky had snapped, her face thin, the little girl ate the grass.

*** * ***

A dilapidated car crawled in front of the Jeep Wrangler. The woman behind the clunker's wheel had gray grizzled hair and wore glasses. The guy with blue earrings who drove the jeep honked his horn, the dwarf car jolted, and stopped. The driver of the Jeep Wrangler blew his horn, the jalopy started and crept up the hill. The jeep horn blared and hooted as the old boneshaker progressed even more slowly. The jeep came to a halt, the driver jumped out of the luxury vehicle, and his companion, a bearded bloke who probably would never be thirty again, rushed out, a baseball bat in hand. He hit the rear window of the dwarf car and broke it, sprinkling the asphalt with glass popcorns. The minuscule vehicle froze to a standstill. The bearded man sprinted forward, stopped abruptly and lashed at the windshield. The glass broke up into tiny crystal butterflies. In a flash, the baseball bat attacked the side window, did a good job of it, and the beard managed to get at the woman, a brown caterpillar writhing on her seat, her chest pressed against the wheel. The other guy gripped the woman's legs.

"Help!" she screamed.

Cars, some new and dazzling, others dusty as old boots, whooshed by. None of them stopped.

"Do you need help, sweetie?" the man with the earrings asked blandly as he slapped her across the face. The woman screamed. The pair of earrings pushed the granny into the roadside ditch, and his bearded companion kicked her by way of goodbye.

"Everybody has the right to live a normal life," he told her. "One must not stand in high-quality people's way."

The two men, their muscles erupting under their shirts, walked past the woman who had coiled herself up amidst glass shards, then they took their seats in a business-like and professional manner. The guy with the earrings switched on the car radio and listened to Lady Gaga's Poker Face. His companion smoked a cigarette. It was a pleasant drive. The jeep Wrangler left all other vehicles in the dust, making a joke of the bends in the road. The sky became overcast and quickly turned into an angry beauty queen. The heat retreated, giving way to a squall of cool air. The jeep drove faster, and the drive was even more enjoyable.

"You or me?" the guy behind the wheel asked in a rich, sonorous voice. A couple of minutes later they turned off onto a highway, an aluminum signpost announcing "Private Road". It was lined with cypress trees, protected bike lanes ran along its sides, violets, azaleas, arctic orchids, and other remarkable flowers bloomed at full steam. A magnificent place altogether.

"I'll be the first," said the guy with the earrings.

"It all depends," the sonorous voice objected. "Maybe she'll choose me."

"I'll be the first," the earrings repeated. The man's voice seemed to have been created solely for the sake of admiring flowers and unforgettable nature scenes, for there was much fine silk in it. The jeep acknowledged the barrier in front of the property with a rumble of gratitude and crept along the lane, a black snail boasting of a powerful engine in perfect harmony with the green landscape. Here, every detail kept a balance between excellence and peace. Politely, the lane vanished, and the wonderful evening descended over the massive door of silver metal. The jeep Wrangler stopped and came to attention, ready to salute. The driver discretely honked his horn, but the door didn't budge. The luxury vehicle waited. The weather was exactly the way poor writers described it: mild and lovely. The cypress trees that surrounded the jeep gave one the feeling of grief and loss, or of Mediterranean romance —depending on the availability or lack of banknotes in the respective person's pocket. It turned out the watched pot never boiled, and the long wait was not over. The sunset was all fire and gold as the earrings dragged on his cigarette.

"Crappy music. Stop it!" said the silky voice. The driver immediately pressed one of the dazzling buttons and Lady Gaga shut up. The driver, too, lit a cigarette. They both — the gold earrings and the mellifluous mouth — behaved in a civilized manner, smoking silently. The guys had lit many cigarettes since they'd arrived, but did not knock at the massive door. It was cloudy and the air was cool and fresh the way writers described it in the most recently published romance novels. The sky broke apart and hurled a handful of raindrops at the vehicle. The rain set in heavily, and the cavalry of the storm thudded against the roof panel of the jeep.

"Rotten weather!" the earrings pointed out.

"What's that worm dawdling over I wonder! We've already wasted the afternoon and the evening. And who does she think she is?" Evidently, the guy with the silky voice was inclined to draw revolutionary conclusions. "She's off her rocker. The worm is off his rocker too."

"Shut your trap!" the earrings snapped.

They took another smoke. It turned out June was the nastiest month of the year so far, searing heat first, then a steady drizzle and sludge. The weather had a screw loose.

Thunder rumbled, sheet lightning flickered among the clouds, the rain and the jeep hugged each other, wobbling like newly hatched swans. At a certain point, the massive door came to life and, languidly, as if in severe lower back pain, sank into the concrete platform in front of the powerful vehicle. A fine figure of a man emerged from the space as two searchlights lit up the wall under the overhang. The guy had long, artistically white hair. He waved lethargically at the two visitors; most probably his bones ached, and willpower alone kept him alive, or perhaps he suffered from the runs. The jeep recovered from an afternoon of poor quality slumber. With regal detachment, its tires licked the asphalt lane, clean and smooth like glass. The two men got off.

"You two smell, and you will be disinfected and cleaned," the white-haired sentry said. "Don't fool around with your shoes," he added as he threw towels at their feet. "Stench!"

"Who'll be the first man on the moon?" asked the earrings.

The white-haired judge of character did not even give him a glance because he rapidly developed an aversion to the total lack of logic in the visitor's question.

"Parallel slalom. Two skiers. It will be a head-to-head contest."

The two invitees exchanged glances. The white-haired weasel made a long arm for the drawer that gaped open behind his back.

"I'll examine you after you're done with disinfection. You'll put on these outfits…" the weasel chucked them ball-shaped objects that hit the floor not far from the towels. The bearded gentleman, the more impatient one, or perhaps a warrior better prepared to deal with extraordinary situations, lifted one of the little balls and unfolded it. A transparent, weightless lace skirt, this was all there was to it.

"What…" the bass voice with the earrings hobbled and dropped unable to reach the end of the sentence, finishing in the quagmire of the ellipsis, a row of three dots.

"The process of disinfection will be over in thirty-seven seconds," the white-haired pillar of strength announced. "Milady does not tolerate delays. She abhors violence and men who run behind schedule."

After thirty seconds, the two athletes — clothed in soft lace provided by the white-haired tower of strength — followed the tower into a brightly lit corridor with brilliantly mirrored walls. Without any warning sign, a large section of the mirror disappeared, and the two men hung their heads submissively as they fell to their knees.

A woman sporting remarkable muscle mass and stately ankles sat on an ordinary office chair, a rickety and rather old-fashioned thing. For a fraction of a second, she glanced at her visitors, then looked out the window, failing to acknowledge their presence.

"Well prepared for the game, are you?" the white-haired tower said.

The two gentlemen took their places. The white hair held up his hands as if conducting Swan Lake; however, the dance of the little swans would not play a substantial role in this elegant room. The white-haired manager in his elegant black suit tossed two transparent items onto the floor, the first one dazzlingly crimson, and the second emitting magnificent white radiance: two bridal veils with tiaras. The elegant suit didn't bother to provide any explanation or offer the guests chocolates from the superb box on the coffee table. The newcomers didn't seem to mind; they both looked neither pained nor distressed. Obviously, they were very well acquainted with the goal of their visit to this cozy place. Simultaneously, the two men put the veils on their faces, the earrings more nimble than the silky throat. They both were ready after eight seconds — disinfected skin and nails glowed, shoulders radiated potency under the soft femininity of Brussels lace.

Ten minutes later, Milady with the impressive ankles turned to face them. She wasn't smiling.

"You are totally getting in my hair. I accept no excuses. You're late," she said. "Take me by surprise. I'll have some honey cake. Now!"

She was barefoot, her toenails gleaming under a layer of enigmatic luminescent nail polish. Wrapped in a gold oriental robe — this was Okay. But why did Milady sit on this primitive, insultingly cheap chair? Has this moron, the white-haired worm, made her fly into a temper? She let her hands wander towards her waist, and that made everything clear. Simultaneously, the gentlemen fell to their knees making best efforts to perform the dance of the storm for their queen, creeping energetically down to her, two massive naked butterflies bathing in the golden radiance of the transparent lace, their stomachs shivering, fluttering like the eyelashes of a boy in love in the wonderfully fresh air. They were no butterflies, far from it! They were nightingales! Magnificent birds! A moment after the queen's index finger caressed the rosewood flooring, the feathered songsters embraced each other. The queen's palm flew off to the ceiling. The nightingales' veils, torridly entwined, conveyed the impression of harmony and warmth of a fire; however, after a short while the birds parted. Between them, something seemed to have died as the queen's thumb impatiently pointed at the floor. In a jiffy, the winged duo perched at Milady's feet. Her arms moved towards the headrest of the chair. The nightingales immediately gave up the ghost and were no more. Two assiduous bees replaced them, the two insects already working hard on the lady sovereign's sandals, the pair of earrings enveloped in white radiance tilted towards the perfection of the left leg; the purple flame, much softer and more graceful, set ablaze the mystic toenails in a tornado of quick, small kisses. The bigger insect's earrings clanked on the floor, but the noise didn't interfere with the wonderful havoc the honey cake had wreaked so far. First, the cloud of the polished toenails glowed crimson, then the pinky toe and its neighbor, the ring toe, lit up like candles with the alchemy of the bee's thick lips inclined to explore the softness of the skin. The insects kept on looking for nectar further up and further up. Through their soft insistence, they made the volcanic protuberances of the ankles and knees burn red hot; the tender wings patrolled carefully the innocent, very healthy thighs, two white islands of joy in the salvo of the queen's pulse. The bees had retraced their route a number of times in an attempt to find the right ratio of bliss, explosion and wisdom, always an honest contest, a parallel slalom event, from the foot of the mountain to Mount Everest. And, oh, the queen! A miracle occurred as the bees warmed to their eulogies of her nectar!

Honey is a sweet sticky substance used as food. Honey helps queens boost their immune systems. The white-haired sentinel, an epitome of loyalty, sat in a chair in front of the door.

"Oh, love is handsome and love is fine... the sweetest flower..." he recited with a warm feeling of fidelity. It was not his responsibility to announce the winner of the competition. Milady would give preference to the insect with a particular qualification or feature. She would write the champion a check, a large one. How much? He would like to know. After the event, the two bees would sure agree on how to split the money. The white-haired warrior did not bother to brood over revenue and expenses. His obligation was to provide a few lines of great poetry as a means of building strong relationships. "Build me a boat that can carry two. And both shall row, my love and I..." his voice trailed off pure as a mineral spring. The Bulgarian theatrical scene had lost exceptional talent and triumph in the shape of this white-haired man.

At the end of the poem, the urbane poetry lover gave a formal bow. Even the butler in *Vanity Fair* by William Thackeray couldn't compare to the white hair's delicacy and refinement. The Bulgarian butler believed he'd make a good impression on Milady if he offered her freshly squeezed cranberry juice, so he discreetly withdrew from the battlefield. His back touched the imposing mirror on the wall and it sank noiselessly into the floor. The polite aristocrat of the spirit disappeared in the corridor, and within seconds the mirror slid back into place.

A big black Jeep Wrangler was parked in front of an impressive building. A tall, white-haired man, practicing his poker face sat behind the wheel. A girl, six or seven years old — one could never be sure with kids these days — sat in the middle of the backseat. The girl was crying and wiping her tears that caused no problems. A huge woman in a faded floral dress stood some yards away, her coarse hair tied back in a ponytail. She held a skinny boy by the hand, a walking patchwork quilt — pieces of tattered cloth stitched hastily together. The boy was whimpering. He broke free from the big woman's grip, charged at the jeep, crashed into its door and hammered on the window with one small fist. The glass was black and didn't allow him to see who sat inside the vehicle. The kid pressed his puny chest against the glass and screamed, "Annie!"

The expression on the white-haired man's face remained unperturbed as he started the engine. The jeep drove off neither too slowly nor too fast. The boy fell onto the asphalt. The mountain in the floral dress lifted him. He seemed Okay.

"Shushomir!" whispered the girl who sat behind the driver.

The black vehicle drove along the panoramic road that was smooth as a shell of an egg.

"Carrot-cruncher, tie my shoelaces!" ordered the taller girl. The country kid boxed into a corner, her pink T-shirt crumpled, her potato-shaped head bent low, didn't dare to lift her eyes. One would think they were made of wood and someone had nailed them to the floor. She was small and her bones were cobwebs hardly able to keep the pink T-shirt in its place. The cobweb bones bowed over the trainers of the girl bursting with energy — and slowly as if the shoelaces were snakes, the moppet attempted to tie a basic knot.

"You are ham-fisted all over the place." The muscles of the big girl rippled beneath her tunic as she spoke. "Move it!"

The skinny child fell on her knees, almost lay on the floor, and started rubbing the tiles in front of the bigger girl's feet. The big one had strong ankles. The peasant girl shook, then sprinted to the table where mineral water bubbled in a crystal carafe — or was it a diamond bottle? Next to it, a gold glass sparkled. Very carefully, the yokel — surrounded by treasures and hardly able to catch her breath — poured water into the glass and dashed off to the pink princess, then her eyes returned where they belonged, to the floor.

"I don't want water," the athletic fairy said. "Do I make myself clear?" she added and splashed the contents of the glass on the floor. "Look here, you ruined the tile. It costs a fortune. Your mother must pay for it. And you'll learn you mustn't mess with me. I told you to tie my shoes, didn't I? You are stupid."

At first, the unschooled hick bent down to take care of the shoelaces — one could say a frog plopped into a pond to dodge the boot that was going to trample it underfoot. Then the frog seemed to have made up its mind there was no use running away. The poor bugger would better stretch its neck and croak loudly. The crumpled T-shirt darted forward and stopped in the corner. The small kid pressed her back against the paneled wall. Her wooden eyes flared, dog's fangs flashing in them. Her black hair was a mess as if it had been on fire. The flames had eaten a tuft here, left long wisps there, and singed everything to the bone elsewhere.

"I am not stupid," screeched the runt loudly as if her old shoes were in her mouth. "If you insult me one more time, I'll rip your head off."

The brawny child howled with laughter, stomach muscles jumped, and blue eyes brimmed with happy tears.

"O, my God!" the healthy child exclaimed. "You are not only stupid. You are brazen-faced!"

"What does 'brazen-faced' mean?" asked the girl with the badly shorn hair.

"'Brazen-faced' means 'dumb' and 'sassy' rolled into one."

"Now I know," nodded the runt.

The rosewood tiles trembled. Darn it! Where do all those pink apple trees grow? They must have cut a forest to make the floor of this room.

The old pants suddenly swooped down like hawks, noiselessly and savagely. It didn't become exactly clear what happened — did the cobweb bones smash into the sturdy blonde chest? Or had the fists — cuts all over the place, dirt under the nails — sunk into the blue-eyed belly? The gorgeous girl, a head taller than the runt, ended up lying prostrate on the floor, her willpower and brawn as good as a bowl of soup.

The scraggy kid, lost in her wide-leg pants, bent over the blonde one and said evenly as if the wall had spoken in a human voice, "Next time you insult me, I'll break your left elbow."

A sudden silence fell over the room. For a while, as long as it took you to check if you had a fiver in your purse, nothing stirred.

"Mommy! Ivan!" the blond girl screamed. The blonde lips couldn't produce any statement or maybe they did; however, the scream was so high-pitched that the whole sentence drowned in it with the exception of the vowel sounds, "Ow! Ow! O-o!"

For sure, the provincial weed couldn't scream like that. The big girl did.

The tall butler in his elegant suit rushed into the room brought to the boil with anxiety.

"This foul… This cheeky…" for the first time the robust girls had used comprehensible words; prostrate on the floor though the kid was, she looked really impressive. "She hit me! I'll die. Call Doctor Petkov! Call the urgent care center. If I breathe my last, my mother will chop you up and you will stew in your own juice. Mom will feed you to the dogs. Ivan! Kick her, you fool!"

The runt, a turtle that had just crossed a busy highway without getting crushed by truck tires, retreated to her corner. Her bones of hoar frost — or maybe she didn't have bones at all — clung to the wall and stayed put — a fishing rod prepared for an outing. The fishing rod, however, had eyes that watched the white-haired virtuoso. He came up to the runt, taking polite steps of a man in an expensive jacket who, parallel to his loyalty to Milady, could probably cut throats.

"If you cut my throat," started the little one, her ribs jittery, "or if you say I'm cheeky, I'll break your left elbow. Then I'll break your right elbow too." The kid's words were smooth as the floor under her shoes.

The suit burst out laughing and was soon bent over double with guffaws, but a butler even a talented one, shouldn't take the liberty of chortling with delight.

"You're fired! Idiot!" shrieked the blonde girl as she rose to her feet that looked more impressive than Mount Everest.

* * *

DEARR ANNIE

I AM OK

BUT tT'S AIN'T OK WITHOUTT YOU

ITS BAD WHEN YOU'RE IN SOFIA

VERY BAD

I WILL COME.

I'LL COME TO SOFIA

I'LL FINDE YOU

DARINA TOLD ME

WE LL TAKE YOU BACKK HOME

ME AND DARINA WILL

WAITE FOR ME

YOU DON'T KNOWE ALL LETTERS OF THE ALFABET
ASKE SOMEBODY TO REED YOU WHAT I WROTEE TO YOU

ANNIE
ESCAPE FROM PRISON

SHUSHOMIR

✳ ✳ ✳

A tall man, a beanpole so thin the breeze might snap his spine in two, sat on the scorched grass. He was clutching a bottle on account of which the universe smelled of plumb brandy. The man didn't care a fig about the universe as he drank from his bottle, a stream trickling down his neck. Thus, the triple distilled thunder, the source of national pride in Staro, went to the dogs. Only God in high heaven knew how the wild damson trees managed to blossom in the sand and where they stole water from to survive on. The guy didn't give a tinker's damn about the damsons, sour snakes that ripened on the trees. A boy sat close to the man, curled up into a ball, a scrawny thing, his red hair cropped close to the skull, and his skin badly sunburnt. A tear heavy as a potato beetle trickled down the man's cheek.

"They took Anna from me," the man said.

The scrawny thing reached out his hand, plucked a blade of grass, rusty in the heat of September and chewed on it. After a while, the kid's mouth went rusty too.

"They took Annie," the boy said. "I'll find her."

"When pigs fly," muttered the man.

At that point, in the dry backyard, a man came into view, tall, his head hitting the wild grapevines, his eyes as sour as the grapes. How could these vines squeeze any moisture from the poor soil, which out of habit village folks called "land"? It was all cinders and stones. The newcomer, ginger-haired like the scrawny boy, was cinders and stones, too. His shoulders looked bigger than the barn across the street, an unshaved wolf of a man, his red beard shaggy and horrible.

"Dad, don't hurt him!" the child said. "Please, dad, don't beat him up!"

The ginger heap of muscles flopped down onto the yellow grass. Now he was a length of a rope strong enough to hang someone, his huge knee almost touching the beanpole's tattered pant leg. Keeping mum, the ginger-haired mountain took the bottle from the hand of the other man. He was silent for a while, then poured liquor into his throat, coughed, waited, coughed again, and drank fiercely as if he hated the damson trees and the brandy which was as hard as the hill.

"You're not going to die," the beard, a huge red anthill on the burly guy's face, muttered. "Stop sniveling. You are not a woman."

Another potato beetle, bigger than the first, slid down the thin man's cheek. His eyes were a dark deserted road.

"They took Anna from me," said he.

The boy didn't say a word, his ginger hair trimmed so neatly you'd think: they must've given Tano the barber two sacks of potatoes to spruce this kid up. The head that Tano the barber had turned into a hairdresser's masterpiece drooped. A thistle in the field it was. The boy, a future man, was silent. The grass, old and patient like the stones under it, kept mum. The red beard had harvested more hay than all trains in Bulgaria could carry in the rocky valley gnawed by the sun. The kid sobbed.

"Shut up!" the beard ordered and hit the boy on the back of his neck. "You're not a baby."

The boy who until that moment was a future man suddenly became a child thin as a moonbeam, a mite broken into two edgy halves.

"They took Annie from me, dad," the boy said.

His father caught him by the shoulder. This big hand patted the boy on the back, slowly as if drops of autumn rain sprinkled the scrawny T-shirt.

"No one can take your girl from you, son," said the ginger-haired mountain. "Drink!" he said as he passed the bottle to the gangly man who had buried himself in the grass. "Come on. Drink!"

* * *

"Tub of lard, drop to your knees! I want to ride you," said the girl who had the brawn and good blonde hair. A dazzling solar explosion in the immaculately clean room she was. In the corner, a mushroom eaten by worms through and through, the same age as the blonde explosive, my daughter waited, her eyes nailed to the carpet on the floor. I imagined what it would be like: I sink to my knees, making myself convenient to be ridden. A blonde girl sits proudly astride me, and my daughter watches. I'm on all fours, neighing, and whinnying.

"Would you like to race with me, Elizabeth?" I asked the girl's powerful layer of muscles as I smiled sweetly at her.

"No. On your knees!"

"Let's wrestle," I suggested trying to avert a catastrophe. I knew Elizabeth's fists left bruises in their wake. This time, she didn't care about bruises. The blond fairy bit me through my pant leg. Her teeth didn't set me free before I started to bleed.

"I'll box your ears if you don't behave," she said, razor blades clanking in her throat.

I could feel my daughter's eyes on my face. They were dark and wild.

"My mother's hired you to amuse me. She's paying you seven times as much as a high school teacher gets paid. You don't amuse me."

I needed the money. I wanted to break free from Sofia, from the drab blocks of flats and the exhaust fumes. Where could I go? I was looking for a job. An old woman wanted me to run her market stall for her, 20 euro per day, working seven days, Monday through Sunday, until "the end of the season". I was a skivvy, yes, but they had given me a roof over my head and room in the servants' quarters. A clean place, next to the gym which belonged to Elizabeth, the lassie who had twice as many teeth in her mouth than us lesser mortals. Ivan often sent for me; believe it or not, the princess was afraid of the dark. She shrieked and twitched in her sleep. Wrapped in her duvet, she leaped out of bed and rushed to me, terrified. She scratched me and made me sing to her. If the mademoiselle didn't like the song, she dashed into her mom's room in the middle of the night to voice a complaint against me. Madam Percha dolled up to kill, her gold nightgown from Dusseldorf magic in the dusk, swooped down on me. Milady made me croon cradle-songs until the crack of dawn. I thought of Hush a Bye Baby as a terminal disease. In the morning, my eyes looked puffy and swollen. The only verb I hated in my life was "to hush".

I still hadn't sunk to my knees when the blonde grenade pounced on me, and my belly hit the floor. The lassie straddled my back, her iron knees flattening me, her fingers gripping tufts of my hair.

"Neigh!" she ordered.

I didn't neigh. I kept seeing my daughter's dark eyes in the corner of the room. At a certain point, my blonde charge produced a hundred-dollar bill from her pocket and slowly waved it under my nose.

"You like it, don't you? Neigh!" she said as she jabbed her heels in my ribs.

I neighed. She immediately stuffed the bill in my mouth. I choked. My stomach heaved.

Then — like a black mudslide, like gravel of a swollen river — the corner wrenched itself free. My daughter — a mole gone mad, a worm cut in half, advanced and fell on the blue-eyed princess. My girl, desperate blood oozing from an infected wound, flew at me. After

Annie arrived in Sofia, she refused to put on light-colored clothes. She scribbled the letter D on any scrap of paper she could lay her hands on — old newspapers, train tickets, love letters Mrs. Percha received on a daily basis. It was I who paid volunteers to pen torrid epistles to Milady.

My daughter, the scrawny letter D, flew from the corner yellow as jaundice and gripped the blonde hair. Elizabeth, strong Elizabeth with her pearl-white teeth, was wallowing in the chastity of the carpet like an old sock. My fearless T-shirt that had no beginning or end straddled Elizabeth, grabbed her by the scruff of the neck, and yelled, "Neigh, Elizabeth!"

Elizabeth bit her lower lip.

"Neigh, Elizabeth! If you don't start now, I'll break your left elbow!"

Even before the sentence reached its exclamation point, the blonde mouth made a wild, ear-rending neigh that hit hard he walls of the gym. The sounds were shrill and deafening.

Elizabeth was neighing.

✳ ✳ ✳

A situation arose. To be honest, I didn't know what the meaning of the word "situation" was, but I'd heard you had to always remedy it. A woman white as the ceiling of my room made me watch as she kneaded and squeezed the backs of well-fixed people. I wondered what "well-fixed" meant, most probably it was "grumpy". The woman whose face was an expensive white bar of soap rubbed heels, asses, legs, and everything well-fixed you could think of. She insisted she was my grandma.

"I don't have a grandma, woman. Go knead those backs and keep quiet. Don't you pull the wool over my eyes! How come my grandma massages fools' asses? I don't have such a lowly grandma. If I had one, she would have planted peppers and tomatoes, my grandma would. She must've weeded strawberry beds and started the petrol pump to bring water from the river to her tomatoes. If you, lying woman, rub folks' bellies, you can't grow peppers! And if you can't, you're not my grandma."

"I am. You look like me. Your eyes are brown, too," the silly woman said.

"Frogs have brown eyes as well," I said. "Are frogs your grandchildren? They can be, but I'm not." She said nothing. This woman had no backbone, then where did she keep her nerves and all, I wondered. She had no face; she had soap. She had a cold draft in her mouth and no words.

"I have my Darina," I told her at the very beginning, and she knew the truth. "Darina is my mom in the village of Staro. I have a friend Shushomir, the smartest kid in the world. And I have my aunt Vera, Shushomir's mom. She's fat, but she isn't shifty like you. You have no eyes. You have two freezing buckets of paint instead."

"You talk too much, Annie."

"I do because you're weak. I can beat you up any time I want," I told her honestly.

Darina had explained to me everything about being strong. I called her "mom", and she called me "Annie" or "sweetheart". No one had ever called me "sweetheart" before I met Mom Darina. "Annie, sweetheart, if you beat their pants off, nobody will yell at you."

✳ ✳ ✳

The blonde caterpillar says she'll give me the thrashing I deserve. Wait a minute! She approaches me slowly, sliding along the floor exactly like the sideboard dad pushed towards the kitchen door some time ago. Mom said it was no good and she wanted to get rid of the mold smell. I won't let the blonde tank touch me, not a chance. She's all thumbs.

"You are dumb. Come here!" she orders. "I'll teach you a lesson."

"Why don't you come up to me if you're so smart? You don't dare to lay a finger on a dumb girl. What would you do if I was smart?"

Her chest is hard as a skateboard, I know. She hurls herself at me. I dodge to the left. The blonde shell collides with a chair and collapses on the floor, a heap of muscles and teeth. I jump on her back and dig my old trainers into her ribs.

"Hi, Elizabeth! A stupid carrot-cruncher is teaching you a lesson. Don't forget to say 'thank you.'"

The blonde girl's screams are shrill and echo through the house. Here comes Madam Percha — I've dubbed her Wooden Percha - seething and wanting to know, "You are trampling her to death. Why? Tell me! Now!"

"Because she said I was dumb. I whupped her ass. What do you think she is? Smart?

"Mom, tie her up! Tie her quick!"

"Tie her yourself. You are two twice as big," says Percha. Her words taste sweet, but her eyes hate me. If she could, her eyes would drown me in the glass aquarium in which her pet fish are jailed for no reason at all. Percha wants to make me glug all the water in the aquarium the way dad swilled brandy all day and fell into the river blind drunk. Mom Darina whispered something in his ear and he braced himself for a rough landing. There's no one in the house to whisper anything to me.

"This is for you," Percha says. She puts her hand in her pocket and produces money, not coins I've known for years. A big fat bundle of money it was. "Go buy yourself a posh phone. I hope Elizabeth will allow you to trample her underfoot tomorrow again. She's a lame duck, and I'm ashamed of her."

I reach for the bundle, but even before I pocket it, Elizabeth — I don't know what a "lame duck" means, it must be something like "soft-headed" or thereabouts — the lame duck breaks herself free from my sneakers, grips my legs and hauls me down to the floor. Her fists hit my eye as Percha breathes happily, watching. It's too early to rejoice, Milady. Maybe I'll knock you off your perch.

"Elizabeth, your cheek's bleeding!" I shout before she treads on my neck. "Look!"

The duck cranes her neck, and I bash her on her big head. All my fingers hurt. Elizabeth bawls and swims in a blonde lake of spit and tears; I get off to a good start. As I take a furtive step away from Percha her eyes tell me things I wouldn't like to hear.

"Stupid! Ugly!" the blonde eel whimpers, brokenhearted.

"Elizabeth! Don't forget that a stupid and ugly girl beat the living daylights out of you under your mom's nose in your own room," I speak evenly tying the words with the cold and long thread of fear.

"Mom, punish her!"

Percha says nothing and if Percha keeps quiet, Ivan the white-haired petticoat will soon show up. His name is Ivo; however, the blond miracle and her mom think it's too unsophisticated (kill me if I know what this one means; in my view, it must be something like "Hey, bitch, come here") so they gave him an attractive name — Ivan.

If Ivan shows up, I'm in for a kick, so I take it easy.

"Mom, beat her!" the blonde crate screams from the floor, and there's no more air to breathe in the room. Elizabeth's voice puts on weight, the aquarium and the fish in it shake. Elizabeth, drool smearing her chin, mentions a word I haven't heard so far. She's familiar with things I've never seen, but I'll see all of them for sure.

Ivan, in a black suit, comes running like a puppy. In Sofia, asphalt and paving stones are all over the place, so I wonder where they'll bury him if he cashes in his chips. Or will Milady drop him into the waste bin?

"Tie her up!"

Ivan will be the moon in the sky at noon before he ties me up. He carries a coil of rope, but I am not scared — the rope's thin as a bottle of sore throat remedy. The butler bends down to bind my hands and feet. Give me a break! I remember well, "Take aim with your fist where it hurts the most. Take good aim, and he'll howl with pain for a week, Annie, sweetheart." I know pretty well what gets Ivan into trouble. I give him a kick, a big one, and the next thing I see is an expensive suit lying prone on the floor. I'm not clear about the meaning of "prone", it surely has to do with guys finding you stretched out in your best black pants, your face on the ground. The butler keeps quiet, his white head close to the blonde worm's as I sprint full speed to the corner.

"If you try to tie me up, I'll break your left elbow," I say and my voice is all knives and tripwires.

Percha's gaze has no good news for me, I'm sure of it. Her eyes smell of roasted almonds.

"My Goodness!" Percha says. "She's made a woman out of you, Ivan, my dear friend!"

Ivan in a black suit on the floor…

We had a ewe that Darina slaughtered and dragged a 9 inch-long flatworm out of it. Ivan writhes exactly like that worm. The blonde duck jumps up. She'll bite me if she catches me, and she'll catch me when Ivan's white shirt takes root.

"Percha, death lives in your eyes," I tell her.

She stops staring at me and coughs instead, a frog in her throat. She's coughing her head off the way I've never heard her before. Yesterday, Elizabeth told me that the glass box in which the pet fish lives was called aquarium. I believed her. I shouldn't have. The blonde flatworm lies every time she opens her mouth.

✳ ✳ ✳

"You are not my grandmother," I tell the woman who doesn't have eyes. She has two slits instead and she paints them every morning with a tiny brush. You cannot see her skin, she has a jar of pink mess that she daubs on her nose and ears. The old battle-axe looks light-green around the gills, so I wonder — does she smell of roasted almonds? Does she invite death, my old friend, to dinner? Death treads ash into the carpet under mom's bed. It's a big bed, I have my side of it, and mom has hers. Mom can't die twice, so I think that my side of the bed is an oven, and I sleep in it with a bag of almonds.

"I'm your grandmother. You must not feel hostile towards Elizabeth, my child. You should not rub her the wrong way."

"You can't tell me what to do. You have taught me not one letter of the Bulgarian alphabet, so you are nobody."

Her white face dissolves in the white color of her teacup as she says, "You are a wolf cub adrift and isolated in the city."

"If you say I am a wolf cub, I won't believe any word you say. I am not a wolf, I'm a child, woman. "Cut adrift" means "crazy as a brush", but I'm not crazy. I can pick up a trail of a rabbit and I can kick a hawk if he swoops down to kill a chicken. I can catch a snake with my hands. A snake is ten times smarter than you, woman, especially a horned viper."

"I am your grandmother, and I love you."

"My grandmother doesn't smudge her cheeks with pink clay to hide the lines around her mouth. My grandmother doesn't knead old farts' backs for money."

"You are like me," the confused woman says. "I can smell death, too."

"Hey!" I cut her short. What was the white bar of soap, the sneaky shrew, thinking about? "Death talks to everybody, to you and to me."

"Your mother loves you. She stays in Mrs. Percha's house for your sake."

"My mother died," I told the woman white as aspirin. "Mom died long time ago. She showed me the suitcase she'd shoved her death in. If mom had been alive, she'd have never allowed fat-assed Elizabeth to ride her."

"Your mother puts up with Elizabeth because she has no money. She needs money to buy you a T-shirt and new jeans.

"I'll sweep the floor of Fedo's second-hand shop. I'll bring him water to drink and he'll give me black jeans. I will let nobody ride me. Nobody! You, woman, can smell death as long as you want. It's none of my business. You knead rich oily butts and that's why you're oily like them."

The old woman's name is Lena; I am Annie, and she's getting ready to knead Percha's belly. The tomahawk, clean as an ambulance, will be beaming at Milady all the time. This is the clearest proof she isn't my grandmother.

"I don't care about you, or about death," I tell her. "I care about Shushomir."

* * *

Mom sat down at the table. Why? Percha, mom, and an old geezer — mom led him to his chair as if he couldn't walk by himself — were all beaming faces and sugar. Another guy, thin as a thermometer, more of a donkey's tail than a man, showed up. There was not a drop of color in his face as he told the old fogey, "Dad, dear, after you!!"

The woman, who lied that she was my grandmother, brought everybody coffee and things to eat. She beamed at the geezer, purred, "Mr. Vasilev, please be seated," as she pointed to the soft French easy chair. She went on kissing the floor before him, her voice a bar of chocolate stretching for miles, turned to the colorless one, "Mr. Vasilev Jr, please take a seat. I dedicate this dinner to you: rabbit pie made to a traditional Bulgarian recipe — my late grandma's best choice, God rest her soul. <u>Bon appétit!</u>"

I peeked into the room. No one noticed me. Alas! That was what they said on TV if they couldn't convince you to buy the best shoes ever or the softest mattress.

I was sure it was Percha who declared, "I wouldn't like to tax your intellect, gentlemen; therefore we'll be having an adults-only dinner."

Mom grinned so hard I was afraid that both her front and back teeth hurt. I felt like sprinting full speed to her.

"Have no fear!" was all I wanted to whisper in her ear, but the woman who fibbed she was my grandma slammed the door in my face.

* * *

"Don't go to Sofia, Darina! The city's bigger than you, you can't beat the snot out of it. Darina, don't go. In Sofia, guys are double-dealing mouths, their tongues are made of fraud, and their purses are full of scams. In Sofia, they don't look you in the face, they look at your pockets. In Sofia, your neighbors' words are honey, and their hearts are mud. Don't go to Sofia, Darina! Without you, they'll steal all the roof tiles over our heads. They'll bump off the old women and they'll be ripping the undershirts off the old mens' backs!"

Darina, bigger than a bus and taller than the bus driver, said nothing as she stood there in her faded floral print dress. For some reason, the bus was late, some strangers were also waiting at the bus stop, and you couldn't say who was who: a nutcase, a thief, or a guy like you and me. The folks that had come to see Darina off looked at her. Some were hunchbacks, others were limping behind the crowd, still others spat as they spoke, a few heads twitched, nickels and dimes tinkled in most pockets. White heads, gray heads, black, and hazel heads — they all circled around Darina.

"You won't find Annie, woman. Her dad would've brought her back home if it'd been that easy. You can't pick a fight with big money. An honest woman like you gets stuck like a sow in the mud the minute she has no penny to bless herself with. Are you willing to get your hands dirty, eh? No, not by a long shot. Money will be your grave, big gal. 'Hey, flagpole, who are you? This little girl is none of your business. Don't touch her. You are not her mom. Why did you bring your fat ass into Sofia, bulldozer?' that's what the big shots will ask you."

"I'm the little girl's mom."

"Come off it! Did you give birth to her, eh?"

"I taught her to be a child. She won't lick anybody's boots."

"A fat lot of good that will do her."

"I taught her to write seven letters of the Bulgarian alphabet, the most difficult ones."

The month of September was a puddle of boiling water, the day was a bowl of chicken soup, but there was no chicken in it, the sky was scorching hot clouds, but why should you waste the word "clouds" on them? The rain must have beaten it for Sweden and left no drop of moisture behind its tail — as everybody could see.

"Listen," said the tall woman who had bought the most expensive dress in the store since the day the sales assistant opened the commercial establishment. The clothing label said 100% cotton. But how could cotton dig into the skin of your arms and cut it? Was it made of nails? Darina's words weren't words made of cotton either. "If some squirt steals a thing here in the village… if a bonehead pilfers an apple or a pear when I'm not in Staro, I'll break his left hand. I'll do it the minute I'm back. Then I'll break his right hand too."

Behind the clump of trees, an engine roared. Who was driving? A thief who'd stolen a truck, a motorbike its tires thunder and fire, or perhaps it was the bus that trundled through the valley ready to transport you half-baked, half-choked to Sofia?

"Aunt Darina! Take me with you!" A boy, his hair a nosegay of dry red thistles, a scrawny thing, his sunburnt face way darker than his arms, raced to meet her. The kid stopped in front of the woman and clasped his hands around her legs. Another woman, plump and short, chased him along the path in the field strewn with stones. The yellow grass had run wild with the complaints of grasshoppers in the last hot day of the autumn. Some folks wondered where the roly-poly sweetheart had bought her jeans from, simultaneously so short and wide that your thoughts whirled in your head. A round and chubby housewife she was. Perhaps Fedo's second-hand store had provided the woman with that unique pair; it offered you pants and skirts for nothing, an honest shop all normal people purchased their changes of clothing from.

Finally, the rickety bus arrived.

The housewife, a ball of cheese, grabbed the ginger-haired kid, pulled at his shirt as she tried to wrench him from the huge woman in the most expensive dress procured from Fedo, the junk dealer. Honestly, an article of clothing tied around the tall woman's waist looked downright frightening. The boy didn't budge, his hands clutching at her powerful legs and the flowers of her painted dress. Slowly, gradually, he lost the battle, let slip his grip on the strong cloth, but held on to the hem of the dress like grim death as if his whole life depended on it, and not only his life — the universe, its sun, winds, and stars depended on it. The Milky Way and all the neighbors waited in that hem. The universe was a place not far from the post office where the wild cherry trees grew. You could pick cherries — fill your hat with them — and then give all you'd picked to a girl, her hair dark as a blackbird's wing.

The red-haired boy didn't let go of the faded hem, although the big woman tried to push him away as she stood by the electric pole. The short one, round and soft, a bunch of grapes rather than a chubby housewife, wrenched the kid's arm from the faded dress, but he clung to Darina, a boy whose hair was a swoop of cranes and a field of orange crocuses. It was no good. The plump one, this angry unripe bunch of grapes, slapped his hands, smacked his fingers, pulled at his wrists and finally managed to wrest the ginger child from the most expensive dress in Fedo's second-hand store. She rested on her oars for a bit, but the kid was tough, a stinging nettle that pierced granite was that kid. The woman went on yanking at him, she grabbed his arms the way a thief snatched your purse and pulled hard, a plump Madonna who dragged her son through the deserted field. The village of Staro had already lost everything: the grass and the seeds. The wind still waited there but wasn't happy in the oven of the September heat.

The boy was kicking and flailing, his cheeks smeared with mud, his face wet.

"Let go of my hand, mom!"

She didn't let go of the kid, she pressed him to her chest, her face a heap of stones that had forgotten what the river looked like. Salt was all that was left of the whirlpools. There was no mud and no dust. The month of September was weak and hungry; it had gobbled down the fish and the crabs and now was waiting on the road for the old bus.

"Let go of me, mom!"

The woman didn't let him go. She was afraid of the deserted road which was slowly sinking into the autumn. She wished she was a flock of crows that was flying away from this yellow field.

✳ ✳ ✳

That day, I let her box my ears. I had dreamed about Shushomir. It felt like I got a Christmas gift. Shushomir, the smartest kid in the world, the strongest one, almost as nimble as me said he'd baked apple pie for me.

"This dirty black T-shirt again! It smells. You smell!" Elizabeth lunged forward and reached for my throat, but this time I didn't move aside. I was getting fed up with the blonde mat. I was an honest and just kid. "If you lie to folks, I'll break your left elbow, Annie. Then I'll break your right elbow, too," Darina had said to me, and I had no choice. I grew up decent and fair-minded.

"Elizabeth, if you so much as lay a finger on me, I'll break your left elbow. If you hit me, I'll catch you even if Percha and Ivan hire Navy helicopters to protect you. All the ships of the Bulgarian Navy won't be able to guard you closely enough. I'll find you, you blonde worm! You know about your elbows, I've already explained what will happen to them."

Even though I'd never fought against helicopters, the blonde chicken comb flopped over, and her fists were boiled potatoes slowly turning into potato puree.

"You wear the same stinky T-shirt every day. Why? Your idiotic mother bought you clothes, but you're dumb. You go on making an ass of yourself, don't you, carrot-cruncher?"

"You say mom's idiotic. This means you have no brain in your head. You have pork fat instead."

"Your mom's crappy. She creeps on all fours and grovels to my mom."

"My mom was dead, but she weaseled out of death's suitcase and found the way home. Few mothers can do that and come back to their girls. If you call her 'crappy', what will you say about your own mom? She's so evil that dogs are scared and wouldn't bite her."

"Your T-shirt is ugly! Bite the dust, idiot! I'll throw your dead body to Hunter, my bulldog. He'll chew on your bones."

I wore this T-shirt because I loved it. It was Shushomir's, his mom Vera dug it out of a moth-eaten bag. She gave me Shushomir's black short pants, too. I had the most magnificent dress, Mom Darina bought it for a heap of money, I put it on every evening and I spoke to the dress. I imagined I was talking to the big sweet lady, "Hey, Mom Darina, who brings you the long piece of rope after I went to Sofia? Who helps you water your pepper plants? Mom Darina, come to me! I have a new mobile phone. It's called Andro or Droid, I'm not exactly sure. It's on the table. Give it a ring! Come! Teach me another letter of the Bulgarian alphabet. I'll write you a message. Here it is, I wrote it, all the seven letters you taught me typed next to one another, Mom Darina. The thing I wrote to you means, "Please come! I'll call you Mom all the time. You won't break my elbow if I mess up our living room. At times, even good women just shoot the breeze. They mean no harm. At times, even smart women like you get confused and end up sharing a pillow with my dad. He drinks a lot and makes lousy love. All the films I've wasted my time watching on TV tell the same story: you die of love and broken heart. But if you hadn't got confused, Mom Darina, how could you have found me? How could you become my mom? You taught me to beat the socks off thieves, liars and stinkers. It's good you showed me how to duck down. I do it well and my enemy's fists don't clout me across the face. The stinkers shout their heads off, call me names, and always hit the roof. It's the wind they scream at. I hit them where it hurts. You opened my eyes. It's important to know where your hater's body hurts the most because you can bring death to this spot. On the other hand, you can clean the floor in front of a guy. You give him water to drink too. It's up to you.

Mom Darina, it's no good pretending. It hurts. My heart's in my mouth day and night. I dream about Shushomir and I dream about you. Come to Sofia. Come to me, Darina, please."

I was still thinking of my enormous mom when I felt the blonde worm's teeth sink into my neck. I was sure a stray dog was in pain like that at the moment he breathed his last. I was going to die. Could I, like Mom, find my way from death's suitcase back to the village of Staro? To Darina and the river? Mom did come back; that meant I could do it too. I lay dying, but my ugly wound chased away death, and all that remained with me was pain, sitting by my side, sharp and large-toothed.

"You have a lot of fighting spirit, Elizabeth!" Percha said. Her admiration clambered like a lizard over a sunlit stone wall. "Well done, my child! Bravo!" Elizabeth's blonde teeth sank deeper into my throat. It felt bad. Blackness enveloped me. I couldn't breathe. Her teeth led me to death, but I wouldn't be pushing up the daisies, far from it. I didn't catch a whiff of roasted almonds. At a certain point,

I remembered what Darina had taught me, "Your kick is bigger than the pain," so I gave the worm a good kick at the spot where it hurt most. The worm wasn't a guy, I knew, yet this tender spot was sure to give her trouble. My knee was all bones and edges, so the blonde worm shrieked and screamed blue murder after I broke free from her teeth. I felt like an egg that a goose had just laid. Then, oh then! — blood, warm and all of it mine, soaked in Shushomir's T-shirt and his short pants. It stained the worm's clean cheeks and her red trainers. My strong courageous blood was all over the place, drops of it spattering on the floor. If your blood soaks in a thing, this thing becomes yours. Darina told me once. "Bulgarian blood has soaked in this poor land. That's why this land is ours."

The blouse, the undershirt, the pants, and the panties of the blonde egg were smeared with my strong blood. They were all mine.

"Ivan!" Percha shrilled.

The silver-haired broomstick didn't wait for me to aim a kick at the spot that hurt most. He advanced on me, a big cage in hand, and trapped me in it. Blood spurted from my wound and flowed like brandy. Mom Darina had explained to me, "Your throat is made of vocal cords." Now, perhaps both the throat and its vocal cords were sloshing around on the floor. I was sure I could neither speak nor stand up. This meant I was about to kick the bucket. I scanned the room looking for anything resembling cords and saw none.

Percha produced a bundle of greenbacks thick as a slice of bread and said, "Magnificent, my little girl. Over the weekend, I'll take you to Switzerland, and there you'll get some rest. I am proud of you!"

Elizabeth pocketed the money, came up to the cage inside which I was locked, and waved at my nose.

"Now you know what I can do."

"Let me out of the cage!"

Both Percha and Ivan burst out laughing.

"If you don't stop chortling before I count up to seven…" I could only count up to seven, "… I'll break your left shoulder…" I started evenly stiff as the wire with which dad mended our broken picket fence. It did a good job this fence did, stopping Shushomir's tribe of goats from nibbling at our apple trees. Wire mixed with blood before I counted up to four, five… Then the darkness was everywhere.

…The fog dispersed. They had removed the cage, I was in my bed, and the woman who lied she was my grandma was spreading bubbling goo over the wound on my throat. The thing smelled worse than the poison in her bottles she treated her famous clients with. The old one didn't become aware of the awful stench. Her nose must have gone all wrong.

"Woman," I said to her. "Please help me put on the dress mom has bought me."

She brought me a frock sewn without pattern or worse: it was patterned after a baggy nightgown. Its fabric was thick as the asphalt on the road, and was pink all over the place. Pink is a treacherous color, Darina used to say. She'd go off the deep end, even worse, she'd be hopping mad the minute she clapped eyes on this dress.

"I want the dress Mom Darina bought me, woman!"

"But your birth mother paid a small fortune for this little frock of yours two days ago."

"My mom who visited death didn't buy this ugly thing. My birth mom wouldn't come running back to fawn over your friend Percha," I spoke and it hurt. I suspected I had damaged two or three vocal cords in my voice and now I had to tie them up. A nasty job! "Give me the best dress I have. Mom Darina paid for it. I love it."

"Didn't we throw it in the trash can long ago?"

I told her I'd die soon. And I started dying. I didn't know how many days I slept in death's suitcase. It was in my nightmares that I'd found the road that took Mom back to Percha. Mom served Milady her coffee and spoke softly to Elizabeth. I thought the blonde lizard's throat was constantly full of coins that jangled. I'd rather Elizabeth's mouth was filled with gravel; thus she wouldn't be able to shriek at anybody. I was sure that if your throat was full of coins, you of course spoke English.

I still couldn't master that language. It was true I'd made efforts. I pilfered several pebbles from the fish aquarium, put all of them plus two blades of grass in my mouth, and said, "Shushomir, how are you?" But how could Shushomir understand me if he didn't speak English?

The pebbles were small, but they knew all there was to know about English. They didn't speak a word of Bulgarian, and Shushomir, the smartest boy in the world, try as he might, couldn't make heads or tails of what they said. It was a pity I was going to die. I wanted to see Shushomir so much, but the black fog swirled over my head. That was the end. I forgot the pebbles, the fish aquarium, and even the pain scampered up the wall, its tail tucked between its legs. I guessed it ran away from me because it looked for another child to hurt. I could feel death tiptoeing on the blanket. It was fun, honestly. At a certain point, I'd fallen asleep again.

… How come I was back home? I couldn't explain even if my mom's life depended on it. I was with my new dress on, the one Mom Darina bought me; she paid for it with the last 10 lev bill in her purse, I saw. At that moment, I knew I'd get well. I'll get well, Shushomir, and I'll teach you to fight tooth and nail. I will! If a child can't fight, he feels like a man who has no children. The only thing he thinks about and wants is to go hit the bottle.

"Are you hungry?" asked old Lena who pretended to be my grandma. The room was filled with her expensive smell, and suddenly my hands were itching terribly.

"Yes. I'm hungry."

She gave me something to eat, and I sank again into the hole where elderberry bushes grew: between our backyard and Shushomir's. It was good I was wearing Mom Darina's dress. My mother who breathed her last in her suitcase long time ago, and later learned the best way to crawl to Percha, stood by my side, straight as a candle. She wanted to make loads of money to buy me expensive milk. She promised to show me four new letters of the Bulgarian alphabet and teach me to speak as if I chewed pebbles. All this meant that the English kids could understand what I said. I suspected, however, that Mom wanted me to grovel to Percha the way she did.

Death and Mom gave me rich soup to eat, and slowly I felt better, but it wasn't the soup that did it. It was the magnificent navy-blue dress Mom Darina bought me. This navy-blue miracle helped me lift up my head because Mom Darina was strong. At a certain point, I tried to walk on all fours, and death ran away from me. Mom Darina was muscular, and death was scared of her the way the blonde caterpillar Elizabeth lived in fear of my sandals that kicked her ass. The soup lulled me to sleep, and I had a dream about Shushomir.

Only Mom Darina's dress, I and the smell of burnt almonds were in the room when I woke up. Directly from death's oven the almonds crawled to me.

"If Mom Darina has no time to see me, they'll burn me to ashes."

"Who will burn you to ashes?" asked the smell that lived under the skin of the woman who lied she was my grandma.

"The almonds will."

Although old Lena didn't have any aching backs to massage just then, she gave a start.

"You smelled death?"

"They're roasting almonds for me, Lena."

The almonds had been roasting for a day, and I didn't have a day left to reach the hospital in Sofia, so I thought death had come to get me.

Old Lena who had taken it into her head that I was her granddaughter said, "He just came here."

I thought I was sleeping. While I was in death's waiting room, I saw him in my dreams, and we played together.

"Am I dreaming about you, Shushomir?" I asked him because the kid stood before me the way I remembered him. Well, not exactly… Shushomir wore a new T-shirt, new shorts, maybe the best pair in Fredo's second hand shop, no bruises on his knees, no scars on his legs, no hair on his skull. They must've paid Tano the barber double price: awesome head shave, the perfect haircut for Shushomir, no carrot-color hair sticking up on top of his head. We all knew ginger-haired guys were troublemakers or brawlers.

"Annie!"

Was I dreaming or wasn't I dreaming? I couldn't tell, but I could hear it again, "Annie!"

I let death get some rest as I sat up in my bed, but the blanket was too heavy for me. It weighed six tons, this blanket did, but I could count to seven, I was strong enough, so I stood up. Shushomir took some steps towards me. I — slowly, timidly — took some steps towards him. Then he, his pate shaved like a thermos flask, hugged me. I hugged him, and we stood there and stood there for seven ages. Why couldn't I count to ten, the silly kid that I was!

"Come back home, Annie!"

"Okay."

"I've brought you a…" but I didn't let him tell me what he'd brought. I hugged him more tightly. I could hold him like that — pressed against my best dress Mom Darina had bought me — until his hair, red as gun power, reached to his heels. I thought it would be fun if I stepped on his ginger locks.

"Shushomir, dad doesn't let me talk to you," I said, but I hugged him. I held him tight the way the field held the roots of the walnut tree so that the storm didn't wrench it away from our backyard.

"Stay with me, Annie!"

Then I thought happily that the roots of our walnut tree grew and were one hundred feet deep. Its branches were big and tall — from the grass to the sky. They played hide and seek with the moon and with me.

✳ ✳ ✳

"I see you've made yourself comfortable here," said the tall slim man.

He had carefully de-haired his arms and legs. His voice was thicker than his beard, although the man was half-whispering, "No butterface has made me melt the way you did. No skirt has jilted me like you did. I've been looking for you. I'd like to strangle you with my belt."

The paneled wall sank noiselessly into the floor as two athletic young men loomed into view. The shorter one, his head shaved and smooth like the hood of a Mercedes-Benz car, the tall one, his hair permed, his shoulders imposing as a basilica, advanced on the guy. They paid no heed to his hairless limbs. The woman retreated to the corner and froze in her tracks under the shadow of a potted evergreen plant. Making no bones about his plan to harm, the shaved head ran his fingers over the visitor's stomach and stuck his thumb in his mouth. The basilica shoulders took off the guest's shirt, crumpled it into a ball then pitched it into the fire that blazed politely in the fireplace. The guy's trousers, mid-calf dress socks, and his slip went through the same ordeal, after which the long-permed hair produced his iPhone and issued an order: "Don't move!" He took five pictures of the visitor's body, adding different perspectives to its most substantial part, i.e. the one that hurt badly if punched or kicked, and could leave the sufferer dreaming of offspring in vain.

"What are you doing? Why?" shouted the guest with the spotless limbs.

The two employees remained unimpressed by his verbal jewels.

"Disinfection," announced the shaved skull as he sprinkled some colorless liquid over the de-haired individual, waited a minute then splashed aromatic substance on his stomach and legs. "Wipe yourself clean. Use a napkin for your mug. Go wash your butt."

"What do you want from me?" the visitor asked.

No one volunteered to cast light on this issue.

The two staff members kept on taking photos of him, profile shots and full-face images. Suddenly, a silky satin pink robe appeared, compete with magnificent slippers and a brilliant broad-brimmed hat. The figure looked majestic as a cowboy on horseback silhouetted against the setting sun. In the center of the silk splendor, a pair of blue eyes glowed, golden hair glinted as it fell over the back of the robe and waited there, a squirrel that had gone to sleep. The lady held up the index finger of her right hand. The two slim staff members bowed before her, demonstrating amazing harmony as they peppered — in sync — Milady's arm with both tiny and huge kisses. Her skin, white and crystal clear, was an island of goodwill amidst the gray Bulgarian landscape. The visitor, a safety pin stuck into a shabby pincushion, was shaking.

"Mr. Tikov, did my staffers show a disrespectful attitude towards you? Any derogatory comments or disparaging remarks?"

The safety pin remained speechless.

"Did they jeer at you?"

At long last, the man joined the conversation. "My name is not Tikov."

"Oh, your name is Tikov, you've simply forgotten it." The woman smiled as she took a step forward, her nose gleaming momentarily next to his own. "So, Mr. Tikov, did my two boys behave rudely with you?"

"Well…" began the citizen who had just acquired a new family name. "They took pictures of my body without asking permission. I think it is outrageous and extremely…"

Milady did not let him think further on this topic.

"Do not worry, Mr. Tikov, they'll reap what they've sowed," Milady promised, and pronounced a phrase in the imperative mood "Get out! The two of you!" The two employees darted out of the room, a pair of scalded cats who did not drag a de-haired mouse in their wake. Milady wrapped her voice with a thick layer of ice as she looked at the dark woman in the corner. "You! I want a glass of freshly squeezed pomegranate juice. I'll be drinking it and you'll be massaging my thighs. Your mother will take care of my stomach. You are not good enough for it."

The young woman with swarthy complexion — on arriving, the de-haired newcomer had given her food for thought — crawled out of the potted plant's shadow and put the glass of juice on the table in front of her employer. She removed Milady's slippers and smoothly, expending a great deal of concentrated effort, worked on her thighs. A couple of minutes passed and the theater of operations changed: an old, still attractive woman emerged from behind the open door. Making no fuss, she took to kneading Milady's stomach as noiselessly and accurately as if the future of the planet depended on her massaging ideas.

"Can you smell something?" asked the blue-eyed aristocrat. She looked as impressive as her muscular feet partly hidden by her pink robe.

"I can smell fear, Madam," the old masseuse answered.

"And you?"

"No, Madam" answered the de-haired visitor. He didn't know what to do with his hands.

The woman with the swarthy complexion, an expert on thighs and juice extraction, didn't say a word.

"Hey! You are annoying me. What is it? Tell me, or I will make your snotty daughter shriek till kingdom come."

The pretty dark face did not cloud or fall.

"Well?"

"The air smells of…"

"Burnt almonds?"

"No, not of death, Madam. It smells of loneliness."

The Blue Danube waltz sounded in the room as the old masseuse sank her fingers into her client's smooth, abundant flesh. The fruit-straining professional allowed to only labor over thighs was squeezing more pomegranate juice. She was so engrossed in her work one could say she was cleaning a gaping wound.

The blue-eyed celeb turned to the guest. "Mr. Tikov, I hope you enjoy Johann Strauss?"

Her hand, not in a rush, yet not too lackadaisically, bore down on the element of his physique responsible for possible additions to his family tree. However, Milady didn't show interest in trees or other plant life.

Outside the house, the month of September had banished the heat from the streets, but the wind was still too timid to frighten pedestrians away. Behind the windowpane, ten acres of wooded land stretched, Balsam firs, silver, white and black pines, in short, all species of conifers that the universe had created in the course of its evolution. It had worked hard, the universe had, because the trees looked magnificent. The grass was superb and the asphalt parking lot was splendid. Into that relaxing ambiance, the Blue Danube waltz injected a buzzing noise, a steel spike that could stab you repeatedly in the chest.

The pink wall, as it was in the habit of doing, withdrew to reveal a Milady, very attractive in a soft crimson dressing gown. Mr. Tikov, his majestically de-haired limbs gone limp, stood by her side, his head bent low like a big bomb, thoroughly unable to explode. In the refined atmosphere of this building, unexploded bombs, however big, seldom filled anybody with admiration.

The two young staff members entered the room in a resolute, businesslike manner. It went without saying that the first one had invested a fortune in having his head shaved as neatly as a new pin. The second one's hair, gleaming and meticulously trimmed, was longer than the Danube River in Strauss's waltz.

The two pressed and shoved him out of the way, then swooped down on him again, nudged him in the ribs, and pushed him. Mr. Tikov tried to protest, but alas in vain. The able-bodied fellows lifted him off the floor and encountered no difficulty in carrying him like a suitcase out of the room.

In front of the lady, a huge TV screen woke up. A monsieur appeared on it, his limbs perfectly de-haired, his body rolled into a ball on a parking lot paved with asphalt. The poor bugger made efforts to conceal a fact that could not be disguised: the individual was naked.

"You could have given him his shirt back," the muscular lady sighed. "I just wanted to commiserate with him," she added. Apparently, her heart bled for the man. The poor soul, how could he walk back home bare-assed the way he was? Well, this was his problem.

"As you know very well, I will do a TV interview this evening. The crew manager said it would start at 7:30." The robust beauty turned to the two wool jackets, and they stared avidly at the screen. "I will speak on the topic 'Young Generations. What Is the Future of Faith? Challenges and Solutions'. I'd like to know who of you will give me a lift to New Europe TV."

"I will, Madam!" the two employees roared in unison. Their teeth and their eyes gleamed with enthusiasm.

* * *

Two children were playing a game of Jinks in a room facing north. The window offered a view of the highway, Jeep tires, trucks, and smash-ups, the normal thing. The girl's hair was black, she was a walking blueberry in a faded dress, barefoot, although the month of September was everywhere. The boy was thin as a flame, his hair a burning fireplace.

"I've brought you some yellow cheese," the red-haired kid said.

Even before the girl muttered, "Shushomir, I don't like cheese…" two high hills burst into the servant's room. No, those were no hills. Two men they were, the first one's head glistened, shaved and smooth like a horse rump. The second hill looked dreadful. Hair, endless and thick, erupted from his head that looked like a bucket of orange liquid paint. The volcano hair clutched the skinny girl's shoulders. The shaved head grabbed the ginger boy by the collar and dragged him out of the room. After a while, he threw the kid in a narrow back street. The brat fell on the sidewalk. In the mornings, a grocery van stopped there, and the deliveryman sold the cook some of the huge house homemade cheese and sausages.

The little boy fell face down on the concrete tiles. The shaved head used the rear entrance of the building, and walked back home. The key turned in the door lock, and that was all there was to it.

A short, plump senora, more like a loaf of bread than a woman, padded across the street and hid in the shadow of the privacy fence around the house. She knelt down quickly — an almost impossible thing to do for a heavy housewife that she was.

"How are you feeling now, son?" the woman asked, her words abandoned bird nests.

The kid didn't answer. His eyes dimmed as he looked away.

"Annie," he whispered.

He didn't cry. Sometimes little boys were stronger than grown men, but it lasted only while their bones hurt as they lay face down on the sidewalk.

✳ ✳ ✳

Two girls stormed into the pink room. The blue-eyed one was strong as a hammer, the other one, a string of cotton, had a wound in her neck from which, like a line of ants, small drops of blood crawled down her chest.

"I let Elizabeth bite me," the thin girl said, a line of ants creeping inside her voice. "I wanted two golden teacups and she said, 'I'll bite you, and they'll be yours.' They are mine now. They cost two million levs, even two hundred thousand." The girl's words were plain and clear. "I'll buy a motorbike. It will be mine, and it will be Shushomir's, too. I'll buy two helmets. We'll go to Warm Lake. I know the way."

"You let her bite you, eh?" the fair-haired robust woman asked. "It means that Elizabeth didn't trounce you. She didn't knock you down in order to bite you. You simply let her do it."

"You know me, Percha," the string of cotton said. "Look at me, and look at your daughter. Do you think that this pig-iron girl of yours can catch me? Bite me? This can happen if I'm dead, or if death's doing the Conga on my cold grave."

The blond woman didn't pay attention to the babbling girl.

"Elizabeth, you tried to deceive me into believing you beat the pants off her. You told me you knocked her down and bit into her neck. Is that so?" The blue-eyed angel kept mum, her gaze hidden behind her eyelids thick as a fortress wall. "Is that so? You lied in order to sponge money off me. Is that so, Elizabeth?"

The eyelids flickered, the eyes shifted, sharp, blue, and able to shove aside anything that stood in their way.

"Mom, you've told me a thousand times that everyone tramples on honest men. An honest man is a slave," the healthy girl said. "You are honest only because you cannot make use of your friend's goofiness. You are stupid!"

"I am your mother. You must be honest with me."

"No, I must not!" the girl objected. "I'll get used to it and I'll be goofy all my life. They will trample me underfoot. Is that what you want?"

"You!" the blond lady shouted. "You tried to deceive me. You planned to pocket my money! You lost two gilded teacups I bought in India. Will you keep on losing precious heirlooms? You're not all there, I tell you. You are silly, insensible, and…"

"The teacups aren't mine, Mom. They're yours. I'll lose nothing."

The strong girl flew into a passion. "Look at me!" she shouted as she snatched away the gilded cups from the other girl's hands. The athletic belle did not hurl them against the floor because the rosewood was soft as plasticine. She chose to fling the gilded treasures at the central heating radiators and watched them turn into a shower of broken gold sparks.

"Now our little country bumpkin has no teacups. Eh? Who's the loser now? The carrot-cruncher or me?"

The thin girl's wounds, one on the belly at the pit of the stomach, the other in the neck, looked like ditches full of tomato sauce. You could say they were tulips that wouldn't bloom because they bled. The blonde teeth had worked on the dark skin. They had left scars red as the towels in the bathroom, and the skin under the chin looked slightly the worse for wear.

"Who is the stupid one now? I think it's not me," the blonde girl pointed out. She was happy and beautiful.

"We'll soon see about that." The words were barbed wire, ugly and cold. The girl with the dark hair who had just spoken took a relaxed step towards the blue-eyed, still smirking face. What exactly happened remained unclear. The stout girl complete with magnificent blonde hair and expensive jeans rolled on the floor. Soon she stopped rolling and wailed.

It was not clear what the worst-case scenario would be. Near the strong lass, the lady with the golden hair rolled on the floor, her leaden legs kicking in the air.

"Percha!" the barbed wire words hit the blonde lady's face. "Percha, if you one more time… if you make Elizabeth break something that belongs to me, Percha, I'll smash your left elbow! The golden teacups were mine. I let Elizabeth bite me twice. I bought the teacups from her. I paid for them with my blood. Now you pay me!"

The blonde archduchess, or perhaps an empress — she had bought a legal certificate saying she was the sole heiress of an ancient noble family in Finland — shrieked with laughter. She guffawed so hard that the chandelier above her head blared like a trumpet as the blue-blooded personage choked on the secretions of her own salivary glands.

"I'll count to ten," the thin girl said. Her voice was dark as an old Michelin tire. It seemed the knife they had cut their pork chops with had started speaking. "One… two… three…"

Before she said "four", a dark-haired woman, probably a home health aide, came up to the girl, seized her by the arms, and dragged her to the door. The aide didn't speak, just lugged the kid as if the little one were a garbage bag.

"You should've stayed with death in the suitcase, Mom," the girl said. "You turned traitor, Death didn't teach you to be a turncoat. Death is honest. It takes everybody. It doesn't accept bribes. Let me go! Let me show them!"

The woman, dark and thin — perhaps she had put death up in her eyes for the night — kept silent as she lugged the bundle of nerves and elbows down the hallway. The expensive marble floor was silent. It appeared this night would never end.

* * *

"You think I don't know? I'm not deaf and I'm not blind. You abandon yourself to debauchery," said the woman in ultra-soft dance tights that highlighted her impressive ankles. She looked healthy, a shield of iron muscles, not a molecule of cellulite on her. An ultra-soft T-shirt. "Shaved Head declared his love for you," she went on as she listened to Vivaldi's *Spring*. Meanwhile the lady beat time and sipped at her pomegranate juice. "Didn't it cross your mind I made him do that?"

"It crossed my mind, Madam."

"So?" the ultra-soft tights wanted to know.

"Despite the fact that I guessed at the truth, I took his declaration of love in good part."

"A thick rubber sole, aren't you?" the lady in the ultra-soft outfit said, and heaved a sigh, making it impossible to guess if she was disappointed, happy, or enraged. The aide, a gray wolf pelt, offered no response. She went on working on the pomegranate extract as if nothing had happened. It evidently had. The lady's blue eyes exploded. She jumped up from her chair, snatched away the cup from the wolf pelt, and said, "I pay you. I demand to be treated with due respect and reverence."

The dark-eyed home care assistant reached for the fruit bowl, but didn't take an apple or a pear. She poked her finger into a dainty crystal cup of raspberries, caressed the handle, and carefully, taking her time, put three raspberries on her tongue.

"You are impudent," said the blue-eyed lady. "Well. Who? Who did you catch in your mousetrap?" She thought for a while, then put her hand on the dark woman's face. At that moment, this face was a molehill, a small mound of freshly dug dirt under the gravedigger's spade. "Vasilev? Really?" whispered the blue eyes that for a split second turned black with anxiety.

"Maybe," answered the molehill.

The fine blonde hairs on Milady's arms glistened. She bent forward and let out a loud laugh.

"You know what? You are number 17 on Vasilev's list."

"True. As long as I am number 17, you cannot harm me."

"But after he ditches you…" whispered the blonde hungry lips. "Then I wouldn't like to be in your shoes."

"I wouldn't like to be in yours either." The words just pronounced by the dark-eyed woman were worse than a bad toothache. She poured herself a glass of pomegranate juice. She fingered another crystal cup of raspberries and started to eat. She chewed slowly, quietly, handling the cup with perfect ease.

"Get out!" ordered the blue eyes bristling with anger. "You are fired!"

"You can't fire me as long as I am number 17," the dark-haired young woman said. "I can fire you," she added. Silence sneaked into the room like a rat and lasted for all eternity. "Madam, quite apart from everything else you've said so far, I can smell the presence of death."

"I can't smell the presence of death," said the lady with the impressive ankles. "I can tell you one thing, though. Every time you smell the presence of death, be sure to have enough money to pay for your own funeral."

* * *

"Shaved Head," started the woman with the powerful ankles. "Have you professed your feelings… for…?"

"I beg your pardon, Madam?"

"Have you expressed everything you feel — particularly love — towards… somebody?"

"I beg your pardon…"

"For smarmy Anna!"

The immaculately shaved monsieur whose huge skull shone like a laptop screen bowed down to her. His breathing was a busy intersection, rumbling trucks and drivers slamming on the brakes.

"In actual fact…" the man started, but got no further than "fact".

"When?" Milady asked, her face flushed, her hands balled into fists ready to avenge.

The laptop couldn't flee from the busy intersection as Milady poked at his cheek. A minute later, she stared at her right hand to check if her fingernails were broken.

"I pay you. You declared your love for her. Under my roof!" The man could smell a volcano on her breath. Her thumbnail must have sunk deeper into the creep's eye. He deserved punishment and the punishment for treason was death. However, you could inflict more substantial losses upon a traitor at a later stage. "You won't get paid this month," Milady announced. "You might work for me as a volunteer, that is, for free. Let me see… for three months."

"But…" the man bent down. It was not clear if he did it because he repented of his sin, or because his cheek hurt where he'd just been scratched. Milady paid him no heed, and the sinner used this opportunity to wipe her spittle off his face.

"What about you?" The tornado of her gaze swept through the room and hit the man with the abundant hair. "When?"

"I… I tried hard … to… explain…" the beautiful-haired guy sniffed miserably and drooped like a captured enemy flag. "I… you… I should…of course…"

The annoyed lady didn't bother to dig her nails into his shoulders or into anybody else's. She grabbed the crystal vase with fifteen ruby red roses and hurled it at the monsieur's hair. His general situation was desperate, yet he stoically stuck to his guns, his bare chest bearing the brunt of the flying vase and prickly roses.

"I think highly of you. I like you. I don't give a crap about Shaved Head. He's a moron. But you! You! I won't pay you a salary for three months! Four months! Five months… Six months!" Milady coughed, wheezed, and at a certain point, she pulled herself together. "You're not worth your salt. Did you buy her flowers?"

"Yes, Madam, and I'm ashamed of myself," the splendid waterfall of hair said. The man assumed a posture a little short of giving a formal bow.

After a minute of meditation, the blonde duchess issued an order: "Run to my room! Now! Take a shower! You idiot!"

"Yes, Madam," the monsieur said, his voice a midsummer night's dream. His lips looked soft and impatient. "Thank you, Madam! Of course, my dear!" He knelt before her, his love and the red locks of his hair scattering on the floor.

"You've lost the right to call me 'my dear,'"

The tedious evening wore on. Some cretin honked his horn somewhere, the sky twisted the clouds into a knot. The moon tried hard to get rid of the rain and cover the landscape with mud, although people believed this would be the best place in town no matter what.

"Oh!" the blue-eyed monarch exclaimed. This particular exclamation spelled danger. The two men sagged like broken electrical wires.

"You declared your love for… ha-ha! Didn't it occur to you that a similar exercise was already performed by…Who?" Milady's dark pause devoured the full moon of September.

"Ivan, the old codger did it."

The room and its rosewood wall panels had not witnessed such a radiant smile since the house was built. The blue-eyed belle did not shrug scornfully. Nor did she shout. Her face broke into a wide grin.

"Ivan!" she breathed, pleased. After about an age in the course of which the two staff members, the shaved head and the ginger locks, were smiling to the best of their abilities, it transpired that it was too early to for them to beam sheepishly. Most inappropriately, they'd indulged in a little merrymaking.

The sounds of Milady's breathing, controlled and powerful, cut through the air.

"Mr. Vasilev's just declared his love for her."

The family name Vasilev put an end to the month of September. The moonbeams were gone. The evolution of the world came to a close.

"I'll speak on the TV tonight, boys," her ladyship turned to her employees. They looked totally crestfallen but had to quickly raise their heads. The storm was about to blow itself out. The month of September survived again. "The topic of my presentation is "Family Values". It will be a very interesting discussion. Red Hair! Run to my room. Now! You'll have to make me relax a bit before I go."

* * *

"This time, I will not die," the woman said. "Don't worry about me."

"I won't worry, mom," the child said. "You know the way from death back to Sofia. If something wrong happens, you'll call me."

"I'm getting married, Annie. I'll marry Mr. Vasilev."

"I understand," said the girl, her face a heap of cinders. "You don't want to neigh for Percha anymore."

It felt good to be in Carlo's pizza hut. The waitress had given the girl a big dish of veal stew although she said it was Boeuf Stroganoff, and not a pot of ordinary stew.

"Who is Vasilev? The one whose head looks like the tiles in the bathroom? Or the other one with the ugly hair?" the girl asked. "Love is something bad, mom. I've seen you many times. Death's roasting almonds for these two guys, and it is roasting almonds for you too. You've stayed with death for a while. You know it. Death often changes its mind."

"What about some chocolate cake?" the woman asked smiling. She was pretty, dark like a memory of a night long gone. A thin, tall woman. Smiles didn't become her. You might think she was ill.

"I don't like chocolate cake. Teach me the Bulgarian alphabet. Teach me to cast a spell on a bad man. Mom, let's go back home and stay with Mom Darina. She cannot cast a spell on anybody, but the village of Staro is all hers. She protects old grandmas and grandpas. She protects even snotty tots. Thieves hide their teeth deep in their mouths and don't bite when Mom Darina watches them. Dad often speaks about you and..."

"I'm getting married, Annie. I won't come back to Staro, do you understand?"

"Yes, I do," the child answered. "You can leave death any time you want and you can come back to me. You know the way. But you can't leave life, mom. Nobody's built a road between me and Mr. Vasilev." The kid caved in like a roof of an old house. A tear gleamed on her cheek, but the girl wiped it with her fist. "Fools cry," she said. "They let every-body know they have given in. They say 'I'm weak.' The only thing tears know is to give in, but I don't give in, Mom. Can you visit me from time to time?"

The woman, darker than her thoughts of the dark night, clasped the child to her chest, and the big dish of veal stew waited on the table, useless and forgotten.

"Will you teach me three letters of the Bulgarian alphabet?"

At the restaurant where they gave you a bowl of chicken soup and called it something that sounded Greek, a thin, very tall man, white as soap suds showed up. He sported a patchy beard. The girl thought it was like garlic that had sprouted sparsely because the summer was too hot or the backyard was infested with moles. The beasts ate the cloves that Mom Darina had planted, and the garden gaped at the sun empty and brown like caramel custard, but there was no garlic in it. Mom Darina, Dad, and you had nothing to eat. The girl tried to chew at a dirt clod. It was no good. The man's beard looked like a lump of mud, and the child thought that many moles had burrowed into his cheeks.

"Good evening,"| said the child who was thin and dark as her moth-er, a stick capable of talking. The newcomer did not say a word. "Good evening, Mr. Vasilev," repeated the girl, and she stood up by the dish of veal stew that smelled so delicious.

The man didn't say anything. He bent down and kissed the dark woman's hair, then kissed her on the lips. His mouth looked for her hands, finally landing on her left elbow. The girl knew which elbow was left and which was right. The left one was always closer to the heart; therefore, it was weaker.

Another man approached the dish of veal stew: white hair, two cuffs, a sparkling white suit, a pair of new white shoes. Then the newcomer purred respectfully, "Good evening, Madam."

The lady did not bother to look at him. The sparse beard that had kissed her hand, fingers, her left as well as her right elbow, did not respond either. Obviously, her ladyship was busy. Vasilev's index finger touched the woman's lips. He said something. The words sneaked their way through his unimpressive beard: "I love you!"

The new arrival in the designer suit bowed discreetly, which meant that his white hair shook and he dropped his eyes to the veal stew, then, without further ado, he grabbed the girl's hand. The little one immediately wrenched it free of his fingers. The wing-like sleeves of the white jacket fastened around the kid's waist. There, a pink belt with a cat and mouse buckle glowed. It was easy for the newcomer to seize the belt and pull the kid out of her chair.

"Mom," the kid screamed.

For a moment, the dark woman looked up from her wine and smiled at the pale man. Then her dark eyes returned to her lass, and the woman whispered, "I love you."

"Ivan, let me go," the child said. One could hardly expect her voice would be polite. The white suit made sure the girl was safe, let the cat and mouse clasp be, and allowed the pink sandals of the girl to step on the floor. The floor of the restaurant was white marble, and so were the walls. The universe was a place full of stone, a reliable material altogether. The white suit momentarily lost its balance. The girl moved away from the white cuffs and slowly walked to the table where the veal stew was still waiting for her. She beamed at the dark woman, approached the man with the patchy beard, and tried to buckle her sandals, all the while calm as a summer night with its twinkling stars. After the girl was done, she kicked the pale gentleman's ankle. Possibly, his lips still persisted in whispering, "I love you!". The man's gray cheeks drooped. His feet kicked the marble floor, his chin wobbled. It seemed Mommy Mole had bitten him, or perhaps she wanted to tug him to her kitchen and cook his beard for her baby moles.

"But ... but! But!" cried the man, his molehill face outraged. The girl did not lend a sympathetic ear. She leaned over her plate, scooped up some rice, and forgetting good manners altogether, picked up a veal fillet with her fingers. She immediately bit into it. The man in the white suit gave another discreet bow. His head — he'd rather someone had already chopped it off — weighed a ton and seemed to be a millstone around his neck. He grabbed the child's pink belt with a cat and mouse clasp.

"Excuse me!" whispered the man, his resplendent suit trembling, and his shoes white as soap suds. "I am deeply sorry for what has happened!"

The man whose ankle had been kicked, his face a layer of dust on an old cupboard, had no intention of accepting the apology. He refused to waste time. His finger wrote "I love you" on the dark woman's neck that a weak poet would compare to a sad song. The woman also ignored what the white suit had prattled on about. "I love you," her dark eyes answered the man's index finger. It was delicate and slim, an impatient finger that had started painting an autumn landscape on her breasts.

"Mom!" whispered the child.

✳✳✳

"Auntie Darina! Auntie Darina!" A red-haired boy ran like thunder, and so quickly did he race to her backyard, that the woman who was pruning the old apple tree almost dropped the garden shears to the ground.

"What, Shushomir?" Is your mom okay?"

"Yes, she is. Look!"

The boy's hand, as thin as a dog's tail, flew in the air.

"Someone's written ANNA on this envelope!"

"What?"

"A letter! It's real. It's a letter."

The shears slipped out of the woman's hand and fell at her feet, but she paid no attention to the thud. She tore the envelope so fast that the sheet of paper inside it was almost torn in two.

"Look, little Shushomir!"

The large woman in a moon-and-stars dress — in her hand the shears looked like a shaving blade — and the red-haired kid joined the two scraps of paper and stared at them.

The following was written on the sheet:

SH ShU Sh A Anna and Shu

There was a pencil drawing under the printed letters — a woman in a huge moon-and stars dress, and a large woman she was. Her legs were thin as safety pins, her arms looked even thinner, and her shoes were so enormous you'd think they were delivery trucks. The woman's fist, the size of a soccer ball, held a little girl's hand. The child was small, her dress a miserable blue triangle. Several thorn-like streaks jutted out of her head, her sandals had two stripes, and where a heel should have been, there was none. The girl's left arm was a long line and had five fingers at the end. Both the woman's and the child's eyes were black dots. The pencil must have pressed too hard while drawing the child's and the woman's faces, and here and there the paper was torn. The noses and mouths of both faces were short, black dashes. A word was printed below the picture — M A MMM A — such a big and important word that it had taken almost every square inch of the paper. It looked like an aircraft at an airfield. The letters were so crooked and thin that they could barely stay in place. The pencil seemed tired of pressing on them and the paper had probably not been patient enough.

"Mamma," the large woman read. "She wrote me a letter! She did!"

The woman looked even bigger in her brown dress, and you felt like asking her, "Where did you buy this endless thing from, woman? Certainly not from Fedo's shop?" Then you saw her pressing the sheet to her starry dress. She began to breathe as hard as if she were carrying the old bus to Radomir on her back — or was she about to choke to death because there wasn't enough air? But the woman was all right. She kissed the huge crooked letters, kissed the picture of the girl in the blue triangular dress, and kissed the thorns jutting out of the round head.

In this part of the country where the soil was sand and granite shards, people did not cry. If you shed tears, your horse must have died or your house was robbed to the bone, and there was nothing you could do to the thieves. They broke your ribs. You should be glad you hadn't kicked the bucket yet. But you fumed and you saw red. It was not fair. You were weak. You couldn't beat them black and blue. The only thing you could do was let out a sob and ram it down the throat of your nasty life. Now, this big woman, whose blood was made of stone, felt there was a grain of sand in her eye. No, there was no grain of sand. She was about to start crying. She didn't know how to stop it. The boy, ginger-haired like any July sunset, was frightened.

"Feeling sick, Aunt Darina?" he muttered in panic.

"I'm not sick!" the woman snapped. "I'm glad that Annie sent me a letter!"

"Then why are you crying? Does the letter say Annie's ill?"

"It doesn't."

The woman felt ashamed. Her large hands, in which, the boy believed, the universe looked like a penknife, wiped her tears and left not a droplet of moisture on her face.

"Does the letter say anything about me, Aunt Darina?" the boy asked as he bowed his head.

"Keep your head up, kid," the woman said. "Listen to me. Little Annie has written the whole thing for you. Look," her brown finger strong as the hardwood floor in St. Nicholas the Miracle-Maker church pointed to the end of the sheet. "You can count, can't you, Shushomir?" See how many times she's written "SH" to you!

The red hair burned as the boy tilted his head to one side, licked his thumb and began to count, "One, two, three, four, five, six, seven."

"You see, she wrote "SH"— that's the beginning of your name — seven times."

"Isn't it someone else's name?" There was a squirrel in the boy's voice and it gnawed at something very hard with its teeth. In this stony region of Bulgaria, people knew that the hardest thing under the sun was fear.

"Don't be silly!" the woman cut him short. The red-haired kid raised his head and smiled, letting the month of September settle comfortably, in the sky, in the streets, and in the hardest thing, fear. "It's your name, Shushomir."

"What does that mean ..." the kid's voice ended here, and so did the universe. There was only a pair of eyes that any the pencil would find very difficult to draw on paper. Any paper would be too thin to hold the gleam of hope in these eyes.

"Well," the woman stammered. She felt the kid's words were very different from a bad man you could tie to a fence with a piece of rope. You couldn't compare words to a coward — you could scare the pants off a craven. You could tell the jerk you'd break his left elbow if he stole anything, just anything, from his neighbors. But you couldn't tie the words nor could you browbeat them into silence. Words were exactly like the universe, you thought it started in your backyard, but it was everywhere, on the other side of the hill and in your hands. "Well…"

"What?" the boy swallowed painfully.

"Well, she writes to you, 'Shushomir, you're my friend.' She's written seven times: "Shushomir, you are my friend.""

The woman choked because she had never told a whopping great lie like this one before. In that rocky mountain people got into brawls twice a day, drank and stole, but their lies had no legs, so you had to be dumb as a brush if you swallowed them. The woman feared the boy would see the white ropes she'd tied her fib with, and his head would droop as if someone had punched him.

"It's not right, Annie!" the boy cried out. "Annie, I'm not just your friend. I'm your best friend! I want you to know it!"

✳ ✳ ✳

"What will you do with this wash basin?" she asked me, pointing at the thing. I never called her "grandma." You can't be silent like a sink-hole and watch your daughter marry a man who has no blood in him. You can't keep a child locked in Elizabeth's room. You know Elizabeth has teeth to bite folks with. You've heard her hiss to the child, "Stupid carrot-cruncher!" You can't do that and say you're this child's grand-mother. That old woman knew the smell of death the way I did. I believe she made a mistake when she gave birth to my mother. My mother was getting married to Vasilev. Then my mom made a mistake and gave birth to me. But a woman had to give birth to a child who could hear the footsteps of death. Death was so lonely. It visited people who had no friends. Death and loneliness went out and returned through the same door.

"Why is this washbasin here?" The woman insisted on getting an answer. She had a lot of money and counted the notes in the evening when I sat in the chair next to her. I did it because I hated to disturb my mom. I annoyed mom when "Uncle Vasilev" came for a visit. I'd planned to cut his finger in order to check — would blood or oil spurt from the wound? On the other hand, I'd seen parched mud. I watched it carefully for hours, and nothing gushed from the cracks. That was what Uncle Vasilev was, a mud crack in which even nettles and donkey thorns couldn't grow.

"Dropping off to sleep, are you?" the woman snapped her fingers under my nose, grabbed the washbasin and dragged it away.

"Give it to me!" It wasn't difficult to pull the thing out of her hands. They were so weak I wondered how her fingers could trap diseases she stumbled upon in the skins of old wealthy geezers. I'd learned, or was it Elizabeth who told me: "wealthy" meant "filthy rich". I knew what filth meant and I imagined worms crawled in a purse among the pennies. The old biddy was mistaken; she didn't fight off illness. I once examined her hands while she slept and, honestly, I saw no bugs or disease on them. I told her, "Woman, don't touch my washbasin. Don't make me break your left elbow."

I couldn't sleep without this basin. It was green and small. I'd stolen it from Elizabeth's restroom.

"Why are you so fond of it?" the woman asked.

"Mom said that if she would die, she'd send me rain from the sky," I explained to the woman who tried hard to deceive me she was my grandmother. At times, she stared at me the way our country folks in Staro gawped at Damian the idiot. "Mom said, 'Collect rainwater in a basin and use the raindrops to wash your face with. If you are sad, you will dream about me at night.'

"But your mother won't die," said the woman.

"If mom marries the scrawny man who has clay in his eyes, she'll go away, and I won't see her again. This means death will begin roasting almonds for me. I will send raindrops to Mom, too, but she won't use them to wash her face with because she doesn't want to dream about me. That's why I'll ask the rain to go and fall in Staro. But it's not important. Mom Darina dreams about me, Annie, day and night no matter if the rain is heavy or it doesn't rain at all. If she washes her face with my raindrops, she will not be sad for me."

I loved the month of September because it didn't obey anyone. It was cold in the mornings, and the viruses died like ants. In the daytime, the sun tiptoed on your back and you were a sparrow that had just pecked at a truckload of breadcrumbs. That was why in September sparrows became much stronger. They learned what happiness was. It was a washbasin you'd filled with rain for Darina. Trapped in my room, the month of September was lonely; on the street, it was a child like me and had plenty of cars and benches.

"Take your basin," the woman said.

I no longer slept in mom's room. She slept with the skinny man whose eyes were dust. The guy made of mud pressed his finger to her lips. I don't know why he did it. Maybe if a man had no blood and his skin was made of clay, he didn't know how to make love and paid the doctor to show him. I slept in the flat of the soft-handed woman, but I wouldn't call her "grandma." It would feel like calling myself "you, dirty louse!" The folks, whose illnesses she pretended to trap like minnows with her fingers, addressed her as "dear madam." I, too, sometimes called her like that. However, "dear" meant you could never buy the thing you wanted because it was very expensive, You could not put this thing in the shirt pocket above your heart.

"Yesterday you pushed Elizabeth to the floor, so you're not having dinner today," she told me.

"All right, dear madam. I can stay hungry all the way from Sofia to Staro. When the car comes to a halt, I can run from the bus stop to the blackberry patches in the mountain. Hunger won't break me."

"Okay. I changed my mind," the dear madam said. "I'll hide your black T-shirt and your black pants. You will not put them on for two weeks in a row."

"No!" I shouted. "That way, I won't be able to dream about Shushomir!"

She went to the closet where I'd stored all my clothes, pulled out Shushomir's black T-shirt and Shushomir's black pants, and waved them in front of me.

"No! Please, thank you, dear Madam, give me Shushomir's pants!" She didn't budge. "Give me the pants! Please, thank you, Ma'am!" I grabbed my best dress — it was daylight robbery, had costs Darina an arm and leg — and I started wiping the floor at her feet with it. Then I brought dear madam mineral water to drink. She kept mum. She stared at me and didn't give me Shushomir's pants and T-shirt.

"Please, thank you, dear madam! Now I'll show you!" I wiggled my rear end like the weasel that had strangled Shushomir's chickens. It was true his father shot the mean poultry-eater in the head — so I darted forward like the weasel before Shushomir's father shot it, then I rushed to the cupboard where dear madam kept her ointments, aromas, and smells in bottles. I took that pot from which madam poured aroma onto her head every time one particular client with a black wallet walked into her studio. This old man rolled in money, and I feared worms crawled in his bank account, and in his throat.

"Dear Madam, give me Shushomir's T-shirt and Shushomir's pants. Otherwise, this bottle will smell no more! I'll smash it to pieces on the tiles in the restroom!"

A miracle happened. She gave in. I knew what a miracle was. It occurred when mom and I went together to pay some tax or penalty, and we sat down to eat pizza on the way. The pizza on mom's plate was my miracle. We shared it. But this happened very rarely.

"Take your old pants. You should be ashamed of yourself!" said the dear madam. "Give me back my perfume bottle!"

"Put Shushomir's pants and T-shirt on the chair in the hallway," I told Madam. That was how I dealt with Elizabeth. If I didn't watch my back, the blond shark left me nothing and bit my throat. "I'll put your scent pot in front of the door."

I had already hidden the pants and the T-shirt, and madam had collected her aroma pot when the man mom had married, the one with oil flowing under his skin, entered the studio. He didn't talk to me because he didn't see me. How could oil see a child? I knew what oil was — I'd seen madam rub it into her clients' backs — and I was not afraid. The oil had no eyes and wouldn't notice a little girl.

"Dear lady," began the man colorless as the works that crawled in the grass. You wouldn't catch a glimpse of them unless you accidentally stepped on one. "I love your daughter and I'll take care of her. I visit your studio once every two months and on the rare occasions when this happens, I'd like to feel the benefit of a quiet ambiance."

"Of course, Mr. Vasilev," dear madam replied. "I apologize for any inconvenience caused. Should I take care of your shoulders first? I am confident this will have a beneficial effect on your blood vessels and your frame of mind."

"I hope you are acquainted with my extreme noise sensitivity and my intolerance to impolite little creatures."

"Oh, Mr. Vasilev, I fully intend to send the impolite creature to her native village tonight!"

The oil in the colorless eyes of my mom's husband smiled. I felt sorry for her, my poor mother. She would be much better off if she had married death.

* * *

I knew that I was number 17 on his list. The presence of young mademoiselles at Mr. Vasilev's residence was a fact of life. Each one of them had a serial number, and no number lasted more than a year. It made no difference to me. On the one hand, men tended to get fed up with me fairly quickly, on the other, they soon became items in which I had no interest. I enjoyed the short spells when I didn't have to impress anyone. The insults they threw at me didn't break my bones because I no longer cared about the respective guy.

I sensed that my stay in Mr. Vasilev's biography would be a temporary one, and that was okay with me. My husband asked me to call him Phil. He compared me to numbers 16, 11, and 8 who were brunettes like me. Numbers 7 and 2, unlike me, did not like grapes; 3, 15, and 1 were exactly the same weight and height. He was surprised that I did not care about mink coats and conjectured it was my trick to ride longer on the crest of a wave in my capacity as number 17. The invitation came unexpectedly. 11 September 2021 was a gray day, with a few limousines in front of Julius Caesar restaurant where he took me out for lunch.

"Did you read the letter I left on your nightstand?"

"No, Phil," I strictly adhered to the "Need to Know" principle, with which I got acquainted by perusing a spy novel. I listened, paid attention, and commented only on the topic my interlocutor — i.e. Phil — seemed to evince an interest in. I believed that this was the reason why my bones had not been broken yet, and all my teeth were in place.

"Why haven't you read it?" Phil asked. He was tall, quiet, given to planning every step of his to perfection. Surely, Vasilev was a neat freak and an exceptional esthete. His two houses were full to bursting of flowers that were taken care of by a platoon of gardeners. His armchairs were delivered from Vienna, and I lived in fear of damaging them. The mirrors in all his houses and apartments were, as he pointed out, procured from the best London furniture makers. His bedroom suite was designed by a Stockholm cabinetmaker, and each item in it, including his 19 pairs of slippers, possessed an official manufacturer certificate. One of the rooms had been transformed into a museum that housed a rich collection of objects owned by all my predecessors, from Number1 to Number16. Phil did not call the demoiselles "numbers". He used the phrase "physiological surprises" instead. One day he took me to his museum where the exhibits — scarves, bikinis, bras and lacy panties immaculately arranged in long rows, caught me off guard.

"What would you say, Anna?" Phil asked me.

I thanked him for putting his trust in me and for his openness. His next move dropped a bombshell. He took out a sheet of paper, flattened it to perfection, and left it on the table in front of me. The sheet contained the following text written in ugly block letters:

I WANT YOU. YOU ARE GREAT.

Peter, one or Percha's toy soldiers, used to send me scrappy notes like this one. His hair was long and fell to his toes if you bothered to look at it and cared about his flowing locks that didn't flow. Madam Percha adored his mane; on Wednesdays, from 5:00 p.m. to 7:30 p.m., she carefully teased his curls into place, at times forcing me to comb them. Meanwhile, I recited a bouquet of best romantic lyrics. She had placed me under an obligation to select from the Collected Poems, Oxford World's Classics. I had memorized eighteen of these and recited an odd sonnet or ode as I wielded the comb and the curling irons. I couldn't stand poetry. Love was the most conventional method for turning numbers 1 through 16 into exhibit items stored in Phil's neat collection. I chose the shortest possible verses. As I saw it, the poem's brevity was its most valuable quality because less time was wasted reading it. In my case, the misleading love experience lasted four months. Annie's father said he loved me and carried me in his arms to the peak of Bare Hill to prove it. I believed him. He was tall and thin like Phil, and panted as he trudged up the hill. I had a feeling he was going to die after he said, "Ana, you don't believe I care about you." He wouldn't let me step on the ground, not even once; however, we often took long breaks. Love happened among hazelnuts bushes. Hawks flew over our heads, and lizards watched us. Love was beautiful, and love was stronger than the rocks. Maybe this was the reason my daughter could feel death's approaching breath. Death was a part of everything that surrounded me, but it was no part of love.

Love existed only in a muddle-headed lover's mind; it collapsed if confronted by a trivial obstacle in its path, and the sooner you realized that love had not survived, the faster you'd move away from the poisonous brew that men of dubious wit called "devotion". My daughter was a horse of a different color. Sometimes I woke up at night and thought about her. I thought so long and hard that pain shot through my chest and burned my lungs I wanted her to be healthy far away from me because I brought misery to her. She'd been languishing ever since she came to Percha's house. The world kept staring at her with wolf eyes.

"That's why I'm losing weight, Mom," she said. "Your room is looking at me with the eyes of a wolf."

"Your daughter is really giving me a pain," Phil complained. I thought he was pretending; however, as soon as Annie opened the front door on the following day, he did feel sick and threw up.

"I don't want to see her," "Phil spoke softly, and so did I.

Annie's shadow, lost in the autumn, made me imagine I heard the footsteps of a man abandoned in an unknown city. It was easy to rob a little girl and steal her coat. I saw her in that boy's black T-shirt.

"My heart hurts, Mom," she'd tell me.

Didn't this sentence sound ludicrous! The heart was a muscle. What did it have to do with the avalanche of sadness and anxiety that seared through me at night? Logic had no bearing on the insane fear of losing her. She should not love me. Love was a burden on her. It made her weak and sick. That boy's T-shirt seemed to heal her. Well, all the time I'd be number 17, I'd get my money's worth, I'd buy a beautiful house and I'd have a carefully tended lawn, flowers, and trees.

"So, what is this?" I was well informed that Phil was averse to asking the same question twice. The employees to whom he had to repeat his queries lost their jobs on the following day. Those who could not respond adequately were fired on the spot, and representatives of the special category who provided misleading information simply disappeared over the horizon. Where did they go? I can't say for sure. I knew such a person, an expert accountant, who had most unexpectedly acquired chronic kidney failure.

"This is a note Peter wrote to me," I said.

"Who is Peter?"

"The man with the ankle-length hair."

Outside the room, the rain had stopped, the park glowed cheerfully green, the grass was thin and the trees did look impressive. I still received a salary paid by my employer, Ms. Percha, and to my surprise, Madam had provided a fourfold increase in my paycheck since I became №17.

"And what is this?" On the back of a bank statement issued by First Investment Bank, Sofia, one could read the following example of the imperative mood, "COME ON!"

"This is what Todd has written to me."

"And Todd is the reindeer with the huge ugly skull?"

"Todd is Mrs. Percha's employee. The one with the shaved head."

"Aha!"

"Aha" was Phil's entrance to a place that was not shown on any map. I was sure Phil wanted me there, and it would not be the most picturesque peak in Bulgaria. Not by a long shot. Phil's limbs, belly and lips were cold to the touch. His love was a nest where a baby bird would not hatch. The restaurant, the mountain peak, the green eyes of the wind, the worms, the AT, the wait staff, the kitchen, the menu, all this belonged to Phil.

"Am I at the lower end of the scale compared to Peter and Todd?" he asked.

"You are off the scale," I said, and that was the truth. One way or another, I could get along with Todd and Peter. I didn't understand the logic behind Phil's question and I did not know the measurement unit of fear.

"I am interested to hear more about your assessment process," he said. Nothing in his intonation suggested interest. Phil's voice was a layer of soil that consisted of stones and sand. This was the case with the backyard behind our house in Staro. I'd built a shack there and hid in it because I couldn't sleep next to Annie's father. My love for him had turned to sadness. He had broken his back as he carried me to the top of the hill. The poor man.

Phil's words were yellow mud, and yellow was attractive to snakes and lizards.

"This is Mom's magic house," my daughter used to say. "Teach me to cast magic spells, Mom!" She didn't know she was my greatest magic.

"What do you think about guys like me?" persisted the yellow mud that killed tree roots. Fear could thrive in it. Nothing else.

"I don't know anyone else like you," I said. It was the first time that I has seen Mr. Vasilev smile. His smile gave off a smell of roasted almonds, but I had not been afraid of it for a long time now.

"I'm interested in your assessment of me as an adult male," under the mud, his voice had a layer of gravel and bare rock, and it was the rock that was talking to me.

"You are just normal," I replied.

"Never use my name next to the word 'normal'!"

"This statement sounds reassuring to me," I lied, and the smell of amonds was gone.

"I mean the man who has had a catastrophic fall from grace with Ms. Percha ..."

Phil didn't encourage anyone to interrupt his profound musings, so I waited to see where he'd take the action in his story. Was he interested in Percha? I expected an ambiguous, two-pointed question, a slippery trap. But Phil wouldn't be Phil if he did what he was expected to do.

If you don't know what to expect from someone, don't expect anything, and observe nature's beauty instead. Three unspectacular cherries, a sullen September afternoon, an empty street in an expensive neighborhood perched amidst the pine trees of Vitosha Mountain. A plot of land worth half a billion. The meaning of human achievement, And the crux of the matter was development. Evolution had labored for hundreds of millions of years to create the beauty of nature that Phil bought. Then he erected a concrete fence around beautiful nature, installed NightWatch, the perfect wireless security cameras, arousing jealousy and leaving his business competitors green with envy. On the other hand, would anyone envy Phil a woman like me? Not likely.

"The man you've recommended to Percha on account of his unquenchable carnal desires. Or was it his thirst for spiritual intimacy?" Phil went down the path of his vague intention. I nodded. "I talked to this macho tough guy, your aristocrat in question," Phil dropped me a hint between two bites of salmon. "I was informed that Percha demoted him because of his unsatisfactory performance. The poor devil told me he was still crazy about you. "I nodded again. "I know he had been longing to break your head, roast your favorite cat, cut your middle finger and carry it in his pocket — the one near his heart or anus, depending on the mood the man is in. I can quote more statements along these lines." Another smile crossed Phil's face, a sly leer that took me back to the millions of years related to the evolution of roasting almonds. "The bottom line is that the idiot has never met anyone like you."

To comment on the declarations made by an individual who wanted you to breathe your last was a pointless endeavor, so I decided not to go for it.

"I did my best to find your husband i.e. your daughter's father. This good citizen is actually a wreck, and your daughter, his direct descendant, was the reason I had an asthma attack," Phil continued. "Your husband, a degenerate fella, shacks up with a creature who, in my view, does not lean towards female. His womanlike companion beats him with his own belt. Do you know her?"

"I've heard of her."

"Your daughter is convinced this Tyrannosaurus Rex is her mother," Phil continued. "Your husband got drunk the minute I bought him brandy and mentioned your name. 'Give her this', he said, and stuffed a sheet of paper in my shirt pocket. Here, read it!"

"ANNA COME BACK"

Ten minutes passed. Phil kept silent and he looked at me. I didn't mind. Besides my daughter's, the only other presence dear to me was silence.

"So you boil down your strategies to the essentials — how to make gentlemen, all without exception, appreciate your skills." Phil's hand flew over the grilled salmon, ignored the roasted vegetables, took no notice of the wine, and touched my hand. I'd often marveled at Phil's frugal, balanced movements that reminded me of equations with three unknowns. His silent fingers frightened me. "And you, Anna, what would you say about your omnivorousness?"

I could have answered, "I've lived alone since I was eight years old," but I said nothing.

"You're number seventeen on my list."

I knew this for a fact and believed my opinion on this issue was inconsequential.

"I'll probably dump you soon. I don't like your silences."

It was good there were a number of things I adored about nature. I liked lawns and well-trimmed terrace gardens. It was cool in the back-yard and unexpectedly I thought my daughter had to go to kindergarten.

"Look who's coming to see us!"

No one came to see Philip by pure chance. For Phil, a coincidence was a surgical scalpel that ruined your plans and left your thoughts bleeding. But why should I give any thought to the newcomer? It turned out I had to no matter how I disliked huge ankles had smiling blue eyes.

"My dear Anna! I'm so glad to see you!" said Mrs. Percha, her jeans and short Armani jacket beaming. She wore the dizzying Armani for Mr. Vasilev's sake, I knew. "Honey!" She kissed me and touched my hair. "Wow. You are gorgeous! I have a little present for you," a shiny package, and perhaps a silver trinket inside.

When Annie, a grasshopper in that frayed T-shirt, called me "Mom," I didn't look at her. I would have given ten years of my life to hug her tightly for just a moment, but I didn't do it. I had to teach her how to hate me. Don't expect a hug from Mommy the way I didn't expect it from my mother. But God was merciful. God begins where knowledge ends — an abyss in which Annie was hungry and infinitely lonely. This must have been the meaning of death, the One who began at the end of knowledge. It taught me one thing — I was ready to die for a dark, ill-mannered child, stubborn as a wolf. I panicked when she lost weight. But I had not glanced at her my daughter. I didn't wave goodbye to her. At night I dreamed of her voice; she called my name and slept lightly like a bee. I dreamed that she was breathing on the pillow next to me, and in my sleep, I lit the bedside lamp and looked at her.

God, what a beautiful child she was! How could she live with the almond smell of death?

I didn't bother to look up at Mrs. Percha. I refused to reach for the lavish package. I ignored Milady's gift altogether. She opened the box and put it in front of me, but I continued to observe nature's beauty, and I thought of the universe's futile efforts to destroy fences altogether. Probably billions of centuries ago, there were no fences, and the universe invented a few gods whose task was to rule us, the humans.

If fences did not exist, nothing but our own fears would be able to govern us. Fences raised the banner of property and erased freedom from our minds.

Mrs. Percha was staring at me. What the hell.

There used to be many stones strewn across the world far and wide. The folks began to pile them on top of each other because men and women wanted to climb high and steal a glance at the house of God. How come He has a house and we don't have one? Why has he thrown so many crags and cliffs on the ground and why did He give us so few vegetables? Why hasn't evolution done its job properly? Winter is coming. Why hasn't God provided us with coal? Is He really as smart as he tries to pass himself off? And the primitive people took to piling up the stones and the rocks that the universe had dumped instead of serving meat on their plates. A huge hill of stones rose under God's feet, then a mountain soared and turned into a giant ridge of rocks, but the primitive savages did not stop working. They kept on dragging stones to the mountain.

"Darn it," said Our Lord. "Not only did I make them in my own image, but I also gave them bread in their hands. And now they want to storm my house and hurl stones into my courtyard. Then someone will say that I am not the Lord at all. So many cheeky creatures have never evolved before…"

"How are you, dear Anna? You look great. Really!" Mrs. Percha assured me, a dazzling smile in her eyes. To me, her Armani jeans spoke far more convincingly than her lips. I had personally washed this article of clothing with the utmost care, perfumed it, and zipped up the fly by pressing hard Mrs. Percha's belly. Her belly was powerful. Poor Mr. Armani must have sweated buckets as he chose the best fabric to wrap the avalanche of Percha's abdominal muscles with. I did not answer Milady's questions. When have I become so dear to her? I wondered.

I came back to my musings about Our Lord. He sat down on a bench and thought hard. What was he to do with the impudent people he had created out of nothing? It was true he had nothing at hand, had no particular interest in arrogant creatures, and created them just to pass the time. Suddenly an idea struck Him. What if He let the savages know the meaning of the words "my" and "it is mine"? No sooner said than done. Thus, within one night, the primitive brutes became human beings. God descended to them in Sofia, the capital of Bulgaria, and said, "Look here." Then He started stacking stones on top of each other and built the first stone fence in the world. Maybe the fence around Phil's restaurant was erected by our Lord himself.

The aboriginal buddies scratched their heads, and already knowing what "my" and "it is mine" meant, everyone young and old rushed to grab stones. First, men dragged rocks, using their hands and feet, then they invented bags, wheels, pistols, airplanes, and so on — these folks erected fences that seemed to touch the sky as they tried to distinguish themselves from their more elementary comrades. No one could — not even Our Good Lord — stop them. Only death was able to achieve this feat. Ever since the first fence was erected, people have been roasting almonds. So, at a certain point, the smell of death was born. It is not true that "in the beginning was the Word." The truth was that in the beginning were, and would forever be the fences the humans built.

However, even death could not stop the class-conscious individuals. Within a week, one could find no trace of the stone mountain that people had piled up to climb to Our Lord's house and ask Him why he had a palace, and they were toiling and moiling in dark caves. Why didn't the universe move its ass to give them bread and circuses? Why should evolution put bread only in Our Lord's mouth and fill his eyes with magnificent views? Wasn't that an example of what you called a conflict of interest at work? Everyone plundered rocks and debris, erected fences and fought for more and more stones. Not a pebble, small as a peanut, remained of the huge mountain range. The land was divided into plots immaculately fenced and surveyed. Every time, even before a baby was born, his dad and mom looked for cement and iron to build a fence and mark the boundary between their infant and the rabble of morally offensive savages…

"My dearest girl!" Mrs. Percha exclaimed. I was unable to further enjoy my vision of the future fences. "I'd like to ask you to manage my Global Logistics Company… International shipping, you know the thing," but I did not listen to what deliveries and transport services worldwide she was babbling on about. I got up and failed to beam at Phil; I didn't even go to the bathroom, which might be a plausible excuse for missing a conversation with a transportation tycoon. I left the restaurant and observed nature with a soft gaze — a manicured lawn and asphalt. The mountain, as befitted this part of the world, was well taken care of — the pine trees had been pruned, watered, and waited ready to be part of a postcard. Phil's bodyguards dutifully bent from the waist the way they should when I — number 17 on their employer's list of intimate hygiene wipes — made an appearance.

Enough with nature; many writers had tried to earn a living by providing poetic descriptions, sighing, and admiring every aspect of beauty one could admire. As soon as a student graduated from the Academy of Arts, he grabbed a brush, threw nature onto a piece of canvas, and put bread on the table in front of his wife. Every molecule surrounding me now was nature at its most exquisite — ceramic vases, alpine gardens, and grass protected by nine-foot concrete fences, the core of creation. I went back to the restaurant. Philip was reading his text messages, Percha had also taken out her cell phone, but was not focused on its screen. Milady saw me coming in, jumped up from her chair, and cried out, "Dearest Anna, I could provide you with a neat business plan, the non-ferrous metals, copper alloys, you know. Profitable, progressive growth, a lot of money..."

I passed by her, the scent of her breath on my face, expensive like everything Mrs. Percha used. To be honest, Percha's fragrance was never among my priorities. Looking at the picture on the wall, I did not turn my back on Milady as some ill-wishers would think I did. I was enjoying the artist's relationship with color — a meadow, flowers. I didn't know the names of any of them.

"I wonder why this artist doesn't get the attention he deserves. I am glad his art aroused your curiosity," Percha continued enthusiastically.

Yes, the sunset glowing in the picture should not be overlooked: pink, purple, red-brown, royal colors — all of them. Paintings are an important component of luxury restaurant interiors. I turned my back to Percha, intent on feeling the benefit of the quiet ambiance that had crept into the canvas on the wall.

"But you, of course, could ..." the woman with the feet of iron continued cheerfully.

"Percha, get your ass out of here," Philip said. He spoke evenly as he did every day.

Mrs. Percha swallowed the syllable that was rolling on her lips, leaped up at me — agreeable, ready to cooperate — regaled us with a magnificent smile, and curtsied more beautifully than Todd and Peter had ever done.

"Goodbye, my darlings," she chirped, her lips still smiling.

Philip didn't look away from his phone. He said no word. I continued watching the uninteresting flowers in the picture. Another velvet curtsy and Percha walked out of the restaurant as she waved multiple goodbyes.

"Will you marry me?" Philip asked as he studied his iPhone. He spoke calmly the way he did when he ordered a steak in an eatery.

"Let me see," I replied. I spoke amiably the way I addressed the saleswoman when I wanted to buy toilet paper.

＊ ＊ ＊

"I'll tell you something important, my girl."

"I'm not your girl," I interrupted the woman with the transparent hands who was my mother's mother. Mom had left our apartment and told me she would become Phil's wife. I thought that a mole lived under this guy's face.

The little animal had eaten half of his chin and had buried itself in his throat; when Phil said something you heard a mole's voice, and a mole talked to you. The animal's sharp teeth had been biting off pieces of his heart, and Phil finally had no heart to speak of. Mom's new husband never looked at me, and the reason was clear enough — moles did not like sunlight.

One day, mom made me weed the garden. Suddenly the tomato bed began to move on its own, and I told myself that the earth had learned to walk. When a thing started walking then it was a toddler. There were so many bad men on the earth when it was still a little baby. What would happen after the earth grew up? Come off it. A bad child sometimes became a good grown-up man.

"What about your mother?" the old woman asked.

"My mother said the mole didn't want me," I admitted that, and felt blue. You'd be in low spirits, too, if you were in my old shoes. Mom Darina was far from me, Shushomir hadn't written me any letters, and Mom had agreed to become Phil's wife. She was very dear to me so I said, 'Okay, Mom. I won't stand in your mole's way. I'll pass by your house from time to time, and I'll have a look at you. We won't talk. If you walk quickly, I'll know nothing hurts you. If you look ahead of you, I'll say to myself 'She's okay.' I am a healthy child, and I won't infect you with any disease. I was forbidden to visit Mom and Phil. It was the first time I had admitted to someone that Mom did not want me. I told that old woman, the liar, about it.

"What did you tell your grandfather Jacob?"

"I don't have a grandfather," I told her. "Jacob is sick, but death doesn't want him, and he'll howl in pain for a long time. That's what I told him."

"How do you know?" the woman asked me. She took out a purse full of pennies and added, "They will all be yours. Just tell me how you know that death does not want him."

"I take death to him, but it runs away," I explained to the woman. "You can smell death, can't you? Or do you lie to me about it?"

"I love you, kid!" the woman said.

"Then why do you lie to me all the time?" I cut her short.

"Grandpa Jacob says his stomach doesn't hurt when you visit him, Annie," the woman said as she pulled a chocolate bar from the pocket of her apron. Shushomir and I often dreamed of cosmos made of chocolate. I was ready to stalk the airport guard, and when the guy fell asleep, I'd jump into a plane. I'd sure gorge myself on big chunks of chocolate space, with the moon and the stars in it. After a week, I'd get on the plane and return to Staro with a whole bag of chocolates for Shushomir.

"Don't visit Grandpa Jacob anymore," the old woman said so softly you'd think her voice was hanging by a thread.

"But when I'm not with him, his legs and stomach hurt. You yourself told me as much, woman," I couldn't understand her. The darker her brown eyes looked the more deceptive her conversation sounded. They infected me with sadness, her soft words did, and I felt that Shushomir would never again write me a letter.

"Let his legs hurt," the woman said as she tucked the chocolate bar into her apron pocket.

"But he told me he loved you," I interrupted her. This woman was either off her rocker or was telling fibs again.

"Don't go to your Grandpa's room. Do you understand?" The woman's voice turned to stone. She usually spoke gently as if her words were slippers she'd give to a thief. I wondered if she really wanted to tell me something, or was waiting for the pickpocket at the front door. "If I see you at Grandpa Jacob's room one more time, I'll send you packing. Is that clear?"

"But Grandpa Jacob said he'd taught you to cure sick people. He said because your clients' sweat smelled you could tell how many years the poor fellow would celebrate Christmas," I reminded her. "Grandpa Jacob told me he did something bad to you. But it was before he realized how much he loved you." The liar turned her back on me, an old, skinny thing, her back. I wondered how she lived so long with those gossamer bones of hers.

I was cold. The month of September tried to get its teeth into my feet and infect me with bronchitis. It felt like I got kicked by a horse. I coughed and coughed, and may not celebrate another Christmas. A stiff wind was blowing. It brought rain to the leaves and tried to trick them into taking a bath. Then they'd fall into the big September puddles.

"Go play with Elizabeth!" The stones in the woman's voice were so numerous you could cover a town square with them. Her words were a dark alley where people turned into salt statues. A "statue" was a monument in the park; the metal letters had been wrenched from the granite slab and exchanged for a glass of brandy. Bad guys, too, walked around in the voice of that woman who lied that she loved me. I knew what happened when they lied to you — they put stones in their voices and planned to bury you under their weight.

"I don't want to play with Elizabeth," I said. "I want to see how the autumn cheats the leaves."

"Go play with Elizabeth. Now!" the woman spoke so softly that my teeth hurt.

My throat and even my belly button hurt when she spoke, and her tongue was a vinegar bottle. It was a pity that darling Mom Darina wasn't here. Please come to me, Mom Darina! We'll do our little trick! Bring me a glass of tap water. Light a match above the glass and say, "Let whatever scares this child be eaten by a bull." Then the old woman's voice wouldn't give me the evil eye. Her hair wouldn't trample me underfoot even though it had been dyed golden bronze like a September sunset. Bring me a glass of tap water, Mom Darina! Wash my forehead with it and I won't be afraid of anything.

"Grandpa Jacob says his back hurts when you enter his room, woman. It hurts a lot, he says." And I kept on explaining to her, "It hurts more than death when you talk to him."

"Is that what he says?" the woman whispered, and wasps hatched in her mouth.

"But grandpa says he loves you. He wants you to stay with him no matter if his legs hurt. 'Does it make sense to breathe if she's not there?' he asked me. I admitted that I did not know, but I told him it was better if he breathed on.

"You see how stupid he is," said the woman who was mistaken about being my grandmother. "Let his legs hurt."

I felt bad about grandpa.

Mom Darina was gone, I didn't have a box of matches to light a match over a glass of tap water. I had a stomach ache and it hurt. It hurt so much that my stomach felt like piercing my skin. I suspected it wanted to run away to Shushomir, and I hoped it wouldn't be run over by a car on the road. I didn't want to keep the old woman's voice in my ears. It was a pack of wolves. I left her therapy studio and went to the large living room that was pink as a truckload of sliced watermelons.

Elizabeth was lying on the floor.

"Do you want me to teach you how to ride a horse?" she asked me and suddenly rose, a hill that had four legs.

"No, I don't," I told her.

She stood on tiptoe and looked tall — like one of her mother's crazy assistants, a huge man, almost as big as Shushomir's dad." "Assistant" was a guy with a silly brain. In the beginning, the guy's hair was black as my new boots, then it turned blond, and now it loomed, a red thunder cloud that reached his heels. He often stepped on it, and I felt sorry for him.

"Then come and bite my neck, Annie. I won't squeal on you to Mom," Elizabeth said as she stretched her neck. I thought it looked like a minibus. Here, in Sofia, folks believed minibusses could run over more people than a regular car.

"I won't bite your neck."

She suddenly jumped and stuck her tongue out at me. It was five feet long.

"I'm not going to take this anymore! You think you're the queen after your mother married Mr. Vasilev," Elizabeth muttered, her tongue still sticking out of her mouth. "I'm livid! Your mother was mom's charwoman, you know that. And now I must be nice to you. But don't be under any illusions."

"Illusions" meant potatoes I was baking in the oven while the lying old woman massaged a bigwig's buttocks. I didn't believe she had cured anyone. Grandpa Jacob hadn't really taught her to fight any serious disease. So the "illusion" was to wait endlessly while she kneaded a wealthy belly. No baked potatoes for you; the liar threw them all away, and their smell could not offend the big shot's nose.

"Don't foster any illusions, and don't bake potatoes," Elizabeth said as she spat — not at me really, but you could not be sure with her. On the other hand, I knew a bad carpenter blamed his tool. I'd better be careful with her. "Your mother is number 17 on Mr. Vasilev's list. He'll dump her in a month, and then ..."

"Then what?" I asked.

Her blue eyes burrowed into the floor.

"Mom will pay our dentist, and I'll get braces installed. My teeth will be very sharp," If I didn't keep my eyes open, I could fall into the abyss that the blue-eyed eel left between her sentences. "My braces will be made of stainless steel alloy. If I bite you with those stainless steel braces..."

"I'll be honest with you. You're clumsy, Elizabeth," I told her. "First, you'll have to pay the red-haired idiot to tie me up. Second, sooner or later I'll break your braces. What does "alloy" mean?"

She wouldn't let me know what an "alloy" was.

"Your mom is mean," Elizabeth whispered. "Don't stare at me like that."

I stopped staring at her like that and wondered if Mom was mean.

When I was a little kid, I was scared she would go somewhere, and I'd have to live by myself. The evening would scatter its darkness over my head, and that would be the end. I wailed. Mom used to say, "Don't howl," but I yowled on, long and loud. Finally, mom would mutter to herself, 'I'm not going anywhere. Let me calm this child down.' She gave me ten cents. I was saving up for a motorbike, so if she left, I'd start the engine and ride the thing to her new place. Every night, I was afraid she was going to leave me. Ten cents meant today, ten cents tomorrow — that meant a tiny pile of coins next to my pillow.

I kept watching the night. I was convinced that the Bogeyman wanted to steal my money. He'd sure buy a motorbike to reach my mom's new place before I did. Dad had mentioned that my mother was very beautiful, and I knew the Bogeyman had an eye for beauty.

"If you keep on crying for no reason, I'll punish you!" Mom warned me. "For every minute of crying, I'll take a dime from you."

Of course, I knew what a minute was: the time during which the big hand, the dumb one on the alarm clock, ran like crazy to catch its tail because it wanted to go around the clock face.

I hoped my mother wouldn't take the money she'd given me, but I was wrong. I went on wailing quietly. It wasn't pleasant to screech like the tires of our old Opel car, but what else could I do? I wanted to be sure mom wouldn't accompany the bogeyman and leave me all alone in the empty backyard with her spells that lived in the shed. Just my luck! I howled, and the little hand also went around the clock face. Mom came running to me and said, "Look here. You've been crying for two minutes, so I'll take two dimes from you."

I kept wailing, the dumb minute hand ran madly around the same places on the clock face, another minute ticked by, and mom pocketed one more coin from my tiny pile. The situation worsened; in the end, mom took all my money. So, I lost my motorbike and when mom told me she was getting married, I couldn't start any engine and couldn't ride any bike to go with her. To put it plainly, I was left penniless, mom collected all my dimes and put them in front of her on the table — a mean thing to do, I thought. You not only left a screaming kid by herself, but you also took her dimes. Now she couldn't buy a thing to come and visit you when Phil worked in his office.

"And what's more, your mother is cruel," Elizabeth said gritting her teeth. "She's cruel, she is! She is! Bite your nose off, you little squirt!"

But I didn't bite my nose off. I remembered the best year of mom's life, which is to say of mine, too, because before Vasilev married her, I had only my mother. Mom Darina hadn't come to my father's place yet.

A year ago, mom took me to the sea. Since a very young age, when my brain was a breadcrumb in my head, I'd known what the sea was — water from my toes to the end of the world.

Then I realized what happiness was. It was mom teaching me to swim. She held me, so I wouldn't drink that huge water. It felt good. Mom stopped me from sinking to the bottom. I didn't want to learn to swim, for if I did, she wouldn't hold me anymore. She'd take her hands away to the towel on the beach. Then why should I care about the sea if mom wasn't there to keep me from swallowing the waves?

"Why can't you learn to swim, child?" she wondered.

One day we, both in blue swimsuits, were walking along the jetty. I loved it more than the sea. To me, the jetty was quiet and old. It creaked under the weight of a thousand sunny smiles. Mom and I ambled along this pier, grandfather of all jetties in Bulgaria, and I watched the sea to check if a pearl had accidentally dropped out of an absent-minded clam. All of a sudden — even now I shudder at the memory of that cove; in my mind, it was as big as fear — mom pushed me into the sea. Then water, wet and icy, water everywhere.

"Swim!" mom shouted. "Swim for your life!"

I couldn't swim, but I swam. What else could I do? Fear and the cosmos would fill my nose with salty water if I stopped kicking, coughing, punching and spluttering. I puffed, hit the sea, panted, spat the waves out of my mouth, and reached the shore at last. I swayed, tottered and fell on the wet sand, fuming. I was angry with my mother, and refused to talk to her — clammed up and kept mum for so long that the alarm clock was about to melt. The second hand circled its face so many times that the poor thing became twice as long as before. At a certain point, mom ruffled my hair that was already dry.

"You see, Annie," she began. "You are angry with me, I know. If I hadn't pushed you into the water, you'd have told tales, a pile of nonsense each, and you wouldn't be able to swim. Now all silly words are gone, and you swim like a minnow, my beautiful girl!"

I didn't know if this was cruel or not. Elizabeth pushed me.

"Your mother has no heart. Go shoot yourself, little cretin!"

But Elizabeth didn't know anything. For a long time I slept in a crib next to mom's bed. Her heart beat slowly — thump, thump, thump — which meant, "Here, here I am. I'm with you, Annie." If mom didn't have a heart, then what had I heard? What was Elizabeth blathering about? My ears were as sharp as a razor's edge.

"I can hear the electricity running in your iPhone, Elizabeth," I said.

✳ ✳ ✳

They had tied the big woman to an oak. Here, in the vicinity of Staro, the forest was weak, the oaks were not huge, but if you planned to tether a woman with a strong rope, this tree would do. She was almost as tall as the men, the thinner one's hair a reddish mudslide that cascaded down below his buttocks. The other one was completely bald, and his skull glistened like a lighthouse. The guys were melting some substance on a gas stove.

"Everything will be ready in a minute, sweetheart." said the mudslide man. "Molten lead is extremely hot. Now I'll tell you where I'm going to pour it. You can choose: your left or your right ear?" he spoke quietly, his velvet-soft voice doing the tip toe dance as the man stirred the bubbling concoction. "Wait, I've got a better idea. I'll pour the metal where love takes place, honey. You know how to call this cavity, don't you?" the guy ignored the patchy rain that interfered with his work. "Don't you care to learn where the molten lead will go? It will reach your urinary bladder. The bladder is in here," his fist sank into the tethered woman's abdomen.

"Oh, you're strong, sweetie, but the lead will hit your spleen. Shall I show you where your spleen is, eh? In here. Does it hurt?" asked the man whose shaved head could hardly hold any fertile brain. "One of your kidneys will wither and die inside you. The left one. Oh, but it's nothing!" the bald head said. "We have plenty of time until our lead melts. Will it hurt if I drip molten lead in your eye?" he bent down and grabbed a stone. Crags and cliffs that resembled marble abounded in the vicinity of the wild village, but the chances of coming across veined marble in this rural backwater were equal to finding steamed prawns in the village butcher's shop. It was true it faced St. Nicholas the Miracle maker Church that was built in 1670. The shaved head rammed the stone into her mouth.

A girl tall as common nettle shrieked inside the black jeep Wrangler. Its windshield looked bigger than the mountain ridge. The shriek was dead stubble put on fire, the flames scraping the windows of the powerful vehicle.

"Don't be afraid, child, she'll die soon," said the man who sounded calm and sure under the thatch of his red hair.

"Mom Darina!" the nettle shouted. The girl was tied to her car seat designed for tall Danish children; the jeep had been imported from Denmark. This kid was much more diminutive than the Danish tykes. The girl pulled at the rope that kept her immobile, nailed like a horseshoe to a hoof. She wanted to be a storm and wanted to hug the oak tree. Perhaps the roots would know the price of a storm's love. The child screamed, but the ginger hair didn't hear her. The shaggy locks were bent low as they looked for another stone, a bigger one. The bald head was stirring the bubbling lead.

"My darling," he whispered as he kicked the woman. "You can't give birth to a child, can you? Don't worry! You won't have difficulty conceiving after I pour lead into you. I guarantee you'll love it."

There was a commotion inside the jeep. Was the brat knocking the thermos flask against the windshield? Perhaps she used the ice hammer or banged her head against the window. Mrs. Percha had mentioned the enfant terrible was not all there. The little idiot had eaten a cockroach glue trap, Madam said.

"I hate the sight of you!" the kid had blurted out staring into Madam's eyes. "I'd better die."

"The little imbecile is right," remarked the ginger locks.

"She's a little piece of shit, but she's right," the glistening skull agreed, brightening.

"She'll scratch the window glass, the idiot!"

"She squeals like a pig. I'll go make her shut up."

Unexpectedly the oak tree to which the giantess was tied began to shake. The big woman who by this point should have no spleen, no urinary bladder and no mouth, broke free from the tree trunk. She had somehow managed to cut the rope. It was a strong length of cord that jeep drivers in deep waters used for dragging their out-of-service vehicles back on track. The woman took a slow step forward. She said nothing to the man whose hair was red a dog's tongue. She didn't pick up a stone that resembled marble — you shouldn't expect to blunder on veined marble in this poor land. She didn't kick the gas burner and the bowl of molten lead above it. Her finger touched the back of the neck hidden under the ginger mane. The guy — it was a pity his hairstyle was absent-mindedly magnificent — produced a wheezing sound. The same type of gasping and whistling noises came from the throat of the athlete whose brain and head had been shaved.

"He-e-e-lp!" whispered the ginger-haired hulk whose locks still had a rebellious streak.

"The molten lead will do you good," the woman assured him.

She opened the jeep door, untied the girl, and set her free from the car seat designed for chubby Danish kids. Then she gripped the small hand. The two of them, the oak tree woman and the tyke the size of an acorn, set out for some inhabited place, but where could you set out for in this wilderness? Not a fox or rabbit had survived in these parts, the hunters had exterminated every living thing that had legs and could be sold. Whichever direction you chose, you'd end up in the village of Staro, but before you started for Staro, you had to puncture and cut the jeep tires. It went without saying you had to wait until they all were flat and dead. But even before you punctured the tires of this magnificent vehicle, you grabbed a stone — it was as different from a hand grenade as your pee was from a glass of whiskey. Wielding this stone, you etched all letters of the Bulgarian alphabet on the doors and the hood of the jeep. You were awfully sorry you could not remember all the letters Mom Darina had taught you so far. A, H, E, S, U, and M — you cut and hacked away at the jeep until your hands were puddles of pain. You dug and scraped and scratched the black vehicle, and its alarm wept with all its power. What else could it do? Men had invented the alphabet so that you could kill the jeep in which they tied you with Percha's shawl to the car seat intended for tractable children in Denmark. The car alarm wailed, but if someone scratched the letters A, E, and H on your cheeks, you'd wail too, wouldn't you?.

A little further down the mountain slope, a bog the locals called the Dark Hole sprawled and stank to high heaven. The shore was mud and stones — these were as distant relatives of marble as were the poplar tree and the thistle which grew in its shade. The folks from Staro believed that somebody evil and dark called Teva lived there, and even the thieves from Sofia knew that in fact Teva meant death. The big woman chucked the jeep key into the Dark Hole, and at that moment the funny flowers stamped on her brown dress looked like scars left after an ax blow. The girl, quite shabby, her pants wrinkled as Percha's old shawl, spat in the bog. Then she kissed the stone which had carved the most terrific letters of the Bulgarian alphabet on the hood of the black jeep. This stone had also smashed the windshield to smithereens.

∗ ∗ ∗

The car was waiting for me. I was on my way to the mall. To be honest, shops of any kind gave me a feeling of nausea. In the beginning, I felt intrigued. The shop assistants and consultants welcomed me, a rose in hand, at the entrance of their boutiques. The waiters bowed to me, the general manager of the hotel Philip had arranged for me to stay at made his appearance, bowed and said, "Good morning, madam", his eyes and beard all smiles. The chambermaids changed my towels and sheets three times a day. My masseuse used various sweet perfumes in accordance with the favorable aromatherapy forecast determined to raise my spirits. The astrologer Philip had hired half an hour after our first kiss — at 8 am — reported to me she had drawn up my daily love horoscope. She warned me not to avoid any household-related matters; the lunar lift would bring some distinctly feminine energy with it — therefore, how wonderfully compatible Philip and I would be from an astrological perspective! She would let me know when the moment would be propitious, so our joint amorous efforts would meet with success.

Philip found a primary care physician who visited me three times a week and insisted I should go through a thorough medical examination focusing on all organs, systems, processes, and liquids in my body — blood, lymph, hormones, mineral salts, chemical, and non-chemical elements in my bloodstream. A team of twelve dieticians catered for my proper nourishment, a sexologist recommended the best sex positions taking into account Philip's preferences and artistic biases.

An extremely attractive gentleman had already called on me several times in my apartment on the fifth floor at Venice Hotel (five is Philip's

lucky number in the opinion of his feng shui expert). The visitor offered me an intimate Variety experience whatever that meant, having
assured me he was authorized personally by Mr. Philip Vasilev to perform this mission. I should by no means assume that the whole event
was a joke. The young man showed me a certificate signed by Philip
and certified by a famous notary from Sofia, the capital of Bulgaria.
The young virtuoso had been hired to teach me everything pertaining
to Mr. Vasilev's preferences "in that particular sphere, you understand."
I asked the strapping specimen of manhood how old he was, and he
replied, "Twenty. My name is Radoslav. I will be honored if you agree
to call me Roro. "

"Where are you from, Roro?"

"From Silistra, a little town on the Danube, Ma'am. My youth should
not embarrass you. I have extensive experience and broad general cul-
ture. I am familiar with world literature, Renaissance painting, music,
and in addition to participating in our joint physiological activities you
can talk to me on a wide range of topics. I'm careful, I wear a condom,
and I don't use drugs."

"Goodbye, Roro," I told him. "I hope you will find another large-
scale employer.

"Do trust me, Ma'am! Let's not waste more time."

In less than two seconds, the young Apollo freed himself from his
snow-white T-shirt, his Highlander jeans, making it clear to me he wore
no underwear. The picture looked stimulating if you forgot the Highlander jeans abandoned at his feet. Unfortunately, I preferred still life.
In other words, in my view, nature's beauty was more attractive than a
twenty-year-old muscular male smiling at me without a stitch of clothes
on. Summer had not yet found its autumn makeup, and an odd heat-
wave swept away the fallen leaves.

"Please, Ma'am," said the man from the little town of Silistra as
he began to recite a poem I happened to love. Perhaps he did it by

chance, although of all the things under the sun I hated fat chances most. 'Ay, the pain it cost me to love you as I love you! For love of you the air, it hurts…'"

"You've chosen the poem *It's true* by Federico Garcia Lorca," I said surprised, but it turned out I'd taken the wrong direction.

"I'm very good at the Rooster position, Ma'am. I researched your favorite verses," the handsome young man beamed. "Your mother was so kind as to share some little secrets with me, for a fee of course. She is the best masseuse in Bulgaria, she truly is, Ma'am."

"Goodbye, Roro!"

"Ma'am, you probably do not know that your mother charges an exorbitant fee for the information she provides. I paid her out of my own pocket, and if you send me packing without even letting me demonstrate my skills…"

I stood close to this young man who looked like the Danube River near the town of Silistra; a lot of water, and the risk of waking up with a skin rash if you splashed in the shallows. I looked over his shoulder and saw nothing — no painting on the wall and no window. I liked the lovely wide space of my apartment, the cedar wood floor, the walls lined with yew wood, my laptop plus the immediate internet access. In the twelfth bottom drawer of the desk designed by an Australian cabinetmaker for my future husband, Philip Vasilev, I had hidden a photograph of a girl, a small, thin one like the string of the hat in Federico García Lorca's poem. It always rained in the little girl's eyes.

"Mom, I'll pass by your house. Keep your head up. I'll see you and I'll know you're okay!" But I don't have a house, Annie. I have an apartment lined with divine wood.

"Please, Madam," whispered Roro from Silistra, as he took a step forward. Then he kissed me. "I implore you!"

I left the room, its cedar wood floor shimmering at my feet. I knew I was strong as I walked down the corridor with natural stone marble flooring. It had been supplied from Carrara, Italy — at least that was the information the floor manager provided me with, I went to the bathroom. Marble from Norway the color of smoked salmon was all over the place. "Mom, hold your head up and I'll know you're okay!"

I held my head up high as if I wasn't in a restroom. It felt like I had climbed Mount Everest to the top.

✳ ✳ ✳

"I heard this one a long time ago from my grandmother, Annie," began Mom Darina.

I, Annie the shrimp, held her hand. I held her fingers tightly because Mom Darina had explained to me: a child's hand gives strength to her mother. I was the child, and I'd give her all I had. I knew my strength was great — it began in our house and reached the end of the universe on top of the hill. No one would dare bully her. Mom Darina told me an important tale.

"Annie, little sweetheart, I heard it from my grandmother Dara... if a woman plants a cornel tree with her own hands behind her house, then the man who is more precious to her than her own blood stays with this woman. 'For example,' my grandma said. 'If your man is sick and he's about to meet his maker, you, Darina, plant a young cornel tree. Your man will get well soon and will stay with you for good."

"Yes, Mom Darina, you planted a cornel tree on the very day you came to live with us. Do you remember? I asked you, 'Hey, big woman, why are you driving this stick into the ground here?' You still haven't become my mother, and I haven't become your child. You said to me, "Don't get in my way. If you do, I'll break your left elbow and your right one, too!"

"I couldn't have said that,'" objected Mom Darina.

"To 'object' meant to smarmily tell someone that he was lying to you, but I wasn't lying to Mom Darina. She raised me to be an honest child. At first, I was afraid she would break one of my fingers for each lie I told her. Then I realized it was better to have a broken thumb than to lie to Darina. A lie gets into your brain like a thorn in your heel, but you can get the thorn out. Once a lie gets stuck into you, you lie until you die. Unless, of course, Mom Darina wasn't around to break your left elbow first, then the right one.

"Oh, mom Darina, please tell me the truth. Why did you plant that cornel tree?"

"I didn't want your father to walk away from me, Annie, sweetie. That's why I planted it. And the thing took root. Look what a tree it is now! A beauty!"

"My father drinks, shouts, scolds me for nothing at all. He is weaker than you," I went on counting the chinks in dad's armor on my fingers. Truly, I wouldn't find so many fingers in the whole village to list the bad things in my father's head. "He's skinny as a beanpole, and you are big."

"I'm big, but my heart is small without him, sweetie. My heart is full of your father! He is a good man."

"My heart talks to death when you are not around, Mom Darina. Mother married Phil, you know. I went to see her three times. Her house is big and scary. I can only count to seven, but there were two hundred fifty-five floors above the seventh floor. Now, I can't see if mom keeps her head up. I don't know if she's okay. You're the only one I have — my friend and my mom. But my heart is not full of you alone, Mom Darina. It is full of Shushomir. My mother has taught me to look at nature's beauty when I'm sad. She lives on the two hundredth floor in Phil's big house. I think she married him because she wanted to eat lamb stew. I can't buy it for her because lamb meat is expensive. And I watch nature."

Nature was the forty-two tomato plants in mom Darina's vegetable garden. I stared at them and I said to myself, "You're no good, tomatoes, honestly. If I were nature, I'd hate the sight of you! Hens are always pecking at you!" I made sure I knew very well what nature was when — lo and behold! — I saw another little cornel tree sticking out its green banner — its young green leaves — in nature. It was small, just two twigs, a little bit taller than me, but the sapling — perky as it was — strained every nerve to show it was a big shot.

"Mom Darina?" I asked, wondering if I wasn't getting on her nerves. I could still see the scar where the thug with the red hair and much grease in it had clouted her. Her chin was swollen. She was limping, "Mom Darina, who planted that tiny cornel tree that looks like a leek with a long stem?"

"I did."

"Who for?" I asked digging further into the story.

"For you, Annie. I don't want you to go away from me, my girl!"

Then I said to her, "Please bend down. You are very tall." She bent down and I kissed her. If you kissed someone who had planted a cornel tree for you, you'd have to tell her, "Mom Darina, I will never leave you. I'm going to beat the universe black and blue if it bullies you. I'll dig another bank for the river and I'll plant twenty-five cornel trees on it if I have to, but I will not leave you, mom Darina!"

I noticed them without meaning to — the folks of Staro walking in single file like ants before it started to rain. What were these guys up to? My dad, Shushomir's father, many other men, young and white-haired, their heads pools of molten silver; at a certain point, I spotted what Shushomir's father was holding in his hand — a huge bundle of red hair it was. Other villagers clutched different clothes, all rags. Old grandma Dosta, the baker, squeezed a purple floral shirt in her hands — its left sleeve was torn off, and the other was in place. I knew whose shirt it was — the Shaved Head's. I hoped the two cut-throats had been trampled underfoot in the nettles, or even better, maybe somebody tied them up and dumped them somewhere in the dell.

"What's the matter, Dad?" I asked, not that I expected he would answer me. He thought my brain was as small as a worm's, and, in his view, talking to me amounted to conversing with the mud someone had scraped off his shoes. But this time he grabbed me like I was a carton of cigarettes, and being what he was — thin and long — lifted me to the top branch of the big cornel tree.

Annie!" he said.

Then he said "Annie" again... and "Annie" ... must have been afraid he would forget what my name was. Dad kissed me on the forehead. It was the first time this had happened since I remembered him. I was scared he'd fallen ill, no kidding. He could drop me on the stones — dad wasn't strong, He held me in the air, and my feet touched the highest branch on that cornel tree. Mom Darina had bought it from the marketplace, and even if dad wanted to, he couldn't walk away from her.

"Dad, did you beat the two gorillas? They smashed mom Darina's mouth with a rock.

It was like I was speaking to Grandma Petra who we buried last year. My dad was silent. He looked at mom Darina, looked at her, and swallowed hard as if he was gulping for air and preparing to swallow the mountain peak. Shushomir's father, huge and scary, his hair as red as the hood of Little Red Riding Hood, cut in, "I used the rock they'd smashed Darina's mouth with, and I smashed their mouths. We set their pants on fire. I tied the muggers to the seats in the jeep and left them there," he kicked a rock that lay like a dog at his feet and added, "I cut the bully boy's hair. And I'll scare the crows with it."

I didn't want to know anything about the crows or whether their brazen beaks would be frightened by a mess of greasy red locks. I had to find a cornel bush. It could be as thin as a mouse's tail, but it should be a cornel sapling. I would dig a hole for it with my own hands, and I'd water the small plant every day.

I wanted Shushomir to never go away from me.

Never.
I wanted the universe to know it.
Never.

✳ ✳ ✳

A big woman in a brown dress — they sold them by the dozen in the corner shop which was simultaneously a pub, a bakery, a hardware store, and a pharmacy in Staro — and a girl in a pink frock bought from the same shop, were carrying: the woman two huge baskets full of pink tomatoes, and the child two small baskets full of pink tomatoes, the most wonderful vegetables in Staro. They walked slowly. The weather was neither good nor bad; what else could you say about these clouds, the waifs and strays in the sky above your head? The highway to the Greek border was just a fairytale away from Staro, but the woman in the brown dress sighed, "I don't know any fairytales, Annie."

"Do you know the one about Eliza and the wild swans?" asked the kid who was just a little bigger than the tomatoes in her baskets.

"No, I don't. I can show you how to chew through the rope after they've tied you up," the woman added. "In my native village, everyone wants to tie you up and give you a thrashing. When they're slapping you, you have to fill your lungs with air. Your rib cage expands, they tie you up, then you let the air out, and the rope comes loose. You wriggle out and hit back. You beat them, so they can hardly go back to their wives. You make them remember that if they meet you again and are spoiling for a fight, they won't be able to return to their wives anymore."

"I don't want to beat them that much. Let them go to their women," said the child. "I wouldn't beat even Phil, though a mole lives in his mouth. He's married Mom, and he gives her plenty to eat."

"If you don't crush them, they'll crush you, my girl."

"Can't I love them, so they'll love me?"

"No, you can't. They don't love anybody."

"Stop!" said the girl. Without warning, she put the baskets on the ground and fumbled in the pocket of her pink frock. The pocket had been attached to the kid's chest and looked bigger than the dress. "Look at this. I made it with clay."

The woman looked at the crumpled, shapeless ball in the kid's hands and asked:

"Is that a pear?"

"It is not! This is my heart, Mom Darina! I want to give it to you. You'll keep it better than me. They beat me and I'm not a lizard. I can't get away when they tie me up. I'd rather walk without a heart and have you guard it for me."

The woman put down the baskets on the grass — a large woman, a sun-tanned face with a swollen chin. She seemed to forget the baskets, each one as huge as a suitcase, and lifted up the girl — high, even higher than the sun — kissed her both cheeks and finally her forehead.

"I'll guard your heart better than anything in the world, Annie, sweetie!"

Then they both took the baskets from the ground and continued along the path to the highway. It was the highway that hurried to the Greek border — only a fairytale away from Staro.

"Once upon a time there lived a child," began the girl as she carefully carried the baskets of tomatoes. "The child's mother died, but she remained dead just for a while, some hours, enough to get some rest. She could cast good spells — so that people made a million dollars and didn't quarrel over money. But all her spells were hard to weave. The child bent over backwards to be near her mom and of course got in her way, so the mother decided to go and meet her death. It was warm at death's place, and no one beat you," said the child, then kept mum.

"Hey! What happens next?" asked the woman in her new brown dress with huge yellow stars and moons printed on the back.

"Well, the mother put death into her suitcase and took it to Sofia, the capital of Bulgaria. Death has lived there ever since. There are big shops in Sofia, all thronged with people, so Death doesn't have to search for a long time. It easily finds the man it has chosen — just skips across the street and picks the fellow up," the child explained, "Wherever death stalks a guy, the air smells of roasted almonds, so I know when the end is coming. If you don't want death to take you to its house, bake some almonds and put them on the doorstep. Death will have a bite. "They taste good, these almonds do," death will say. Then it will think to itself, 'This guy is very heavy, I'm not going to drag him all the way to my place. Let him live on. I'll come back for him another time.' That's what Mom told me. She went and met her death, then came back to teach me how to put stones in my mouth and how to talk to children from other countries. When you have little pebbles in your mouth, you speak English. If the stones in your mouth are big and heavy, you cannot say a word."

"That's not true. I put pebbles in my mouth, but your father said he understood what I was saying to him. And he doesn't speak English."

"I'm telling you a fairytale now, okay?" the child interrupted. "A woman from Sofia was so prickly and stingy that even death was afraid of her. This woman said to the child, 'I am your grandmother.' How can you explain to this woman that stingy people don't have grandchildren? I've heard a story about a father who was so bad that he didn't even have a child."

"How come he didn't have?" the huge woman wondered.

"Well, if you're bad, even if you have a child, you still don't have one,'" the little girl explained. "It was good that a woman came and stayed with the bad father. In the beginning, the child thought, 'What is this evil newcomer doing here? She's so huge that even Fedo's second-hand store will be too narrow for her. If she remains in our house and stands up, her head will hit the ceiling, and the house will collapse.' The child was scared of her. One day, she said to the woman, 'Merci, please! I won't make you nervous. Don't beat me. Don't crane your neck because the roof will cave in. A tile may fall and squash me!" The child swept the floor in front of the woman. The kid believed that the giantess was as mean as the leeches that drink your blood if you stepped on them in the river. The beasts crept under your skin, ate everything — your heart, your lungs, and only your face remained whole. The leech drank your brain and kept on living under your skin, so it would look like a person. This happened to most people. The child thought, "This giantess can't be human; a huge leech from the river has settled inside her." However, the child was not a faint-hearted fool.

Any leech — no matter if it was as big as a wolf — would be more stupid than the stupidest child. 'And I'm not stupid,' the girl said to her-self. One day she said 'Mom' to the ogress. The ogress stopped being a leech and turned into a woman again. She began to call the child 'Annie sweetheart.' No one had ever called the girl like that. The child was not that clever, much to the contrary, she was sillier than the cleverest child in the world, a boy called Shushomir.

"His name is not Shushomir. It's Stanislav," objected the tall woman. She did not shake or wobble under the weight of the tomato baskets although they were each as heavy as a helicopter.

"You're wrong," said the child. "When I asked him what his name was, he answered 'Shushomir.' One way or another, the boy's name in my tale is Shushomir," pointed out the child, a walking piece of wire that didn't bend under the weight of the tomatoes. "The girl couldn't tell why she started to love that huge woman. The little one transformed the leech into a mother, and the mother transformed the cowardly brat into a brave kid. The girl loved her so much — from the village of Staro to the end of all fairy tales. So, the giantess who used to be evil became the most wonderful woman.

They walked towards the highway and could hear car tires screeching with impatience to get to the end of the world, but the asphalt always had a mind of its own!

"Mom Darina! One thing is very important. In every house, a child should be growing up. The kid may not be as clever as Shushomir. For example, the girl in my story has broken three beer glasses. She lost a fork once, and her hats seemed to vanish into thin air. This was okay. The girl wanted the sun to play with her hair. So she lost her hats on purpose and was not a very good child. But if a child, even a naughty one, lives in the house, the leech becomes a woman. At first, the woman is evil because she cannot forget what the leech has taught her. But I tell you — the child has trained her well, and she becomes gentle and good within a month."

The tall woman that carried her heavy baskets with ease didn't say anything. Perhaps she had choked on the wind. In September, folks often caught a cold, but fortunately, no one coughed or ran a temperature.

"And what happened then?" the woman, in her brown dress with yellow stars and moons, asked quietly. Perhaps she didn't want the tomatoes in the baskets to hear what her question was.

"Then, one day, the child overheard his father say things. He told the big woman something. She knew she shouldn't lift her head up for she could break the roof of their little house. The man spoke loudly. He didn't care a fig that the girl couldn't sleep. His voice was larger than he was, and dark as the night. 'Darina, I'd have died if you hadn't been there for me.' 'That's true,' the woman agreed. The child didn't know if she shook her head because the little thing pretended to be asleep. But the girl wasn't mean, Mom Darina. To be mean means that you pretend to be asleep. The truth is you're all ears eavesdropping. But the kid couldn't but eavesdrop a bomb in her father's voice."

"And? What did the father say?" asked the woman as she stared at the heavy baskets.

"Well, the big woman spoke quieter than the man. She could beat him if she wanted to. She'd even clouted him one a few times. That's why he was scared. "Darina, Darina…" The father kept on repeating her name. He was a man a bit flighty in his mind and couldn't think of anything else to say. Then the woman asked him, "What about your wife? What about Anna?"

"I love her, Darina! She left me in the middle of the road. She dumped me, but I see her… I see her even if I'm looking at an empty beer bottle. I know she's gone. I dream about her, Darina."

The big woman in the brown dress, with lots of moons and stars stamped on it, was silent. It was a good thing that the highway was somewhere near here, and you could hear the cars roar.

The child was suddenly scared. The big woman could say, 'I'm going to die, Annie,' then she'd pack death in her suitcase. But she couldn't do magic like the girl's mother. Good big Darina wouldn't be able to find the way back to Annie! She didn't know how much that child loved her. When you love someone, Mom Darina, do you know what you have to do?"

"What?" the woman asked.

"You take a handful of mud. There's a lot of it under the big willow tree by the river. This mud is very good. If you leave it to dry long enough, it becomes a heart. The girl turned the handful of mud into a heart — it was her own little heart — and then said to the woman, 'Aunt Darina, I give you my heart. Don't listen to what Dad's babbling! He's a bad man, so bad that he even doesn't have a child!'"

"Your father is not a bad man, Annie."

"Then why didn't he love the big woman who lives in my fairytale?" the kid asked.

They walked on in complete silence if you ignored the fussy month of September that was busy arranging the clouds to make its bed warm enough. This year, September was lazy and often inclined to doze off for a few minutes on the clouds. The woman and the girl reached the highway, put the baskets on the asphalt at the rest stop, and waited for shoppers. Such magnificent tomatoes were good for your salad and your pizza. They could work wonders for your muscles. Hopefully, smart people would pull off the highway to buy vegetables. So, the big woman and the girl could have money to burn, and no, they wouldn't go to the village pub where the owner of the premises sold jeans, bread, rice, and scissors... They were smart, the child and her mom were. They would travel to Pernik on the rickety 9 o'clock bus and they'd hang around the sweetshops in the most beautiful Bulgarian city — until noon! They'd positively get tired of walking around the beautiful city of Pernik, and of course, they would go to San Marco pizza place. Mom Sarina would order the most expensive pizzas in Bulgaria. Oh, didn't the girl pray for numerous buyers of their miraculous tomatoes? Yes!

At a certain point, the kid, keeping a firm grip on the baskets burbled on, "Mom Darina! As long as a kid's heart made of dried mud stays whole in a big woman's hands, everything will end well. A little girl can change everything. The big woman can also change everything. And I'll tell you why — because the woman was a child before she grew up."

✳ ✳ ✳

The gated community consisted of three imposing houses that were actually castles. A ten-foot wall ensured their protection; cameras were installed every two feet and guards tall as lampposts were on duty 24/7 at every exit. A family of gardeners took care of the brightly-colored, fragrant flowers. The landscapers bowed to me every time I showed up no matter where, but didn't talk to me. Both the wife and the husband were paid extra for the detailed reports on my behavior they provided Phil with. I had a personal cook — back when Philip attended the

Italian College of Arts, she used to cook for his whole family. Her face looked like a bruised apple; her hands were wrinkled but clean. She didn't speak at all; the gardeners had set an example to her, and she bowed low to me. I believed this celebrated culinarian described my comportment to Phil in the minutest detail.

I had a masseuse who neither bowed nor spoke a word. The following specialized personnel and assets had been placed at my disposal: a manicurist, a female equestrian coach, a Tai Chi instructor, an art mentor, a shooting range near mentor, a psychologist, a pedicurist, a secretary, a personal luxury lingerie brand, a personal seamstress, a private chauffeur, a personal consultant, and an elderly lady who planned my sexual commitments to Phil. I didn't t have to worry about the phone numbers of arts institutions or the dates when cultural events took place in the Bulgarian capital. The girl who served my coffee in the right way took on this task. She was very pretty, and I wondered why Philip had not made her number 18 on his list yet. Maybe he had.

I told my secretary that I'd rather have a massage or, as ridiculous as it sounded, a chamber symphony concerto. Half an hour later, the orchestra started performing, the musicians lined up neatly in my spacious living room. A committee had chosen three violinists who guaranteed that near-perfect acoustics had been achieved. My astrologer had of course consulted the stars beforehand as to which composer would have a beneficial effect on my psyche. If I felt an overwhelming desire for a capella songs, thirty minutes later, three brilliant tenors burst into "O Sole Mio". I was expected to be nice when Philip got home. I was to never burden him with questions as to where he'd been or why he came back so late. It was unambiguously advised to adhere to the "need to know" principle.

I was expected to behave myself. Well, I didn't. I did not pester my secretary, grinding her down as I was supposed to. I didn't resort to the services of the masseuse, the pedicurist, and the beautician. I swam instead.

The gated community inhabitants had four swimming pools — two outdoor and two indoor ones — available 24/ 7 with a view to maintaining their physical and mental health. I swam twice a day.in the big indoor pool. I had informed the specialized experts that I could not be bothered seeing anyone there. I preferred the Olympic size pool on the ground floor of my house. I'd already gone so far as to call it "my house".

Two other girls lived in the gated community castles. At first, I thought they were numbers 15 and 16 on Philip's list — or why not 19 and 20? I saw no way to get at the truth, nor did it particularly matter to me. Perhaps they were ladies of pleasure toiling and moiling for some of Philip's associates. It turned out that the gated complex was a kind of immaculate dispensary where Philip and dignitaries at his level discussed their ailments and recurring illnesses. I could barely tell what sort of business Philip carried on; on the other hand, I could describe the cars, or should I say the space shuttles that the public figures' chauffeurs drove.

The other two ladies, should I call them my colleagues, were probably artists. I could hear one of them sing at night. Her voice was beautiful, filled with the scent of baked almonds. There was no shore and no end to it. I would have warned her to be careful, but she didn't see me as she hid in the woods surrounding the buildings. There were no words and no melody in her tunes. Her voice turned the air into beautiful music, but I caught the terrible smell and was afraid for her. And for myself.

The other woman drank a lot, and she was no singer to speak of, though she had told me, "Hi, there. I'm a singer. I've been informed that you are Mr. Phil's special handpicked toy. How did you become that successful?"

"I haven't become successful yet," I answered her.

"Modest, aren't we? No one believed Philip would focus on scum like you."

"He'll throw me out soon," I told her.

"Then what's that?" she clutched at my arm. On my finger, a ring glowed. It cost twice the value of the four castles and the four swimming pools, the two outdoor ones, the other two hidden underground, all filled with extremely pure mineral water.

The woman was silent, but her eyes, green, their searing heat hating me, met mine. She reached her right hand out towards my face.

"Doesn't that impress you?" her voice was full of whiskey. The skin on her wrist was almost transparent, the vein — a river cutting through the desert of the white skin — reached the middle finger and dried up there. A ring gleamed on her ring finger, the dam wall that held her blood in place. "Well?" The whiskey on her breath detested me. It shot to kill.

"The skin on your arms is beautiful," I ventured, unsure what exactly was supposed to impress me.

"If there's one thing that disgusts me it's you!" the whiskey slopped all over me. "You're either too dumb or ... even if you are, I despise you. Remember it well!"

I remembered it well. I'd sure make efforts to steer clear of this damsel in distress. She grabbed my shoulder.

"You loiter in front of the buildings dressed as a salesgirl at the Housewife Market," she laughed. "Your ring is twice as expensive as mine. Don't pretend to be blind!"

"Thank God I'm not blind," I agreed.

"I saw hers too, the other slut's" the odor of expensive alcohol hit my cheeks as the woman pressed her face against mine. "Her ring is cheaper than mine. She focused on this detail. She's been vomiting for three days in a row. Grief-stricken over it, isn't she? Can you hear her? She's wailing. Showing him she can sing... Sing my foot! But you... You'd better drag your ass out of here. Do you sing too?"

"No, I don't," I replied. Then I made a mistake. I still could see the purple marks where the hand with a ring many times cheaper than mine clutched my neck. I turned to the woman — the bloody fool I was! Didn't I know it was Philip who asked questions in the gated community? I asked her, "What was I supposed to notice about you, Madam?"

Her hands were strong, and my neck was thin. I could feel less and less air pass through my throat to my lungs. I wasn't particularly afraid when the smell of baked almonds engulfed me. It wasn't a smell; it was thick as mist.

"So you don't know what it is, huh? You don't know! You're a moron. A provincial rag! He proposed to all three of us at the same time."

Yes, I was interested in exactly what had been proposed, who had drawn up the proposal; however, the smell of almonds was no longer just a negligible detail in the relaxed ambience of the park. I could not breathe. No air came to my lungs. Perhaps I was not quoting her words correctly. Roasted almonds floated in the pool of whiskey she had drunk.

"He proposed marriage to all three of us and plans to arrange brawling matches between the three contestants he's selected. Tonight! Whoever crushes the other two in freestyle wrestling will become his wife. I was the winner twice. Survived two rounds of cuts and bruises. You stupid provincial stick! I was hoping it would all be over, but he dragged you to his private suite."

Her words flew like angels over my head. My neck no longer hurt. Death killed all pain. Death was a path to love... There was no air in my lungs.

"He bought three engagement rings... Ha-ha-ha!" Death settled in my throat. "And I secretly cherished hopes. I hoped..."

I'd read somewhere that people were attached to life by ropes that scientists called instincts. I called them "thirst for oxygen". I tugged at her fingers and wriggled free. The gust of air was so strong I couldn't swallow it.

"Your ring is most expensive!" the woman whispered. The whiskey smell fled from her mouth like a prisoner escaping his cell. "What about my ring? Phil sent his dumb secretary to buy it. Then Mr. Phil will wrench the ring from my finger. His secretary will return it to the posh shop."

At that moment, I saw the woman who sang striding along the path.

She said nothing as she withdrew to the perfectly manicured lawn — a tall, blonde woman, slim, in a plain grey dress. I liked her. She had driven the roasted almonds away from my throat.

"Moron!" said the singer who I had never heard sing in the gated property. I didn't know where she'd got a bottle of whiskey from.

The underground pool was fifteen feet deep at one end and six feet at the other. There was a springboard, but I didn't use it. I swam breast-stroke, then front crawl and backstroke. My neck hurt. Where the free-style wrestling winner's nails had dug into my skin, ten reddish holes smoldered, one from each of her long, sharp nails. Gradually, the holes turned blue. I kept on swimming — ten times the length of the swimming pool, which made 500 yards. I planned to swim another kilometer. The masseuse who didn't talk to me — only Philip had the right to speak to whomever he wished in the gated complex. She broke the rule. She told me, "Mister Philip is expecting you for dinner, Madam."

It was impossible to undertake any activities if you'd been informed that "the General Manager is expecting you for dinner, Madam." The table was round, encrusted with different colored gemstones, precious ones I believed. On the walls, lined with red silk, Chinese or perhaps Korean characters shimmered; a semblance of a wooden wheel was installed on the large table. Philip sat in the most imposing armchair and made the wheel spin. Was it made of mahogany? Cedar wood? Chinese walnut? Damn the wood of the spinning wheel, filled with foods I had no idea how to eat. They smelled wonderful though.

The masseuse respectfully touched my elbow, bowed, and asked me to sit on the chair in the central position at the table. The singer with the enormous voice was taken to the chair on my right side — the masseuse did not bow to her. The wrestling champion who had grabbed me by the throat and nearly choked me seated herself on my left side without waiting for a bow or a sign from the masseuse.

"Amelia, I don't recall anyone asking you to take this chair," Philip's words — identical twins, morose and icy — turned her into a statue of salt. "Go away, Amelia!"

The whiskey girl of dubious virtue froze in her tracks. After a minute or so, she turned sharply and appeared to have her finger on the trigger. The woman was not an old armchair with broken springs. Far from it. She did not stare at the floor, neither did her head hang low as she fumbled in her purse. Philip said, "Give me back my ring!" After a while, he added, "Get out, Amelia. Now!"

A hush fell over the room. I was hungry. Swimming had whetted my appetite, but I was afraid to reach out to the dishes on the serving wheel. I assumed it was a privilege reserved for Phil — he had to be the first to help himself to Japanese soups and stews. Obviously, the businessman wasn't thinking about the selections; he was reading something interesting, perhaps a short story, on his phone. Not for a moment abandoning his intellectual pursuits, Phil spoke curtly, "You too, Desa. Get out!"

Phil's latest significant other stood up. Her eyes were very beautiful, and she had everything that made a woman a magical fairytale. She took the ring off her finger and left it on the serving wheel covered with Chinese and Japanese foods. I had never heard of them, but the aroma of freshly cooked fish wafted towards me, and I longed to eat as much as possible from each vegetarian and non-vegetarian dish.

"I like your resourcefulness and the way you've demonstrated it, Dessa. You can keep the ring. Sell it. Deposit the cash into your bank account," Philip said.

The woman who was much more beautiful than me, and her sigh was the universe's beginning and end, did not do as I expected her to do. Her eyes filled with tears and her cheeks, smooth and lovely, glowed red. She did not sob, nor did she say a word. She wore a mint green suit with matching shoes. It was evident she had perfect dress sense.

"Stop!" said Philip. "I hate tears. Give me back the ring!"

Slowly, as if her arm weighed as much as the water in the swimming pool, the woman took off the piece of sparkling jewelry. Her tears dried up. She was dunes and burning sands. Her eyes were the Sahara. The woman lifted the ring high above her head and threw it on the floor. Then very slowly, majestically, she made for the door. The masseuse, who I hadn't noticed in the living room before, rushed in where angels feared to tread, grabbed the ring, and handed it to Philip. Then she bowed.

"Stop her," Philip ordered. "Make her take off her dress, her shoes… her underwear too. She must pay for all these items if she wishes to go home with them."

The masseuse pushed her out of the room. Behind the door, a huge voice rose. There was no melody and no words in it. It was a giant dust cloud from the Sahara. This voice was deeper than the sky. It had no end.

"She's ill-mannered and ill-behaved," Philip remarked. He kept quiet as he looked up at me — if the whitish space between his eyelids could be described as a look — then concluded, "Every impropriety committed in my presence has a price. If she is allowed to stay in my house, she must behave herself. The saying *give her an inch and she'll take a mile* does not work with me.

I was silent.

"Do you think that's fair?"

"What?"

"People must pay if they're being rude to me?"

I would have kept quiet, but my thoughts smelled of almonds.

"Everything depends on your definition of *rude*," I replied. Behind my smile was great trepidation as I very carefully, and making no haste,

I took the ring he'd given me off my finger. The gemstone was the oven in in which live coals smoldered. I left the ring before him. "It is too expensive to wear every day."

The expression on Philip's face didn't change. Neither did the pale space between his eyelids. His fingers that took the ring gave off a heady scent. I knew what it meant.

"This gem is death," I said.

He put the decorative item in his breast pocket.

"I have not withdrawn my proposal," Philip said. "Will you marry me? However, I want to learn something I still know nothing about."

He kissed my ring finger and my wrist, then his lips lingered long on the throbbing dimples that the claws of the lady, the whiskey lover, had carved into my neck.

"That must hurt a lot," whispered Philip. "I can't bear it! It's the first time I've felt someone else's pain. When you came down with a fever a week ago, I ran a fever too. I've never had anything like that happen to me."

"Maybe you were too strong for the virus that knocked me out," I said.

"It wasn't a virus. When you think about your daughter, that horrible creature, you get depressed. Me too," he said. "When you're happy for your daughter, I, for no good reason, don't feel happy at all. Tell me…" Philip didn't touch me, didn't squeeze my wrist, and didn't give me pain.

He took me in his arms. It was the first time this had happened. His lips dug into my hair, studied slowly my forehead and ears. He made me stop in the middle of the corridor, and I noticed how clean the white wood floor was. In the uncertain light reflected off the wood, love happened — perhaps it had taken careful planning — and passed away in a civilized manner as was the habit Phil had developed. I was surprised when he said, "I love you! I've been looking for you all my life."

Then he carried me in his arms. I didn't know there was a bathroom next door. He soaped my body, gently, softly as if I were a statue of sand. He cleaned my skin with a cotton ball and kissed — my body felt sticky and wet like the first snow of the year — every square inch of me.

"I've been looking for you since the first day of my life," he said. "I've dreamed about your face before I knew you. You are a part of me, an organ in my body, the most vital one. If you are taken ill, I will die! Can you understand? But I want to know something."

It was a room with no windows, and the walls emitted subdued light as he whispered sweet nothings in my ear.

"I've asked you that question, but you didn't give me an answer. This is for you," he started dressing me as if I was an infant, careful not to hurt me, the underwear, the blouse, the skirt. I wondered if he had done that to all the numbers on his list, from one to sixteen, and maybe a few more, eighteen, nineteen, twenty... His hands shook slightly, his face was beaded with sweat, his chin and cheeks were flushed. "I feel safe with you. Please take care of me!" Phil said. He kissed my shoes, then gently put them on my feet. His pulse waited for me, his fingers caressed the hem of my skirt. He kissed the buttons of my jacket, my nails, my knuckles, his lips stuck to my wrist and stayed there so long that my blood vessels throbbed. "I love you! Be watchful!" he whispered. "Protect me!"

In a flash, Philip lifted me up as effortlessly as if I were a dead minnow's skeleton. He pressed himself against me, his ribs crashed into mine so sharply I was afraid he'd break my spine. Was he on regular medication? A new type of drug? Ephedrine forte? He said, "I don't do drugs. I found what I've been looking for since I became unable to blot out my memories of you. I've been seeing your face since I was three years old. You've been with me all my life."

"Maybe my face just looks like the one you've seen," I suggested. I wasn't afraid of Phil. The smell of baked almonds had faded.

"Look!" he said as he squeezed my hand. The bone in the middle of my palm crackled. A pain, dark and agonizing as maybe that of a beetle crushed under a shoe, assaulted my senses. I didn't scream. He did.

"It hurts! It hurts me! Because it hurts you. I didn't think it was possible. I believed I was fooling myself. I dreamed there lived a girl whose pains would be mine. I had a stomach ache night after night, and I believed she has a stomach ache too. The doctors assured my mother "He's a perfectly healthy boy." The results of my medical tests were within the reference range, but I was sick. I didn't have much strength to walk, then suddenly I recovered for no reason, and there was no trace of my illness. I dreamed of your face, do you understand? I told my mother my biggest secret. She had waited a long time for a child. She had undergone all sorts of impossible treatments. She consulted fortune-tellers, doctors in Germany and France — her efforts were to no avail. At long last, she stumbled on an odd woman, a masseuse. It was widely rumored this massage expert could detect the smell of death. It was your mother. Once a week, my mother used to get a full body massage at old Lena's parlor. That lasted for three years, and the unbelievable happened. I was conceived in February and born in November. I've been looking for you ever since. I've been looking for you ever since the moment of your conception.

There was some sort of scary eccentricity about this man; he rocked me gently, punctuating his words by quiet laughter — so different from the cold, abstruse calculations and sentences he used to keep other people at arm's length with. Philip spoke to me feverishly, turning his words into kisses.

"I love you," he said to my jacket, to my shirt collar, left sleeve, the buttons, the belt, and the straps of my shoes. "I love you! I was a fool."

"One of your women sang beautifully. She had blond hair and blue eyes," I whispered as froze in my tracks.

Philip could have killed me.

His kisses swallowed my words.

"I found you. Now I'm sure. I want to know something else."

He carried me, and I, curled up against his chest, weighed as much as a cup of coffee in his arms. He took me to a small office. There were three plastic chairs in it. On the first chair, sat the man who had thrown me out of his car in the mountain gorge. Every fifty miles he had pulled over and over again. I remembered the shards of broken glass, sharp, scattered on the side of the highway. The second gentleman sat in a cheap, shabby armchair. He had scary ginger hair, a lot of it that to me looked like a tub full of water in which someone had washed a badly soiled orange blouse. The third visitor's head glistened — shaved, or should I say meticulously scraped off — to uncover the skull bones. The three men jumped out of their seats. Philip pulled my head to his chest. He had by accident — accident my foot — pulled my skirt up. I saw my shoes, black and beautiful, that cost as much as half the shoe warehouses in Sofia.

"What binds the three of you together, gentlemen?" Phil's sepulchral tone matched his haughty face. You're not worth a brass farthing each one of you, his eyes said. You disgust me. "What's your lowest common denominator?"

None of the three provided an answer. The shaved head ventured a sheepish smile. Philip pressed me hard against him. I could hardly breathe.

"We're colleagues," the man with the unforgettable skull attempted to leap into action.

"No!" Philip interrupted him. "She is your lowest common denominator. You've touched her here, and here!" Philip's face loomed over me like a tombstone. "Anna, every time someone has touched you, my whole body ached. Now I'm hurting you!" his hands sank into my throat. "I lost consciousness. My mother called an ambulance every time someone had sex with you, Anna. When your daughter was born, I was hit by a severe neurological crisis. The doctors didn't know why

or where it came from. I couldn't walk for two months. I couldn't eat —
they force-fed me."

The three men, three statues of salt, stared at him.

Philip loosened his grip and his fingers gave me fresh air. His hands
let my chest live.

"Tell me!" he said as his lips sank into mine. I felt dizzy. "Tell me!
How was it with him? With him? Why did you let them touch you here
and here! Why?"

He put his hands around my throat. I stopped breathing... My lungs
burned... I was searching for an answer in a frenzy to get more air...
The cornel tree... It died. I planted it when my daughter was born. I watered it regularly. In the village of Staro they believed that if you planted
a cornel tree for someone, that person would not leave you.

"Why! Tell me!" the cold lips stole my breath and swallowed it.
Philip wrapped me in his arms. The antelope... the python... That was
how the antelope felt, crushed in the reptile's powerful spiral. Death. It
would save my face.

"It is coming!" I said.

Death came. I was alone.

Philip's hands were on my chest. Suddenly, very gently, as if he was
trying to soothe a fussy baby, he started kissing me — the top of my
shoes first, my knees, the hem of my skirt, the buttons, my breastbone,
and the sore dimples the whiskey woman had embroidered on my neck,
my earlobes... I was a little girl when my mom had my ears pierced and
made me wear a pair of earrings, the cheapest ones in the store. I still
hadn't turned four.

The three men in the cheap plastic chairs scowled at me. They
watched intently. The air gushed from their throats like blood spurting
from a gaping wound.

✳ ✳ ✳

"Those three boys are all bacon grease and belly fat," said a girl in a stylish sports outfit, a strong body, and a pair of blue eyes. "I'm tired of them. Look, I whistle just like that," the sturdy girl blew a police whistle three times in succession, and three boys who were the same age as the energetic mademoiselle came running out of the garden. There, to the gardener's delight, the trees had already lost their green manes. The young athletic lass blew the whistle once again. The three youngsters squatted to the ground and stuck out their tongues.

"Bark!" ordered the little one, and the three let out a shrill howl. Their voices had not yet grown up.

"Lie down!" commanded the girl. The trio sprawled out in front of her, then the cubs wailed, their voices hoarse as they kicked their legs in the air.

"My shoes!" the girl shouted. The tallest boy, blond, blue-eyed, a real hunk, crawled up to the young lady's sneakers, barked frenetically, lifted his foot, then rubbed his nose against the girl's left leg. The second boy, a stocky bucket of cast iron, rolled in the grass, grinned and kissed the lass's sneaker. In all likelihood, the kiss had gone wrong for the girl kicked his belly with the heel of her shoe. The thickset muscular fighter retreated, letting out a mournful howl, his tail between his legs. The third lad was long and thin. His T-shirt hung on him like a poster peeling off the wall in the rain. He was, however, the most persistent member of the squad.

The third boy kissed both the sneaker and the sturdy girl's ankle as a result of which he earned a huge slice of bacon that his mistress shoveled into his mouth.

"He who pays the piper calls the tune!" she announced. The three boys offered up a clumsy backbend, their tummies glistening on account of making sustained efforts. The girl slowly and carefully inspected the three gymnasts. On the smoothest belly, the girl left a two-lev coin, she put no penny whatsoever on the stocky boy's stomach. She kicked the boy in the knees and the unfortunate acrobat lay slumped on the floor. The blond boy's belly, which jutted like the Golden Gate Bridge in the air, was rewarded with two fifty-lev notes.

"All three of you are stupid," declared the girl as she turned her back on them. "Can't you see it, mamma? They are dim-witted. I can kick them whenever I please because I pay them well."

The woman, her eyes blue as the sky over a fashionable Mediterranean resort, blurted out, "I hope, Elizabeth, that you understand what this is all about," her voice was all silk and chocolate; however, despite the smiles she had showered on the boys, it was evident she hardly noticed them. "Money, Elizabeth. I give you money and I want you to understand one thing. A boy who can rip your head off kisses your stinking sneakers because I'd paid his mother. She accepted my money because she doesn't earn enough. A stupid woman gives birth to a stupid son. After all, someone has to kiss sneakers and bark like a dog for a rich girl like you, Elizabeth."

"I'm sick of these three idiots, mommy!" cried the child. "Pay their mothers to get them out of here!"

"I am trying to show you that the difference between the dumb and the smart is money, sweetie," said the blue-eyed woman. "The smart folks have everything they need. The dumb losers kiss much dirtier things than a pair of sneakers. Do you understand now why I fund this appropriate behavior guidance for you?"

"To get used to coping with losers. But those three are boring me to death."

"Boys, I'll give one hundred bucks to one of you. It will be the one who throws my daughter Elizabeth to the floor," the blonde-haired lady announced. "Now!"

Her statement couldn't inspire the three lads. They did not shift in their chairs.

"Doesn't anyone want a hundred bucks?" the woman asked, and her ankles, powerful as cannon salvo, fidgeted in her beautiful slippers.

No one wanted the money. Small red sores glistened on the necks of the three boys.

"I warned you not to bite them," the woman remarked. "You don't listen to me, Elizabeth. I didn't pay their mothers for this sort of activities."

"You didn't, but I did!" the girl objected.

The month of September was an old man who slept in a cradle of gray cloud banks. A light wind blew, and the sky was patiently waiting for the autumn. In the past few years, winters had come early, eating away at the autumn days.

"How much did you pay?" the woman asked frowning. "Who do you think you are? Have you done any... bad things?"

"No, I haven't!" said the girl. "I asked your assistant with the red hair for money and got it. He gave it to me."

"He did?" the woman heaved a sigh of relief and seemed to remember something important. The month of September and its clouds kept nagging you. It was as unbearable as your mom. It would be better for the elderly to buy a one-way ticket to Australia and die there. Then they'd stop getting in the way. "Elizabeth, didn't you think I'd have to pay Uncle Peter back?"

"I thought you wouldn't pay him back at all," said the girl. "Stand up, stallions. It's time to eat," the three boys jumped up in a flash and stuck their tongues out at her. The sturdy girl in a pink dress, pink socks, pink hat, and gloves, pulled a pink sausage out of her pink leather purse with Mickey Mouse embroidered on its beautiful flap. With her thumb and forefinger, Elizabeth tore off a piece and placed it on the first boy's thick tongue. "You, fat hog! I don't like you. You won't eat anything," the pink lassie didn't let the stocky lad have a bite. "Keep smiling. I like it. The whole sausage will be for you," the girl shoved the thing in the mouth of the third boy, thin and tall as a rolling pin. "Get lost all of you! Now!"

The boys bowed low, rather woodenly, to the powerful girl. The tallest one who had kissed both his queen's sneaker and her ankle, bent, glued his lips to her strong hand, and crooned, "Ciao, Elizabeth!" his voice gentle, spilling over like hot chocolate.

"Bye, Bobbi!" Without further ado, the girl who loved dogs so much slipped a folded bill into the gallant lad's small jeans pocket.

The boys, all smiles, walked away facing their tough mistress, scared to turn their backs on her. The one who had received the note purred, "Have a nice day, Elizabeth! Your dress is magnificent. I love you!" Elizabeth disregarded him altogether as she scratched her leg, and, calm though she was, suddenly her narrow eyes brimmed with tears.

"Mama! I want Annie! I want Annie! I want Annie!"

The woman's silky, blue-eyed face peered at the girl.

"Annie? Why? Don't you want a stronger and a more handsome boy, Elizabeth?"

"I want Annie!" the sturdy lass kept on watering the floor with her tears.

"Why?" asked the woman, and her brilliant ankles twitched uneasily. "Maybe Stefan or little Tudor?"

"Annie won't let me bite her. She calls me a 'fool'. And if someone insults you, you have the right to beat the shit out of her, don't you?

"I'm so relieved!" said the lady. "But... It will be difficult to bring Annie here, Elizabeth."

"I want Annie! I want Annie!"

The wind picked up, then struck like a thief snatching brown leaves and dust from the streets. It would sure bring a nasty rain.

"You must not bite Annie... You have to carefully cope with the new situation..." the woman began as she tried to stroke her daughter's cheek.

"Mustn't bite her? Why?"

"You must not wage war on her," replied the blue-eyed fortress firmly. "Annie is the daughter of the woman who can pick up the smell of death. She's a foul rag, but she married Uncle Philip."

"So what?"

"You know who Uncle Philip is, dear. Now the woman's tall tales about death are bigger than me, you understand? The rag is more powerful than me. You must not bite Anna, my dear girl. You must not hit her. You must not even call her names!"

The street, as befitted this neighborhood, was perfectly clean. Two bodyguards, clean-shaven and looking very spruce, kept watch on the only entrance to the property; meanwhile, another bodyguard, neat and large as the Eiffel Tower guarded the only exit to the north.

"By the way, Elizabeth, your friend Annie and her grandmother intend to kindly visit us tomorrow. Then you will see your little friend, dear."

"Her grandmother... the crone's hands look bloodless as if she's been dead for years," remarked the child. "'Her eyes are as hard as nails. Fire her, mamma!"

The rain set in steadily. Swift as a spider, it hurled a volley of lightning bolts at the Canadian pines, the oaks, and the aspens. A torrent of water flowed down the street. The sky challenged the trees to a duel, and the rain, a deft fencer, used the sharp sword of the raindrops to conquer roofs and squares.

"I can't fire her, Elizabeth," said the woman with the sparkling blue eyes. It was the first time she had used the negative form of the verb "can". "The old massaging bag is the mother of the woman who carries death in her handbag."

"And Annie can catch the scent of death," said the girl who looked as tough as a curbstone. "So what? Annie wets her knickers and says death smells like smoke."

✳ ✳ ✳

That's what I want. God, I hollered at Him. If You don't set their house on fire, I will! I hate him so much. When I see him — my neighbor, Anna's husband — I grab a knife, and it's a good thing that Vera, my wife, lives under my roof. Vera looks like a molehill to me, a short and fat thing she is, and I say to myself, Georgi, they laugh at you because of that woman. Georgi, you're worth as much as a leaking roof, man. Water drips from the ceiling onto your head, and you pretend you're dry as dust. Vera's overweight and that's the reason I walked ahead, far ahead of her, when we strolled through Staro. Young and old knew me there.

"You're short and you're stubby!" I told Vera. "Okay, I'll close my eyes and I will not look at you. But when I go down to the pub, don't saunter along the street near me and don't call me. I'm ashamed I tried to pick you up."

"All right," she said. "It is okay, Georgi."

But she is, nevertheless, a sensible woman — my home is spick and span, and you wouldn't believe how spotless and neat the kitchen and all rooms were. She plastered the walls all by herself, and I could hardly believe my eyes when I saw them. She was round and oval, tall as an armchair, so I didn't believe a barrel-like wench could plaster a square inch of anything. Well, she coped with the walls within a week. I couldn't have done it, and I am a man big as a hill.

I couldn't stop thinking about that little girl, the daughter of Anna, the village witch. All women in their family went by the name of Anna, so they named the little one Annie too. I looked at the tyke and wanted to hate it, but God had shaped me in such a way that my hands and my eyes could not hate a child even if she was Ando's daughter. Even if she was the spitting image of Ando! Every time I happened to catch a glimpse of Ando, I looked for a knife or grabbed a stone. Do him in — that was what I'd always craved. I dreamed of burying him, and his shoes, and his shoelaces. God had probably used the wrong dough to make me with, so I turned to Him, "Dear Heavenly Father, come to Staro someday soon, and finish Thy work. Knead my dough once again! Bake me again! Check what Anna the witch is doing. She's not a witch. She is my Anna. I cannot sleep at night after I hear what folks blab about her. Knife blades glow under my eyelids. Ana is not Ando's wife anymore. She's thrown herself into a bigshot's arms, a fool from Sofia. A filthy rich one. She's not Ando's woman, so what do I care?"

You had to plow, you had to make money and work your fingers to the bone while there still was land to plow and seeds to sow. I wanted money in my pockets. Money made you twice the man you were yesterday. Without money, you were an infamous geezer. Look at Ando, I said to myself. He's thinner than his own shirt. But I was still looking for a cleaver every time I saw him. He was shorter than his second wife. I'd seen her tie him up with a rope. And I'd seen her leave him to lie tied and trussed up in the backyard to sober him up. Then I said to myself, "Well done, dear God. You didn't make an exhibition of yourself. Not by a long shot! You lived up to your end of the bargain! Thank you." Ando was a tractor driver and a garage mechanic, but drinking had driven mechanics out of his head. If it hadn't been for his huge gal, the municipality would have probably buried him free of charge by now. Then, you, dear God, you might have thought of me, "This man bites worse than the dog that died of rabies a month ago. Dear God, I'd have given the big gal two hundred leva to buy him a cheap tombstone. Ando, Take it, you scumbag. I'd scream. I'll stick this cross in the ground over your head. You stole my Anna from me!

But this never happened. On Saturday, a cold and windy day, the giant woman showed up at my door just when I was gnawing on a chicken drumstick. Little Shushomir, Vera, and I were having lunch together, and Vera roasted the meat so well you wanted to eat the pot she'd cooked it in. The huge dame rushed into our kitchen, and said no "good afternoon".

"You!" she shouted at me, slamming her fist on the table, "Don't carp at my husband! If you find fault with my husband, you're finding fault with me. I'll punch you!"

I sat on my chair and kept on gnawing at the chicken drumstick. I gnawed and chewed and came down hard on it because if I didn't, I'd have to grab the knife to cut something off: her head or her leg. Then they'd throw me straight into jail. It was not myself or Vera I was thinking of — I looked at the little thing across the table, my son — I cared for him. The thought of his weak arms, small chest, and thin neck was always at the back of my mind. I'd put a picture of him in my wallet and I carried it everywhere with me. One day, I lost his photo, must've tucked it away somewhere, and couldn't find it. The kid got sick. He coughed so hard like he had a truckload of sand in his chest and couldn't spit it out. His forehead burned. And I said to myself, "Dear Heavenly Father, save him! He's the best thing I have. I will take You, God, in my arms and I'll carry You on my back to the Black Peak, I will, God! If You want, I'll build You a church, so You'll have a place to stay when you're homeless and they chase you from these parts." But God did not hear me, he'd gone away and could not help my son. The Doctor couldn't help either. At a certain point, I remembered: Shushomir's photo wasn't in my wallet and I didn't carry it with me.

I immediately took a picture of him and stashed it back where it used to stay. Then I put the wallet in my shirt pocket, above my heart, so my strength would go to Shushomir, the little one. And my strength did go to him! I hugged him. I held him close. He had a fever, and I took it from him. I gave him peace. The boy gradually calmed down and fell asleep. Then Vera, no matter she was as short as the night lamp in the bedroom, kissed me on the forehead.

"Why?" I asked her, and she said, "You soothed him, Georgi."

I'd carried it with me ever since — Shushomir's photo, a three-year-old tyke thin as a cigarette, his hair so red you'd think his locks would singe your fingers if you brushed them. His eyes were blue like Vera's. At times they pierced yours and made you shudder. I had no fear of anything Vera would say or do. She was as meek as the old slates I'd tiled the barn roof with. These slates wouldn't budge or bend, nor would they let a raindrop fall on your head. They'd been slates for two hundred years, and after two hundred years they'd be slates too. Your room would be dry and warm. My wife Vera could scrape out a living with any guy in Bulgaria. If I hadn't let her live under my roof, she'd have fallen for a widower, an old bachelor, or a divorced dad. She'd say to him the same thing she said to me, "Take me with you," she'd mumble. "I will cook, I'll keep the house clean, and I won't make you angry."

Well, she kept on living with me. The attic was neat as a pharmacy, the basement was tidy and shining with cleanliness, and I muttered under my breath, "Look here, man. The ramshackle house your mom left you isn't ramshackle anymore. It's handsome." Vera painted it. She said to me, "Georgi, I'll try to keep it in good shape." She plastered the walls all by herself. Wasn't I a disgrace to the family! A woman as big as my leg was applying lime to the walls herself, and I was watching! So, I made my mind to help her.

"Pass me this bucket, Georgi," she said.

"Listen, woman," I said. "I didn't bring you here to order me what bucket to pass you!"

"Okay. Excuse me!" Vera breathed as she grabbed a shovel. I looked at her and thought to myself — a mouse with a shovel in hand! She dug, dug, and dug, so I got angry at the end. I went and wrenched the shovel out of her hands. Within half an hour, I did the whole garden, and the woman said, "Thank you!" to me. Nobody in this house had ever thanked anybody else. Neither Mom nor Dad. They were both big. A strong and sturdy couple my parents were. If they stepped on a rock, it would turn into a dewdrop, and that meant they were strapping and tough, especially Mom. She didn't speak much, Mom didn't. If she slapped me across the face, then I'd deserved it.

She busted my lip once, and rightly so. I had jumped from Vidibog peak, that beastly rock, into the whirlpool and I'd broken my head. I knew I'd have barely enough strength to go crawl to our house, and when I finally reached the doorstep, I waited to see what Mom would say. If she shouted to my father, "Vasil, bring Priest Dimitar to read the burial service for Georgi, we'll have to bury him soon," I'd know, and I'd take the rough with the smooth. I'd lie down in front of the house and die then and there. So it would be easier for you, dear God, to take me to the place I deserve. I am a tough boy, I said to myself. I can plow and I'd plow dear God's fields. I'll plant Him a linden and then He'll see what a gorgeous tree it is!

However, Mama didn't say a word and priest Dimitar wasn't sent for. They didn't bury me. Mom slapped me across the face then she washed my blood away and said, "Next time you break your head after you've jumped from Vidibog into the damned whirlpool, don't come to me whining like a puppy. Die on the road back home!" I did jump from Vidibog thousand times more, and I did not break my head. Therefore, if mom slapped you, you were a picture of health and solid as a rock. Dad knew it too. When he saw her staring at the ground, especially if she kept mum, Dad feared things were going badly with us. Mom would make the feathers fly. So, Dad looked at the floor, silent as an eel, hoping the storm would blow itself out. He even took the broom and swept the kitchen. That was what soothed Mama the most.

Mama had thick, coarse hair, so red you'd say a fire burned on her head. I had orange hair and she liked me a lot. Mama had proved her mettle a number of times. She didn't forget or forgive thieves or liars. My father knew all about how tough she was. To tame her and soften a possible blow, he tried hard to eat all the grub she had cooked. My mother, bless her soul, was in heaven at Our Lord's place now, and I was sure she gave Him strength the way I did with my son Shushomir.

Mom, however, was no good at cooking. She never stirred in the suet and hated to cut potatoes, so she dropped them whole in the soup, explaining that she didn't want to kill all their vitamins. At the end of the day, mom gave a command, "Eat!"

I couldn't chew or swallow her delicious meals. She'd look at me, and I'd rather she boxed my ears. I sat behind the bowl of soup for hours. It looked greasy and tasted like gasoline. My father, the poor man, kept on eating and slurping, sweat collecting on his brow and trickling into his dish. He made his best effort to gobble up everything she put in front of him. Mom came to check on him and after a glimpse at the bottom of his bowl, she took a glass and poured brandy into it. My mother's energy in front of the electric stove spelled cooking disasters for us, but her brandy was magnificent, more valuable than gold, and known far and wide. It was the biggest firebomb a man could brew out of damsons and plums. Mama used to pour it into a little glass for Dad — I still had it, that glass, a thing no bigger than a thimble. And then, after he drank the thimble of her wild concoction — I could still see him in my mind — Dad was smiling!

His eyes were blue like Mama's, but his hair was quite normal, brown and quiet, not an orange volcano constantly on the verge of erupting on my mother's head. Is that what happiness means, I asked myself. A man smiling at you, his mouth, beard, hair, shoes, and shirt beaming at you and he says, 'This time, you've hit the bull's eye, woman. It's a good thing you gave me that little glass. Now I know what Our Lord was thinking when He created happiness for us, people. Well done, Lord, may you be glorious and prosper in all your ways! Your work is up to the mark. You have class, I tell you!"

That was why I kept this glass and I often said to myself, "In a year or so I'll propose to Anna. She studied in our school, and her Bulgarian teacher was Ivan Georgiev. Mr. Georgiev used to punish me every time he spotted me, but I didn't bear a grudge against him, not by a long shot.

I was naughty and noisy, and I wouldn't listen to anybody, so I wasn't angry with our Bulgarian teacher, may he be strong and well in heaven. I hope he stands near our Lord's desk and tells our Lord all about Shakespeare and Vazov, the best Bulgarian poet! Anna used to recite, "When I consider everything that grows…" and I remembered only what Anna said, the first line of Sonnet 15 by old Shakespeare, and not a word of what Georgiev tried hard to drum into our heads, may Our Lord in heaven have strong plum brandy, for Mr. Georgiev liked it that way, and a large measure of it, the way we drank brandy in Pernik.

I said to myself, Anna's as small as a newly hatched turkey chick, but when she told you about "everything that grows", you felt like playing truant from school and running back to your mama.

"Mom," you'd tell her. "I'm sorry I jumped from Vidibog into that whirlpool." Mum would nod her head bewildered. "I'm sorry."

Nobody said "I'm sorry" in our house, so she'd take me to our GP medical center. "That kid's not all there," she'd whisper. "Give him some pills to get his head back in place."

And because Anna was so weak, her bag of notebooks and textbooks three times as big as she was, I would take the damned thing and carry it from their place to school and from school to their place. At first, Ana would give me her breakfast.

"Take it, Georgi. Thank you for all you've done," and that was all I waited for, her cheese sandwich. I polished it off in a bite, but then it dawned on me: you're a stupid boy, Georgi. She's a feeble thing. If you eat up her cheese and butter, she'll trip over the smallest stone in front of the school, and she'll kick the bucket.

"You'll trip and fall in front of our school. Then you'll die," I told her the following day. "Sit down here in front of me. I'll let you go home after you eat all the cheese, butter, and bread."

Anna obeyed. She struggled hard to eat her sandwich. The poor girl chewed and wiped tears from her eyes. I felt sorry for her. Nobody in my family felt sorry for anybody else. If you did, mom got busy and tackled the problem. She clouted you across the face to send pity packing, and that settled it. After a minute or two, Anna stopped chewing altogether, her face contorting in ripples of effort to bite into the crusty bread. I turned to her, "Okay, enough is enough. I can see you're having a bad time."

And she said, "Georgi, you are a good boy, and I will tell you a fairy tale."

In my family, nobody told you fairy tales, because the tales were all made up by smarty-pants who wrote thick textbooks, and I was brutally tested on them by schoolmaster Georgiev. Anna's tale, however, was not a hoax. It was about a king's son who killed a dragon, then slew another monster — not quite a dragon, a serpent it was. The prince then had to break, rip and tear a pair of iron shoes. Iron shoes my foot, I thought. A whopping great lie if you asked me, but come on, I let it pass, because the guy ended up marrying the princess.

"I can cope with a serpent and a dragon, Anna!" I told her. "Just show me where they're hiding. I'll bump them off. I'm strong."

"You're the strongest boy in our school," Anna said, and I thought, 'That's how Dad feels when mom pours her volcano brandy into his thimble glass.' Not just one dragon, two hundred dragons would I wipe out, if only Anna told me one more time I was the strongest boy in school.

"If you are the princess, I'll do in all fire-breathing dragons and serpents in the village of Staro and I'll marry you," I told her.

"I am not a princess, Georgi," she said.

"O, you are!" I objected. "If you are not a princess, Anna, then no princess has ever lived under the sun all over Bulgaria and all over the world!"

I used to pick strawberries and raspberries for her from our garden. Mama was very good at digging gardens and planting trees. Our Lord must have made her hand so firm to match the abundance of fruits He gave her garden. If mom sat down to get some rest in the shade of a tree, the tree would grow six inches during the following night. Perhaps its leaves were grateful to mom.

One day my father began, "This Anna of yours, you know..." — and did not finish what he meant to say. If Dad, who was six feet six inches tall, left his sentence unfinished, then something was brewing, and it would take him an hour to tell me what exactly it was. I had enough time to collect my wits, make a good fist, so I wouldn't feel flabby like a boiled chicken in a bowl of soup. Mom too had enough time to get up and grab hold of something heavy: the rolling pin, the cutlass, anything dangerous enough to frighten any burglar away. "This Anna of yours, I mean your classmate… You gave her ten pounds of our raspberries so far..."

"Dad, look here. I'll go to the Bare Hill forest and I'll pick fifteen pounds of raspberries for her. I'll give you back every berry I've picked for Anna from mom's garden!' cried I. — "I hate to do it, but if it's raspberries you want..."

"I don't care about raspberries or no raspberries, son..." he didn't finish the sentence, and I didn't know what the future had in store. "Women are no good in Anna's family. Her mother can tell you exactly when you're going to die. Annie, I mean the girl you care about… she had a grandfather, you know. He didn't like all this and couldn't stick out to the end. Got scared, the poor bugger did and took to his heels. I don't know if he's still alive, or they've buried him somewhere. To leave Staro, the best place in Bulgaria! The guy must've been crazy. Totally off his rocker. Staro is a magnificent village. Don't you listen to what Vazov the poet has scribbled in the fat textbook schoolmaster Georgiev forced me to read and analyze! Analyze my foot. Vazov knows nothing. H's never set foot in Staro, and above all, he's never jumped from Vidibog rock into the Struma. Excuse me, Vazov, you're wrong through and through!

So, one way or another, Anna's grandfather made himself scarce. Nobody knows where the wind took him. He had a huge orchard, hundreds of acres, you know — his plum trees produced plums as big as my fist, and his apples seemed to sweat golden droplets. The fruit trees made the guy filthy rich. That was the honest truth. He had pear trees too, and the pears he picked tasted better than honey. He didn't even sell his business lock, stock, and barrel. He simply vanished, disappeared bag and baggage. He used to love his wife, they said. Come off it, man. Love's nothing. Great love is great sorrow. The brandy you've poured into your thimble glass is the truth. They say that two hundred years ago a fortune-teller lived in this village. She could put a curse on you or she could make your wound heal. It's wrong to say a curse, it's either you help a man live on and plow his field, or you bury him. Just an old wives' tale it is, I guess. God forbid you should be a woman born in the village of Staro — your mind is constantly in turmoil. You can feel when death's creeping in, and if your neighbor is your friend, you tell him, 'Now watch it, brother. The black night's coming to put you in her black basket.' If the neighbor wishes misfortune to the this woman, she says nothing, and no one will hear or see the ill-wisher; only his gravestone will jut out like the old fence in front of the town hall. Come off it! The town hall is so shabby you wouldn't think it deserves a fence at all."

"I don't care about the fortune-teller, Dad," I told him, "I want Anna."

My father hid his face between his knees. He did that when he didn't want to say something in front of Mom, but he said it anyway. He didn't look her in the eyes — hers were more intensely blue — and she kept staring him down.

"Georgi," my father began. "Just so you know, I am friends with God. I didn't tell your mother about it because she'd have made me ask Him for money. She wants to buy the garden next to ours. But I tell you, son — if I say something to Our Lord, he listens to me. We get along very well, Him and I. Ginger-haired guys are Our Lord's pals because I believe His hair is red too. I don't go often to church, and I don't know how they've painted His image on the icons. Listen, Georgi. I'll ask Our

Lord not to let you marry Anna. Let Him beat you back to where you were before you met her."

Yes, my father told Our Lord what he had meant to let Him know, and Our Lord listened to him. He beat me back to where I was before I'd met Anna. He carried away all autumns, summers, winters, and springs from me. Our Lord took my heart, my liver, my blood then he gave them back to me as cold as the frozen fish you bought in the village convenience store. Although Our Lord is holy, all-powerful, and all saints are directed by Him, He did not drive me away from Anna. He drove her deeper into me. Only when I thought of Anna, I, a hill of ice, felt warmer.

Anna, Ando, my trusted friend, and I grew up together. Both Ando and I received training in engine repair so that together we could make jalopies and old tractors last longer. If a combine harvester broke down in the fields, Ando and I set its wheels in motion. Weak and skinny was Ando — his granddad and his pop were like him, you'd say their asses were small cushions filled with straw. Would you expect a cushion to flex or tense its muscles? Not by a long shot. I called him my brother. He got sick. He coughed so hard that I could hear him in our house. My mother, God bless her soul, gave him honey she used to gather from our hives. She took care of our bees. She could very well look after the world if she was in charge of it. Mom would give the poor a tiny glass of her brandy, and they'd be strong enough to earn their daily bread. Mom used to give Ando's mother dried thyme, dried chamomile, and white yarrow. All herbs that we had dried would my mother give Ando, for we didn't get sick. My family didn't know what the word "sickness" meant; mom and dad died of old age in their sleep. Please, dear God, take good care of them in heaven. You will tell me everything about what they've done when I join them. Please try to comfort Mom when she feels blue. Tell her she will be okay. Please, if you have something sad to say, don't let her listen. You'd better not say it at all.

Give her some time to get her breath back, God, and she'll fix everything, trust me. She will give You a tiny glass of her brandy and You will say to her, "Shusha, dearest! Your plum brandy is the work of the most wonderful master hand in the world! Thank you with all my heart!"

Unfortunately, Ando, my cleverest classmate, didn't get well. Old Anna, the village fortune-teller, came to check on him. This happened a month or two after her husband left her in the ditch.

"Are you catching the smell of death in my house, Anna?" Ando's father asked.

"Yes," she said bluntly, and they all shuddered. "But your boy could hide from death if he climbs the Bare Hill."

How could Ando climb this awful hill? He was thin as a chicken feather? The worms that crawled among the clods in the field were much stronger than him.

"Come on, Ando, stand up!" his father and his mother pleaded with him. "Totter to your feet, boy! Bare Hill is not far from here. You'll make it. And you'll get well."

But Ando could not crawl. He couldn't even open his eyes. Three days passed. Gray-haired Anna said the room smelled like roasted almonds, and that meant the end was approaching. Death only ate roasted almonds, and nothing else, she said. I didn't go in for such stories, and no one tried to give me that baloney, but what the gray-haired coffin-dodger told you happened all the same. If Anna, the old biddy, said, "Someone is roasting almonds here," in the following afternoon I saw an obituary note glued to the door of the town hall. I was scared I'd read my friend Ando's obituary in the paper. Priest Dimitar came to read out a sermon of hope to Ando, but Ando's face remained pale and yellow as lemonade. Then Anna, my little Anna, visited Ando's house. I had chosen the best raspberries for her, I'd brought her pears that had honey and the color of gold in them, and I'd given her the tender cuts of beef mom cooked for me so that I'd become a strong man.

"Ando," Anna had whispered. That was what my mother told me, and if my mother told you something, then it was the truth. Mom didn't concoct clever tales, didn't embellish her words with gold threads, didn't conceal anything, or shorten the distances between people. I knew truth was high and mighty. It could smack you across the face if you were guilty. Truth poured brandy into your tiny glass and gave you the taste of joy. My mother spoke the truth.

"Ando," Anna had said. "Hold me, Ando. Carry me to Bare Hill."

I thought to myself, how could Ando — skinny as a withered bunch of sorrel — lift her from the ground? Perhaps he'd said something sweet to her, the kind of nonsense schoolmaster Georgiev never failed to dig up before he brandished his fat textbooks. "Magnificent eyes..." — I didn't know how the poem went on, but Ando did. He could blabber on about eyes magnificent or not until he turned blue in the face. He used to jot down some crazy literary contraptions, and after Schoolmaster Georgiev read them to us, I sometimes felt happy as a clam at high tide. I said to myself, look, look — Ando and I grew up together in Staro! I knew his mom had bought his pen from Sofia, the capital of Bulgaria. Was it possible he wrote such beautiful things because of this pen from Sofia? No way. Mom bought me the same pen, and I wrote nothing at all. Ando didn't complain when they made him scribble essays and things. Nor did he grumble when we had to write research papers. Good for Ando! Maybe, I suspected... Was it possible that Ando had written *Magnificent Eyes* for Ana? If only I had known! I didn't understand poems or lyrics. They gave me a headache.

So weak and sallow was Ando that if you threw him in the Struma, the whole river, poor thing, would turn yellow. Ando got up. He swung from side to side like a pendulum, it was true, but he managed to stand upright. He hugged Anna tightly. My Anna! She weighed as much as a chicken, the smallest one in the brood, and so he carried her all day long up to Bare Hill.

I didn't know if he read any poems to her. Every time I heard "magnificent eyes" I got sick, and after I learned who wrote that damned thing I hated the poet's guts. My heart was in my mouth when I passed by Anna's house. The two of them, Anna and Ando, climbed down Bare Hill. After a month or so, Ando got well and married Anna, my girl. Much later, years after Bare Hill, a girl was born to them. I already had a son, Shushomir. For Shushomir's sake, I believe that You, God, are everywhere, in everything on earth and in heaven. No one else can create such a wonderful boy as my Shushomir. Dear God, once I close the earth behind me, I will fix all your farming machines — tractors, combine harvesters, harrows, and grain drills — so you'll be able to gather your crops from the fields and sow without fear of accidents. You can take my word for it. I'm Shusha's son, she was tall and tough, and if she slapped your hands away from the candy, then you'd earned it, God. Thou hast made her, and my mother Shusha never lied to me. That's why I named my son Shushomir after her. It's hard to twist your tongue to say his name, but we all love it. The boy has red hair like mine and my mother's, God, and you should know that we, redheads, are your friends. We don't suck up to anybody. We fight, we don't lie. We're straightforward, plainspoken folks. If you are our friend, we won't dump you in the middle of the road.

I wanted to kill him, Ando the scrawny goat. At times, I felt like murdering him on the spot. "At times" happened often — every day, every night, and every hour. Just looking at their house made me grab a knife or clutch a big stone. You could find no stones in my backyard no matter how hard you tried. My wife had collected them all and made a long pathway. At some time or other, I took to muttering to myself, "Enough is enough. Look at his new wife, a heap of muscles and mammoth bones, pouring into his bedroom! She's going to tear their house down." I saw her tie Ando up, then she left him in the backyard. A sack of manure — that was what he looked like. He'd really had a rough trot lately. In the following week, I caught a glimpse of Ando stalking across the street scared to go home — to step inside his own house that his poor father and mother had built for him. They dug a mountain of clay from the river and they baked a hill of bricks. His mom cleaned the houses of many families in Staro to pay the bills on time. My mother lent them money too. Ando's mom sold the tomatoes she'd grown in their garden — no fertile soil there; pebbles and sand all over the place, so how would you plant vegetables there? She did, and she produced tomatoes out of stones. The couple built the house working their fingers to the bone. The huge woman, an avalanche of brawn, broad in the beam like a boat, a mountain with tits, settled there like a weasel in a hencoop. If she was my wife, I'd shoot her dead. But I looked at their house, and I kept turning my eyes to Anna and Ando's child.

I'd been watching this tyke closely, and the more I looked at her, the more she resembled Anna, the girl from my childhood. The little one was quiet. Not a child — a doorknob, a trash can — she was. I watched her walk in the street. One day she told me she was afraid of trees, of grass, of the wind, and most of all she was scared to be alone. Her father, Ando, lay sprawled across the floor, bombed. Because of this child, I wanted to shoot Ando dead. Can't you see she looks like your wife Anna, you moron! She looks like my Anna!

Ando didn't care a fig that there was no food in the house. The girl was starving, I'd seen her bent double, pressing her tummy with her fists and sneaking through a hole in the fence between my backyard and Andon's unkempt garden. Overgrown elderberry shrubs, nettles, and thorns grew there. I'd planted them on purpose and applied sheep dung to their roots, so I wouldn't look at Ando kissing my Anna. At first, I said to myself, "She's Ando's child. Let her starve to death!" I had a thousand evil thoughts, that was true, but one day I took my scythe and cut down the nettles, all of them, young and stinging. Now the little girl could slip into our backyard. Shushomir showed his mettle, a tough boy; his fists were stones through and through, and I hoped he'd beat the tar out of Ando's skinny rag of a child. Well, Shushomir was a chip off the old block — he couldn't beat the child who was my dearest Anna's daughter. I saw my son give the girl baked sausages his mom had cooked for us. Then he gave her raspberries. I thought to myself, I used to pick raspberries for her mother. Is he going to torture himself like that?

It was because of Shushomir that I believed Our Lord existed. Perhaps he lived among the stars and the clouds. Vera, the boy's mother, was quiet as a cat. She'd let a sparrow peck at her nose, and she'd let me hassle her, she would. My mother would see me from heaven, and she was a woman of courage and justice. She would hear me scolding my wife Vera as viciously as if I was chiding my ox, and Mom wouldn't restrain her anger, no, Sir, not Mom. She'd slap me across the face, and I'd deserve it. My mother would never smack you on the side of the head if you were a decent man and if you didn't lie to folks. Vera left a bowl of soup for Ando's kid near the hole in the fence, but it was a porcelain thing and broke, so nothing was left for the girl. If I caught a glimpse of her father, Ando, I looked for an ax, but... I ran to our village store instead. I am not lying, I cross my heart — I went and did it — bought some iron bowls and left them right on the cupboard in the kitchen. I'd been making good money as a mechanic, and I didn't leave anything on the cupboard. I put things in their proper place. An idea crossed my mind. Vera would see these little iron bowls and she'd pour soup for the little girl into them.

My wife was so timid she'd let a duck pluck out her eyes and she would move out of a lame mutt's way to let the beast pass by. I, however, was sure that after she saw the iron bowls on the cupboard, she'd know what to do. Even before she read the top news headlines on TV, Vera would pour soup into the iron things. She'd surely choose the best pieces of cooked meat and potatoes, my wife would. All went according to plan. I watched as she trotted, a gal as short as an armchair, to the hole in the fence where I'd cut all nettles.

"Annie-e!" shouted my wife, and the child drew near to her. "There's some soup for you, Annie."

And I said out loud, Thank you! I thought, "It's a good thing I have red hair like you, so you're my friend, God! I was lucky I met a woman — short as a mushroom — I give you that — willing to cook soup for this little child and bring the iron bowls to the hole in the fence for her."

At some point, I stopped looking for a knife when I saw Ando. A gaunt face, stringy arms, knobby wrists — a skeleton that guzzled brandy from the bottle — that was what Ando was. One day, blind drunk, he saw me and sobbed, "They took her from me! They took my daughter! My little Annie..."

My son Shushomir ran a fever. The paramedic who came to check on him was at his wits' end. Vera got into a panic, I didn't know what to do. Completely puzzled, I took my son's photo out of my wallet and taped it right over my heart. I hoped against hope that his temperature would come down. It didn't.

"They took Annie from me, dad" my boy gabbled. His hot forehead put my shirt on fire. What was I, a man as big as a boat, to tell him? I knew what it felt like when they took Anna from me.

"No one can take Annie from you, son. Don't you be afraid!" I lied to him and I thought, now my mother would reach out from her cloud to slap me across the face "What are you lying to my grandson for, you miserable cheat!" she'd shout at me.

But she didn't. Shushomir fell asleep. The silly red-haired cockerel believed me. What was I to do? What?

I chose a big glass bottle. I'd learned to bake damsons and plums and I made plum brandy the way my mom did. Whoever drank a drop of it, no longer called me Georgi; the guy opted for Georgi master of his own fate! Was I a master of brandy? No, far from it. My mother was the mind and soul behind the brandy magic. She was the one, fair and square. I poured my thunderbolt brandy into the bottle, then I went and kicked down the fence between my backyard and Ando's messy garden. I'd built it so I wouldn't have to watch my Anna walk in front of his house. I spat on the fallen fence and leaped over it. Then I sat down beside Ando.

"They took my little one from me,'" he muttered. "The bastards from Sofia did."

"Pull yourself together!" I said.

How would he pull himself together? I couldn't tell him how to do it.

I didn't want a knife. I didn't bend down to grab a stone.

We drank together. We drank so much. You couldn't tell if we were guys or piles of mud. Piles of mud…

❋ ❋ ❋

"This is the chair for our guest of honor! Isn't it magnificent?" Percha took me by the hand, wearing such a wide smile on her face that her upper lip seemed to touch her forehead.

Once I tried to yawn as widely as she did, but the corners of my mouth cracked and bled. I could try to write something in my own blood if I knew all the letters of the Bulgarian alphabet. My mother, even before she accompanied Death to Sofia, had told me, "He who wants his story to be remembered has to write it in his own blood. Then all children will love it no matter where in the world the sun shines on their heads."

"Is there a place where the sun doesn't shine?" I had asked her.

Mom answered, "Where no one loves a little child, there is no sun in the sky."

"That's why there's no sun in our house, is there?" I ventured.

Back then, I tried to invent a fairytale to make the other children love me. I scraped my knee and had blood enough to write a story, but it hurt so much I couldn't think of anything. Mom explained to me, "Annie, the Bulgarian alphabet knows all the fairytales in the world. Learn the Bulgarian letters, and the alphabet will tell you all tales." I took my ABC book and at night I told it, "Hey, book, teach me your alphabet. I'm a well-behaved child. I'll say 'thank you, Sir' and 'please ma'am'. I'll sweep the crumbs from the table on which they put you. There will always be a glass of clean water in front of you, ABC book."

I opened it on page 2 where the Bulgarian alphabet was printed, then put the book under my pillow, and slept on it. So, I was hoping I could dream about the stories that lived between the book's covers. If the worse came to the worst, I would write fairytales in my mind. Could another child read the yarns I spun in my head, I wondered. So far, I'd learned ten letters.

Elizabeth's mother not only reached for my hand, but she also kissed my cheek.

"Annie, sweet!" began Mrs. Percha, soft as pajamas. "Look what a smashing chair I've procured especially for you." To be honest, I didn't know what 'procured' meant. It sounded like 'I call you 'Annie, sweet', but I think you're a pig. "I bought this exquisite piece of furniture from Venice."

In kindergarten, I used to play with a girl called Venice. It turned out that my kindergarten friend had a chair and Percha bought it from her. The thing was made of gold: a red seat and four pictures of Mickey Mouse painted on it: you could prop yourself up on one elbow and the Mickey Mouse smiled at you. You could rest your head on the mouse's ears. Percha kissed me on my forehead, ruffled my hair, all her fingers sharp as nails, and said, "Your hair is so lovely, Annie! Beautiful and shiny! Well done, my girl! This is for you," she took a gold gift box out of her pocket and popped open the lid. At that moment, the lid began to sing, a sparrow flapped its wings and said, "I love you!" The other folks in the room: three boys, several women, and two girls, clapped their hands.

"You look so beautiful, Annie!" Percha started spinning her usual yarn of big fat lies. "Dearest children, this is Annie, Mr. Philip Vasilev's daughter."

"She is pretty! Pretty! Pretty!" the kids squealed.

"She is simply magnificent!" chimed in their mothers. "I'm sure Mr. Vasilev adores her!"

I thought beauty was a bad thing — something like a screw driven into your head and everyone could see it. I'd go and have my hair cut to the bone, then I'd jam a hat on my head. A ragged thing it would be, my hat, as old as the cowsheds in Staro, so no one could see any of my foul magnificence. In my view, beauty stuck out like a red pimple on your nose. Everybody looked at you, and you fretted about it.

"Tomorrow I'll get a haircut," I told Percha.

There were no corners in her house. The rooms were full to the brim of beds, tables, pictures, chairs, and sofas. You couldn't hide anywhere. There were no shadows you could sink into. So I put the ABC book on my head and listened to my telephone repeat the Bulgarian alphabet — A, B, C... My telephone was clever. It spoke and gave me a lot of pictures, so I wouldn't forget which letter looked like an animal. I immediately knew whether I had to run away from it or feed it. The telephone told me in a human voice how the letter was called, and I thought: if a letter of the alphabet had its own name, then it was a living being. "Please tell me a fairytale!" I asked the alphabet politely, but it said nothing. It kept on pouting silently and I believed some Bulgarian letters hated me or at least were ashamed of me.

"My sweet girl, let me take you to my hairdresser. What do you say, Annie?" the lipstick Percha wore creased into a broad smile. How come the corners of her lips didn't crack or bleed? Her lipstick kissed me again — this time on the cheek — and filled it with a sharp smell that hit my nose.

"Oh, dearest Annie!" Elizabeth came hurtling towards me like my father's tomcat that swooped down on a bowl of fried fish. He's was a bully, dad's Puss-in-boots was, as he caught pigeons, sparrows, mice, rats, and bulky as a tractor, barged into the kitchen. I was a little scared of this yowling mugger. One day, he clawed at me and scratched my arm from shoulder to elbow. I bled, and when he came again growling and spitting, I grabbed the broom and shouted at him, "Hey tractor, look what I've got in my hand!" He kept clear of me, but his sharp eyes were on my back, hoping I'd trip over my slippers. Then he'd lunge at my neck. That was how Elizabeth hoped against hope I'd trip over my slippers, but I didn't even look at her. I hadn't looked at the thieving tomcat either, so he wouldn't think I was scared of his claws.

"Annie! My dearest friend Annie!" screamed Elizabeth as she threw herself into my arms. I sat in that chair all made of gold, with four images of Mickey Mouse behind my back. She kissed my cheeks, forehead, neck, and my hair, and I nearly shook with fear that she was going to pinch me.

"I love you, Annie! I missed you so much."

"Missed you" — what did she mean? My dad said once, "I miss my old hammer." Was Elizabeth thinking I was an old hammer? Okay. Why did sturdy Percha kiss me, and, even more confusing, why did Elizabeth kiss me if she believed I was a hammer? I could only think of one thing: their kisses hid their biting teeth, and after a minute the air would be filled with the smell of roasted almonds.

"Annie! Annie, I missed you so!" Elizabeth cooed. What was she trying to hint at? Did she really like hammers so much? No, impossible. She grabbed me tight to her chest as I and the four images of Mickey Mouse sat peacefully together in the gold chair. She quickly got me out of it, pulling hard at my shirt — the way a mama-dog snatched her whelp out of an old comfortable basket. Elizabeth clasped me in her arms, kissed me on the cheek, and carried me to the door.

"Where are you dragging me?" I asked.

"To my room. I bought you something special from Venice."

How come Elizabeth knew Venice, that thin little girl? Did they go to kindergarten together? How come Venice got expensive things in the first place? Her parents used to buy her socks from the second-hand store like everybody else. Elizabeth carried me the way our neighbor Jelka, a smart gypsy woman, one of Mom Darina's friends, carried her baby boy — proudly as if the suckling was a combat flag. I also carried him like a combat flag because the little one was very cute indeed.

I tried to extricate myself away from the dangerous situation, but Elizabeth cornered me, and I said to myself, "Now she'll bite me and she'll suck my blood." She didn't, though. I knew her room very well: pink wood from top to bottom — the floor, the walls, and the ceiling — pink as a songstress's nightgown; a pink bed, pink sheets, and Elizabeth's pink dress. The only exception were her gold chair, and a gold royal crown lying on the floor. Elizabeth pulled it out for me and did not bite my neck. She kissed my knees, my shoes, then took the crown from the floor, and put it on my head.

"You are my princess," Elizabeth said. "You are beautiful! You are lovely! I love you!"

What happened to the blue-eyed tortoise? She must've lost her marbles; if you told lies and were a snake oil salesman, sooner or later you'd go nuts. Mom, for example, had stopped talking and kept mum all the time. That happened long ago — at that time the moon was a newborn baby. Now it was leaping from cloud to cloud, made eyes at the stars and wanted too jump into the night the way I jumped from Vidibog Rock into the Struma River.

"Are you sick, Elizabeth?" I asked her.

"I love you more than anything in the world," she said. "How lovely your sneakers are! This is my present for you — look at it."

It was a pink lace dress. I'd seen a dress like that once — Elizabeth's prettiest doll was wearing it. "Now burst with envy!" Elizabeth cried to me that morning. "You are a stupid peasant, a yokel, and you'll never have a dress like that." Now she tried hard to give me the dress for free.

"Try it on," Elizabeth urged me, smiling sweetly from her knees to the pink ribbon in her blonde hair.

"I don't want to try it on."

"Oh, you do. Please! I love you!"

The dress suited me perfectly. I was an honest child. That dress was pink gold! I immediately became a princess after Elizabeth helped me to put it on.

"Thank you, Elizabeth," I said, and I was deeply grateful to her.

She kissed me again and said, "I love you. And now look at this," She started barking and stuck her tongue out.

"Do you like it?" she asked.

"No,"

"What about this?" Elizabeth lay down on the pink floor and kicked her legs in the air.

"No."

"And this?" she crawled on all fours over to her bed and suddenly started bouncing in circles around me.

"I don't like it," I told her.

Elizabeth stood up, grabbed my left arm, and kissed wetly my wrist, my elbow, and my shoulder.

"Did you like it?

"No."

She was very strong and her teeth were long, so I feared that if she bit me, the black and blue mark wouldn't disappear by the time Mom Darina dug up our potatoes in the field. Elizabeth started licking my fingers — the thumb first, then the index finger, the middle finger, the ring finger, and the pinky.

"Why are you doing this?" I asked.

"Because I love you. Don't you understand?"

"I don't like it."

"Then I'll carry you in my arms," she cried. She seized me by the waist the way I snatched the smallest kitten in the litter of a stray cat I called Mia. Mia ate everything she could get her paws on, and mom Darina didn't like her at all.

"I hate being carried!" I managed to escape Elizabeth's grip, but her iron elbows squeezed me tight again. That meant, "Annie, I love you, but if you believe what I say, you're a fool. I'll slit your throat, you slow-witted yokel."

"Actually, Elizabeth, I love you too."

She gaped at me surprised, her mouth so wide open that a sparrow could nest on her tongue. Her hands, amazed, careless, let me go, and if I hadn't been a lithe and lean child, I'd have fallen flat on the pink floor. I jumped to my feet, looked her in the eye, and said, "If you kiss me one more time, I'll beat the snot out of you! I don't want your shitty dress."

I took off this miracle of pink gold, and deep inside me, my heart wept. No one would ever buy me a frock from Venice again. And where should I look for Venice, this skinny girl? Did she still go to the kindergarten in Staro?

I darted out of Elizabeth's room and could hear her scream, "Mommy! Help! Help!"

I hid behind a huge pot in which a tree grew, its white blossoms kissing the ceiling — I'd seen no such trees in Staro, Percha must have bought it from skinny Venice. The poor kid stammered, and when you asked what her name was, she said. "Ve…-ve…ve." So, we called her Veve.

Mrs. Percha came running, and every time her great mind ran in the channel of wisdom, the pink floor shook under her feet. The pot with Veve's tree in it trembled.

"What is it, Elizabeth?'" whispered Miss Percha as she put her finger on her mouth.

"Mummy… that little hick…" Miss Percha jumped up and clamped her hand over Elizabeth's huge mouth. "Mommy..." Elizabeth's tongue seemed to stretch for she was talking very fast indeed. "Mom... get richer than Philip! Way richer than him! Then I'll knock the hell out of *her*. If I can't do it, I'll pay the boys. They'll beat her up. I'll watch. I want you to be richer than Philip the wimp, Mom!"

Percha stroked the sturdy mole's blonde hair.

"Easy, Elizabeth, easy. Mr. Vasilev will soon divorce the dumb yokel's mother. Hold on, my child. Clench your teeth. Be patient. It will be over soon."

"I don't want to be patient!" whispered Elizabeth.

Madame Percha smiled, but this time it wasn't her neck that did the smiling. I knew that a closed mouth gathered no moss, but Percha didn't believe in mouths or feet. She whispered, "Everyone is allowed to think, my girl. Only a fool tells his friends what he's thinking about."

I rolled myself up in a ball as big as an almond, and waited in the shade of the tree they'd bought from Veve. I expected death would soon light its gas stove to roast me, but it had decided against it. "I will roast this girl another time. Now she hasn't any pink dress and looks like a worm. Let her get some rest behind Veve's pot."

"Okay, mommy," squeaked Elizabeth, "I'll go and kiss the yokel once more. I'll kiss her, I promise you."

✳ ✳ ✳

They were holding hands, two kids who wore black pants and black T-shirts they sold in the pub in Staro. There, you could also buy beans, pork chops, bread, a brown dress with flowers printed on it, a hoe, a knife, and tenth-hand-clothes. Bestselling clothes brands from Switzerland were cheap as the dirt on the streets because the owner of the shop had worked in Switzerland until recently. One of the kids had a peculiar haircut on account of which you could mistake his smooth skull for a jar of sauerkraut. Oh, come off it! The boy's red hair glowed like a heap of embers. The girl had black hair. The children didn't talk. They walked, jumped in the air, ran hand in hand, and laughed hard. Their laughter sounded a little scary in the empty street, on a September afternoon in the village that had closed all its windows, but the two kids were only interested in the road to the forest.

"Annie, there's a wooden shack not far from here. The field-keeper stayed in it around the clock and kept us from stealing strawberries. I know where it is."

"I know it too, Shushomir. What will we do there?"

"Nothing. They took you from me, Annie. You lived in Sofia with your mother. I hid in that shack and sat there all day."

"Why?"

The boy took a long time to answer, then suddenly stopped in his tracks. The girl with the black hair that looked like a parachute on her head also stopped.

"They'll try to take you to Sofia, Annie. I won't let them," said the boy. "You came to stay with us at our place, remember? Mom cared about you. Your dad was drunk. You sat on the bench in the yard. You said nothing and did not move — like an old grandma. They took you away from me. I sat there, on your bench. It felt like you were with me, and they hadn't taken you to Sofia. I even slept on that bench. It grew very cold, it really did. One night, the autumn came, and it got very cold no matter that it was still September.

"I didn't know that autumn comes at night."

"I didn't either," the boy admitted. "But I was watching for it. I sat on the bench and saw the month of October throw cold winds on the ground. Dad wanted me to come back home, but I didn't. I waited. I sat on the bench right where you used to sit. It was like you were beside me... like it is now. Dad got angry. He chopped the bench into little chunks. I don't remember what I said — he went off the deep end, and lit the chunks on fire. I couldn't sit there anymore. I couldn't listen to the cold wind. I knew it found fault with the grass, though."

"I see," said the smaller black shirt.

"Listen," said the boy with the shaved head. "We'll have to run to the field-keeper's shack. Don't be afraid. Dad won't pull it apart because it's been built by the Town Hall."

This happened at noon, but the clouds captured the afternoon and tricked it into becoming a cold night. The river was spinning duckweed on its hundred spindles, and the water slept in a cradle of yellow nettles and elderberry leaves.

"If they plan to take me to Sofia again, you know what we can do? We can hide in the field-keeper's shack and live in it forever! It's not near your place. And is far from my father's house," the girl suggested happily.

"Yes!" the red-haired mushroom agreed. "We'll take clothes from your house and from ours. All we need is two old forks and two old spoons. We'll keep the bread in a shoebox."

"Shushomir, you're the smartest kid in the world, never mind that they've shorn you like a lamb," whispered the girl.

"Okay," said the bigger black T-shirt. "Let's go."

As they paddled down the river, its pools meek and quiet after the summer heat, all of a sudden the two children dashed across the grass up the hill. Two stone buildings stood there, both square and strong; actually, there were more stones than mosquitoes in Staro. Two stone boxes the houses were — narrow windows, no terraces, no hint of mercy at their closed doors, stout and solid walls thicker than those of the town hall. Their courtyards were surrounded by unshakeable stone bulwarks, brown and ugly, intended to frighten away all living souls. In these parts, both villagers and townsfolk would steal a penny off a dead man's eyes. A pack of weasels was what those guys were. Imagine you saw someone in the street after the autumn wind had dumped the night on Staro — you were lucky if that individual was blind drunk. If he was not well-oiled, then he'd gone stealing. You'd better beat him up and take to your heels. Otherwise, he'll beat you. There was another option if you were in the village. You might take your time — it was known throughout Radomir district that huge Darina, Ando's fiancée, lived here. She grilled the thieves like sausages, tied them up, and left them dangling on a string to meditate upon their criminal behavior. Then the big woman dragged the thieving characters to the village square. She told them, "Don't you dare steal like that! Or I'll cut off your balls."

"Merci, Madam. Thank you, please! I haven't stolen a thing for a month and a half, Madam, Miss Darina. Merci, please! Honest to God, I haven't! Thank you, please!"

One of the kids, the small black-haired T-shirt, slunk past the larger house, its walls painted white, as if the building was a bridegroom determined to get married as soon as possible. The other house had also been plastered, but its walls were painted crushingly yellow to scare off the budding hoodlums. After ten minutes — that was the time two pairs of young feet took to go up in the white and yellow attics — something important happened. The houses looked tired and indifferent. Their stairs were heavy as women who would give birth in a month's time. The black T-shirts dragged out two plastic bags of clothes from the attics of the unfriendly buildings. The garments were very old — dating back to the time when your dad weighed 155 pounds; yesterday his weight was 243 pounds. Your mom back then used to wear a tight-fitting dress that today would be too narrow for her cat.

"Mom," whispered the girl to the ancient dress. "Don't worry about me. It's going to be warm in the field-keeper's shack."

The red-haired T-shirt chanced on a brown, moth-eaten coat.

"Grandma, you know what? You are the best grandmother in the world. I, Shushomir, tell you that and I never lie. Your name is Strasimira, and mine is Strasimir Stanislav, but it's very hard to get your tongue around my name, so they call me Shushomir. Listen, grandma! The wolves won't eat me up. They'll be afraid of your scary coat in the field-keeper's shack. Annie and I will live there until they come. They want to take her from me, but I won't let them. Her mother's husband has a jeep, and he's a coward. He'll say to himself, "The field-keeper's over there, in the house. Maybe he has a gun, and maybe he will shoot me." So, he'll give our shack a wide berth.

I will marry Annie, if in the meantime she grows up enough and is ready to be my wife. I am ready. I have already made up my mind to become her husband. That means I'll do as dad does — he doesn't let mom lift a large bucket of water, he digs the garden beds when the soil is hard like a roof tile. It also means that when Mom starts painting the walls of our house, he goes, gets the brush, and says, "You're a short girl, Vera, go cook me bean soup and smoked ribs. I'll finish this wall." To be a man means to buy Mom Vera a chunky knit cardigan at Christmas. That way, she'll be tough and won't go down with flu. She won't be coughing or sneezing, I'm sure. She's picked chamomile, lime, and elderberry blossoms for tea. To be a man means to know where the elderberry blossoms are, and you tell her, "I'll make you a cup of tea. Pull yourself together, woman. You'll be fine." It is enough for a husband to say, "You'll be okay, gal," and Annie will be okay.

With the utmost difficulty, the smaller black T-shirt dragged the plastic bag she'd taken from the attic of the white house. In it were old shirts, one (but huge!) velvet skirt, untouched by moths. Annie remembered what her father had muttered, "Darina, take this skirt off and throw it out in the trash. You're like a helicopter wearing a dress." By that time, Darina had not yet become Mom Darina; she was a helicopter that was pulling down its skirt. Darina didn't say anything. She was like that — she boxed your ears first and then questioned your motives. It was exactly what the woman did — she hit the little black t-shirt's father on head. The man immediately said to her, "Merci, please, madam, thank you," but on the other hand, he wouldn't let the sleeping dogs lie. He made a rod for his own back instead. When a fool in Staro didn't care about his back, it never rained but it poured. Dad was asking for trouble.

"Darina, take off that black skirt. A woman wears black when someone dies. I wore black pants when Anna, my dearest wife, ran away from me. She hadn't died, you know, but I wore black all the time. I was in a lot of pain. I still am. When I see you with that black skirt on, Darina, I grieve for Anna."

At that time, Darina didn't look like a mother at all. She was a bus stop shelter, its roof ripped off by the winds. The bus stop slapped dad across the face. The shelter didn't protect him from the downpour. The rain had as many hands as were its million raindrops, so Dad let himself get soaked to the bone.

"If you wear that black skirt, I will die, Darina," my father said. "I'll be sorry I won't see my Anna before I kick the bucket."

Darina was cutting up a chicken. She had just chopped its head off — the huge woman did the job because the girl's father in his black shirt couldn't cut off a flea's head even if his life depended on it. Darina had chicken blood on her hands. ("Oh, how I wanted to eat chicken drumsticks roasted in butter!" the girl thought to herself. "Merci, please, Darina, Madam, thank you! Give me something to eat, a soup pot for me! Give me the pot, and I'll sweep the house seven times a day. I can count to seven! I'm not lying to you, Darina.") Darina hurled the knife, bloody as it was, through the window. Her hands were soiled and greasy, droplets of blood all over the place. She looked at dad and pulled her skirt down — a skirt so huge that you'd get scared. A mountain could put on this thing!

Now, the mountain's skirt was in the trash can.

* * *

Darina became my mother, good for you, and thank you, thank you, God! You know which woman is good to be a mother, and you know which child to give her to. For Mom Darina's sake, I believe that you are up there, among the pine-tops. You've made the sun, God, and I know Mom Darina and the sun are brother and sister. Please send us a ray of sunshine while Shushomir and I are in the field-keeper's shack. You'll make the place warm. If I look at the black dress my real mother used to wear, I won't be sad for her. Dad used to say, "My favorite color is black. It takes away your sorrow," but he didn't have anything black. "Go steal me a black shirt, Annie! I keep seeing your mother — right there, at the table. Is your mother there, Annie, at the table? Or isn't she?"

The girl's father was drunk most of the time. One day, the child walked to the second-hand shop and spoke to Aunt Dima, the shop-keeper, "Merci, please, Aunt Dima, here's some water for you. It's mineral water all the way from the bottom to the cap of the bottle!" The girl took the broom and swept the shop floor. "Don't give me a black shirt, Aunt Dima. A black shirt stops my father from seeing my mother on the bench in the garden, but I don't want him to stop seeing her."

Dima had a long stick which she used to frighten the thieves away. She was about to flog the child with it, but then she dropped the stick and grabbed a shirt — so black that the shop grew dark.

"Give it to your father, the drunkard," said Dima. "And this is for you — the smallest dress in the shop. It's yellow and it will look good on you."

"Will I dream of Mom in it?"

"Yes, you will," Aunt Dima said. "But I hope you won't dream of her. She doesn't deserve it."

The two children met not far from the main street. It was a lazy and old street. Perhaps its legs hurt, and its asphalt put in considerable efforts to climb up to the yellow house. There, the road sank into the ground and turned into a field. The field had many legs and every blade of grass was a step nearer to the mountain — right there, in the meadow, all covered with September mist, the kids stopped. The red-haired kid, a head taller than the little one, but not particularly strong, reached out and took the sack off the girl's hands. Her hair was black as the mud in the river that had nearly run dry in the summer heat.

"Give this to me! I'm a man."

It was hard for him to lug the two plastic sacks stuffed with household goods and chattels, all old and tattered, but the boy strode forward. The girl could hardly keep up with him.

"Wait, I'm a gutsy girl. I'll help you, I can do that. Fear is my friend. Even if I'm scared, I don't give a fig for creepy things."

The two houses, the white one and the yellow one, looked like rocks. They had backyards that had not been cleaned for years, and between them a stone wall rose, a black one, terrible, thick and frightening. The neighbors hated each other's guts and this was quite normal. Most of the folks in Staro couldn't stand one another, and the massive walls did a god job. However, there was a hole in the wall between the two unkempt backyards and the two large, menacing-looking buildings. A woman in a floral dress came out of the white house and ran like a howling blizzard towards the spot where the wall had been knocked down. The stepmother... Why have you coined such an ugly word for Mom Darina, God? I tell you honestly — this time you made a big mistake!

A tall, skinny man, twisted like your grandmother's towel, staggered slowly as he followed Darina towards the hole in the wall. He was the girl's father. Another man, taller than the wall, bigger than a hill, came out of the yellow house. His bristling beard looked red-hot as a string of Chili peppers. It would've been much better if he'd been the huge woman's husband, despite all the flowers painted on her dress — this garment was worth nothing because the summer had badly bleached the violets, the poppies and the snowdrops. A woman, short but quick, full-figured as a bottle of thick red wine, padded along the path behind the gingery beard.

"The children!" said the short plump woman, and happy red wine flowed in her voice.

"Shushomir is a plucky kid," said the man who was thinner than his flannel shirt, an old and very clean one.

"My little Annie..." sighed the woman in the brown floral dress she should wear in July, but her blood was so warm that it helped the flowers, though faded, bloom on her back and shoulders even now, in the autumn. "My little Annie..."

Then everyone fell silent.

"The field-keeper's shack," muttered the beard as gingery as grated carrot salad. — "I'll cut my head off if the two tadpoles haven't hidden there."

✳ ✳ ✳

I have everything — everything if you are foolish enough to imagine that your bank account is the center of your universe. A man could be an antique piece of furniture, a flame of jealousy, or a venomous word. I own a prestigious massage studio; clients I have been painstakingly taking care of for years hold the future of our country in their hands. Death stays in my fingers. Its presence is a commonplace example of a delayed train.

In the night when Jacob beat me black and blue, I must have whispered to death, "Come. Wipe me off the face of the earth. Please be the end of me. I am racked with pain. Pain will not frighten you." Jacob who had turned me into a puddle of apathetic lymph and muscles left me in darkness and terror. He had broken my fingers one by one, cut off a piece of my right ear, and still — though I don't care a fig what or if my glamorous clients think of me — I wonder if any of them has noticed that the earlobe is missing. Jacob severed it with a chopper, and after he boiled the bloody piece in front of my eyes, said. "If you don't eat it, I'll kill you — but don't get your hopes up. I won't shoot you! I won't do you that favor."

He heated a chisel — I've hated iron tools ever since that day. I feel nauseous whenever I walk past anything resembling a chisel. He heated it over the blazing fire in the fireplace and said, "Eat! Now! Or the iron will sink into the hole which gave birth to your daughter."

Panic seized me. Did he want to kill my child? You splash ice-cold water over a baby, leave her naked on the snow-covered street for ten minutes... I ate my own earlobe. I had swallowed it. I had swallowed hard. Jacob let the tip of the glowing chisel touch my thigh. To this day, I have an ugly crimson scar. In my mind, I saw the baby freezing and writhing in the cold. The weather is uncertain and wet in November, and the first snow of the season falls at the end of the month. Snow would put a newborn baby to sleep. It would destroy her lungs. However, the snowdrifts did nothing wrong as they thawed peacefully. Every time I opened my eyes, Jacob was bending over me. I hoped I would die soon — I couldn't see things clearly, and it was painful to breathe. He showed me the little one. Perhaps he had decided to kill her before my eyes.

I couldn't explain what happened to Jacob. He didn't touch the baby, he hid the knives in a drawer and threw the chisel in the corner of the room. He cleaned my wounds meticulously. When I felt I was dying, he would bring my daughter and lift her over my head. And I survived.

At times, I detected the smell of roasted almonds. After a month, or three, or four, I knew it was death. When that odor, at first quite pleasant, drifted to my baby, though my hands and feet were puddles of slime, I managed to sit up and caught a glimpse of her face. My nipples dripped milk mixed with blood. My child's eyelids twitched and she put out her hand to touch me. It happened after I suckled my daughter for the first time — I learned to discern the footsteps of death. I understood why my daughter knew what the smell of roasted almonds meant, but why should my granddaughter know it? Death had put shackles on her young blood. I fear for her. Death talked to my granddaughter and turned her face into a frozen lake. At that time, her eyes were bone.

When the little girl visited Jacob, she did not touch his hand. She whispered to him, "Yes. It is close to you, and it's sitting on your bed. Easy. Don't be afraid. I'll lure it away from you."

One day, I heard Jacob say to her, "Please, Annie, let death take me. It can make a mistake and snatch you. You are a child."

"I know who death is roasting almonds for," Annie said. "But don't be afraid, I'll kick it out of your room."

Why did they call the little one Annie? Annie... Perhaps that dark ability to feel the approaching end goes with this name.

"I love you, Annie," Jacob whispered.

He shouldn't have said that. I wanted him to die.

Jacob published my obituary in *The Daily Star*. Officially, I died a noble death. But day and night, he rubbed my arm, legs and back, brewed a snake's milk potion for weeks, and I grudgingly drank it. He covered me with four quilts and wouldn't let me eat butter. It was four months after I gave birth to my daughter when he allowed me to stand up for the first time.

"Your child is well," said Jacob, "She's a healthy girl. A very beautiful one."

He had learned to take care of her. He washed and bathed her, made her baby cereals, bought her expensive baby clothes — pink and green blouses, tiny pants and cardigans, all spotlessly clean. My daughter beamed and cooed, clean and charming in his arms

"Daddy's little princess!" he babbled. "Daddy's little girl!"

His hands, strong as guillotines, had heated the chisel. Now he dressed my daughter, made different soups for her, and the child smiled at him. Human hands are death's home, but only human hands are patient enough to help the baby when she learns to walk and when slowly and painfully, she recovers from her illnesses. Jacob put the roses back into Anna's cheeks.

Jacob took good care of me. He recognized and encouraged my ability to guess, judging by the smell of one's sweat, when a bilious attack would occur; when gout would flare up; when one's brain would stop ticking over, and how you could, with cunning and perseverance, turn that brain away from the path to death. Jacob taught me to hide behind a mountain of silence and revealed to me the most important point: if you spoke too much, sooner or later it would become clear how unpleasant was the person you had helped pull through.

If you loved a man and tried hard to get him out of the skillet in which death roasted almonds for him, woe to you, and woe to that man. Your hands would cease to feel the end. Your mind, your bones, your blood — all would be love, and love would not see the truth. Love sought no paths. It was infinity that recognized no end and no shore. That was the reason I could not cure my granddaughter. I could not reach her. The same thing happened when my daughter was young. I could not break her high fever, and I could do nothing for her after she came down with pneumonia.

Then Jacob fell sick and slept in that room that had turned the blind eye of its window to the north.

"Come and talk to me!" he begged. "Come!"

I thought of the scar on my leg. My reflection in the mirror did not let me forget my right ear was shorter than the left. That taste returned to my mouth... It had transformed me into a pile, a belly full of food capable of producing only waste products. After Jacob, I could not have children. I watched the little ones on the street and felt a dull pain in my lower abdomen. I believed I had contracted the worst disease and was ready to go away, but the truth was different.

Death had not yet roasted almonds for me.

I chose streets in Sofia where I rarely met young people. I had developed the worst kind of allergy — an allergy to children. The sight of my own daughter caused aches and pain all over my body. I loved her, of course, and saying this was an understatement. I love her — she was everywhere: in the air, in my books, in my room, in all pictures I kept in the safe in my apartment, on my desk, in my hands, in the sand, in the leaves of the trees. I thought of her all the time. But it was not my thoughts that were important. It felt like I was giving her my strength, my health, my energy. And every time I looked at her, my abdominal pain became intolerable.

"I'm going to die, Anna," I told her. "Tomorrow I will be no more, but you need not fear. I'll protect you from heaven," and I showed her the stars.

I cannot forget how she cried. Crying children don't give me pain. Crying children... When I see a child with tears in her eyes, the hatred that has settled in my bones thaws, evil thoughts do not hit me, and weakness is a word written on melting snow. Afternoons and evenings are generous to me. I can ease bone pain, and I can make one's enlarged spleen return to normal size. I don't know why this happens. Maybe it was because of Jacob's red-hot chisel and the purple scar on my leg. I think death stays there.

Jacob lay on his bed in the smallest room as I, with my own hands, installed a window to the north. I didn't hang any curtains, so all the time he could see a shabby block of flats. When I was sick and unable to walk, Jacob kept telling me that death was a wall, but "you will climb over it, Lena." It was his apartment, of course, a huge one, and when he fell ill I left him in the lumber room where I used to keep his dirty socks. Two years ago, he used to be strong and protected me from the world as if I were an egg on the verge of falling from a table. After I'd massaged my sick clients' backs for hours, Jacob would give me a hug and would carry me in his arms from the ground floor, where my studio was, to his apartment on the fifth floor. "I know how tired you are, Anna," he would say. He used to be so tough, I still can't believe how quickly that disease shriveled him. He'd told me "I love you" before. When he got sick and I opened the door to his room, he didn't look up. He just whispered "I love..." and didn't have the strength to finish saying it. Even today, I feel nauseous when I catch a glimpse of the dark scar on my skin. The hackneyed phrase "I love you" gives me the creeps.

I was never going to give birth again, and the thought of it drained me of energy. I lost track of the weekdays, and words like "eagerness," "anticipation," "celebration" meant nothing to me. I met single men who claimed to be lonely. Loneliness was their proper name. I maintained intimate relationships that did not interest me. I was not impressed by gifts or exquisite cuisine. If I could point to anything that attracted my barren womb, it was to invite my next admirer to my house. Jacob was down with his chronic disease. I'm not a pushy person, I don't seek out or sustain interest in unavailable men, so I made only two amorous excursions to the world outside the peace and quiet of my massage studio. Pitiful diversions that offered no way out — that was what I called them. My first paramour was a doctor, younger than me, Jacob's attending physician.

I could describe the pleasure under my skin as instant gratification in the cases when I kissed Jacob's attending physician in the huge parlor, keeping open the door to the narrow room where my husband lay on his sickbed. I've never believed men could fool themselves into standing arrant nonsense, but the young medico did. He swore I was the most beautiful thing in his life; it was the first time he had felt warmth and kindness; my presence calmed his shattered nerves and awakened the wild desire to live.

Give me a break.

"Please have a look at my ear," I said.

He stared at it, exclaiming, "It's beautiful," and after I told him that I hurt myself as a child and lost my earlobe, the fool fell into the habit of kissing me right there, on top of the wound that had long festered before it healed.

I did not expect Jacob to survive the visits paid by his personal physician to his own apartment. I remember how my daughter Anna and Jacob said goodbye to each other. Jacob was crying and whispering, "Don't be afraid, beautiful girl! Heaven is close to the brokenhearted. Mommy will look at you from the clouds!"

"Is heaven Mommy?" my daughter had asked. She did not cry. She was a tough little girl, a rock covered with moss. You'd be fooled into thinking of something soft, green, and inviting, but under the moss, granite waited for you. A million years had to elapse before the rock gave you a grain of sand — my daughter Anna was like that. Maybe it was because instead of getting breast milk, she got her mother's blood first.

In the past, when Jacob, my husband, was healthy and very strong, I didn't dare to even think about escaping from the large and sunny apartment in Sofia. Jacob had earned it as a reward for his faithful service to the brute who had ordered him to bump me off, the obtuse gal. Jacob quarreled with people, many hated his guts, managers fired him, threw him out on the street, but they did not know Jacob. They couldn't even start imaging the barbed wire ball his dark thoughts had woven. He tried to lock horns with me too, but after that chisel no one was able to make me fret or admire anything. My scar had turned dark red. My allergy to children worsened, and Jacob's brawls left me indifferent. Perhaps he believed that if he could make me scream, I'd forgive him for what he did. Maybe he was smarter: I wouldn't like to underestimate the abyss of his hard-headedness. I was convinced that if you didn't give a thug what he deserved, you'd die like a dog. I couldn't figure out what was eating Jacob. It must have been something serious, and that was why the onset of illness knocked him down.

I regard revenge with loathing. To take revenge on somebody means to live in the past. I am interested in greed only when its face is hidden. A guy needs his face in broad daylight to be able to pretend he loves his native land, his wife, and his boss. The truth will out. This happens at night — you can steal anything you like or build up a relationship outside the family. Big lies blossom at midnight. Then you try to rest your weary bones, but you are a stronghold besieged by your loved ones. You hate them. They hate you. They are fed up with the boots you have licked.

In addition to Jacob's attending physician, I invited a math teacher home for a barbecue. I asked myself what I saw in him — he hadn't met Miss Right his whole life. He took long walks by himself wearing a full dress suit, dazzlingly clean and perfectly pressed. His genuine leather shoes sparkled, his latest model iPhone a pool of light in his hand. The smell of shockingly expensive cologne wafted up from this man. I met him in front of Costa Café and after our second chance encounter, I followed him as he strolled down to the City Art Gallery. I stopped near the benches where loners played chess and bet money on every game. A woman had to be patient.

I waited.

His eyes seemed glued to the game. I stood beside him and watched him, thinking about my granddaughter. She told me once, "Your fib telling is disgusting, woman. You're a bad lot!" No word has been invented in any human language capable of describing what I was ready to do for that girl. I'd give her everything I had. I'd agree to roast a skillet of almonds and I'd lure death, my old friend, into snatching me. I'd readily meet my maker whispering "thank you" in death's ear. I missed my granddaughter, I liked her clam-like eyes and her arms of frost. She was a little hound, her tongue lolling out as she waited for her mother's car to come to a halt in front of my building... I hated that fast black automobile, so I thought about the man in the ridiculously expensive dress suit. He was a funny crow perched on the bench next to the men playing chess. His silence seemed to calm me down.

"I've baked fruit cake at home," I told him. "I've got good coffee. Come with me!"

"I don't know you," the man said brusquely. He had a cloud of curly brown hair, plus glasses. His eyes of pale blue fear made me think of freezing water; his sharp profile had probably been carved from a discarded piece of wood.

"You don't need to know me. I'd like to treat you to some cake and coffee," I said. "Please come!"

I took his hand and gave it a slight tug only half expecting him to follow me. Then I held his fingers the way a woman would grip her granddaughter's unwilling hand. The granddaughter, alas, insisted she had come into the world in a suitcase and believed that there had been no other women before her capable of chatting with death the way the silly girl did. I gently supported the man. He walked stiffly beside me as if he was about to march another mile or two. He stopped several times, though — without adequate warning — and took a deep breath.

I didn't say a word as we hurried to my studio. I didn't talk to him as I gave him cake and coffee. He told me he taught mathematics at an obscure provincial university. He dreamed of proving a theorem that had remained unproven to this day, then said he was done with empty chimeras. His students had no heart for mathematics. "Oh, mathematics! It is not a science intended to entertain fools, Madam! Mathematics is an adventure for beautiful minds!"

I took him to the fifth floor and felt sorry I was unable to carry him in my arms the way Jacob used to carry me before he was taken ill. I couldn't imagine how someone as tough as Jacob broke down. Actually, I could, but I dreaded the thought of it.

I expertly help my clients undress. All I have to do after that is look carefully at their skin, feel the pulse, catch the smell, and then I know. I know how to ease the pain, alas, temporarily. The mathematician who had failed to prove the so far unproved theorem trembled. His skin was pale and cowardly. Slowly, silently, and persistently, I eased the tension in his body, allayed the fears bubbling in his blood vessels, and he relaxed in my arms — quiet, exquisite as the most expensive luxury yarn. I'd always wanted to knit, and it was the only reason I read fairy tales — sometimes they were about a good grandmother that I'd never had. I loved it most if the fairytale grandma knitted a scarf for her granddaughter. I had started knitting a scarf for little Annie. I'd been looking for months and finally I found the softest yarn I could lay my hands on in Bulgaria. My granddaughter... let her think that I was deceiving her, let her say I was a mean and crooked crone. The shawl I was knitting for her would tell her the truth.

The mathematician, stuck with students who had no heart for mathematics, was to me an old, submissive sweater. I watched him calmly, without interest. I'm used to massaging naked bodies, healthy and confident, brazen or sick bodies waiting for a miracle. He looked healthy, but his body was waiting for my assistance that I was unwilling to give. Well, the door of my husband's room had been left ajar; there Jacob lay in his bed, his companion, the chronic illness, cooing in his ear. As usual, love happened smoothly, went off without a hitch as they say. It always did with me. The mathematician declared he owed me a huge debt of gratitude.

"Thank you!" he said. "You were good to me."

If a mathematician says you've been good to him, he by no means reveals all that is on his mind. I didn't ask questions; his skin wanted to tell me everything, it felt warmer and moist to the touch. And indeed, "This was my first time with a girl," the man said. "I thought I was going to die. I have not proved the theorem. I have not met a woman."

"Please speak quietly," I whispered. "My brother is sleeping in the adjoining room. He is very ill."

"Ill? Your brother?" asked the mathematician. "I am so sorry."

He stood up, a moonbeam kissing the wall, put on his immaculate black 100% wool suit, knocked at the open door to the narrow room and bowed slightly. It was amazing how easily mathematicians made friends. I was never good at math or at having friends. My guest started speaking in a deep voice. Most probably, this was the way in which he told his students about theorems, lemmas and all sorts of other mathematical mysteries. They all used to inspire awe in me.

"Sir, I beg your pardon, I didn't realize you were sleeping!" he told Jacob. "Your sister is lovely. You can be proud of her."

After a minute, the mathematician was gone. Jacob made no sound. For a moment I thought he had met his maker, and death had forgotten to bring me a bowl of roasted almonds. I rushed into the narrow room where I used to keep Jacob's old clothes, and tiptoed to the sickbed. Jacob's face was wet. He was weeping.

I had never seen Jacob cry. Tears filled me with disgust. Every time I saw a crying face, I thought of my ugly scar.

On the following day, I invited the mathematician to my fifth floor room. I held his hand, and I dreamed of my granddaughter's fingers. The man who could not prove the mathematical theorem had become my grandchild. I took him to the candy shop. We ate ice cream there and kept silent. I gradually got into the habit of telling him funny stories, and he listened, carried away with delight like a child waiting for the happy end. I took him to toy stores and he bought me a new jigsaw puzzle. We spent hours together on the fifth floor. I closed the door to the narrow room because it was cold, and love fell into place, but I didn't care about it. Love was a lie that got in the way and left you shattered. Pimps made big money using love as a multipurpose tool. Fame-seekers produced awful films and wrote rotten poems about it. Yet love was beautiful even when it was desperate.

"Thank you," the mathematician said. He was my friend, my grandchild, and my warm autumn. "A couple of months earlier, I had no one to buy gifts for. Now I have a woman. I can buy you the whole world."

* * *

"Grandpa," my granddaughter Annie said to Jacob. "You are a very good man."

I watched his sick face relax. At last, the month of October put a smile on his face — warm sunny autumn with golden paths in the park and a smart black-haired kid in his room, my granddaughter Annie.

"Jacob, you're my grandpa. Will you be my friend too?"

"Yes, my girl," Jacob said. "I'll be your best friend!"

"Oh, but you can't. My best friend is Shushomir, a boy from the village of Staro."

"Okay, pretty girl. I'll be your second-best friend after Shushomir."

"I love you, grandpa!"

I listened.

No one would say to me, "I love you, grandma!"

* * *

It was just an experiment, dear Anna. Nothing more than a simple test. My mind is looking for challenges, you know, for cleverly hidden, meaningful details. Minute details are dangerous traitors, my dear. What you cannot wring from a man under torture, details he let slip would turn into a loudspeaker that makes a confession of treason he has committed. I am in love with any bold experiment, my dear Anna. I am burning with impatience to see what the outcome will be. My experiments are the mirror that most accurately reflects my mind, and I, incapable of living without you, would very much like you to learn everything about the quirks and fancies that rule my life. Certainly, I do not wish to pass my life without you. It sounds melodramatic like cheap song lyrics, but often truth about life is cheap and repulsive.

How could you even start imagining that I would banish you from my house, my blood? It's impossible! If you are not by my side, the buildings I enter collapse, and that's the truth. If I accidentally scratch myself with a razor, the wound festers if you are far from me. I lose my voice when you're not at home. That's why I beg you... you know how hard it is for me to beg anyone. Thank you for being part of my life. Now, I can beg a human being's forgiveness!

I want you to know one thing. I've been dreaming of you long before I saw you in the flesh. I've been dreaming of you ever since I became aware I was human. I believed, and I am still convinced that friends brimming with fervor could do nothing but enthusiastically betray you. Hunger for money is the reason behind every step they take. Money is the most convincing proof of superiority. Believe me, I have no talent, and no particular skills, except my amazing ability to dig up information and make it available to individuals holding distinguished positions. I knew — how shall I put it — where a secret would prove to be most advantageous.

As a kid, I got into the habit of helping myself to some of the money I found both in my mom's purse and my dad's wallet. Mom did not punish me on these occasions. She begged me not to tell my father about the stranger dressed in black who had bought her an opal ring. My father didn't punish me either. He only insisted that I not reveal to mom the truth about his adorable Thursdays when we were supposed to go for a walk together. We'd both kiss mom and he'd take me to horseback riding lessons. He used to leave me in the care of a fat girl — I've hated fat creatures ever since, dearest Anna — and I long for your subtlety, your humility, and discipline. I love the footsteps of yours that must have been born before you, and your blood became their home. No other woman could walk as calmly and quietly as you. Dogs, forgive me this comparison, use their urine to mark territory.

The air that has touched you speaks to me of your smile. The path you go along becomes my favorite haunt. There, I feel gravity cradling me with tenderness. But I was speaking to you of betrayal, dearest Anna. My father lived for his Thursdays — no beautiful women met him or had anything to do with him, Anna. My father's Thursdays were called Vladimir, a tall and slender young man who would give me a cup of raspberries, grated apples, or a cup of blackberries — it was always some cup of delicious fruit that the fat girl gobbled down. I hate fruit, you know — it's a weakness I have to overcome. Vladimir was the reason my father let me take as much money from his wallet as I pleased, and pleased I was. I preferred notes to coins; I had a drawer full to the brim of bills since I turned six.

Money substituted for the talent I didn't possess, for a certain amount of finesse that would never brighten up my day. One-hundred-dollar bills were the explanation my friends needed to do what I wanted them to do. I'd known those boys from a very early age — our friendship existed only in theory; in practice, they were after free horseback rides, candy, and the old clothes I'd got sick and tired of. But do you think that my dear pals got all these for nothing?

No, dear Anna! Nobody does something for nothing — they crawled to me, fawned over me, and wrote poems in which they claimed I was a genius.

You never told me I was a genius, Anna. Women did everything I wanted. Those belles did twice as much of what I couldn't think about without wrinkling up my nose in disgust. It was so distasteful. Of course, I told Dad all about the gentleman in black and the opal ring he bought mom. I described to Mom my father's feelings for Vladimir. This set off a great uproar. In addition to the drawer stuffed with bills I had stashed away, I acquired more bills and filled more drawers — money has been my only friend ever since I was a little boy. If I did not see you in my dreams, if you were not in my thoughts like medicine to a patient recovering from bronchopneumonia, like air to a man whose head had been submerged by rising water — I should probably not wake up in the morning.

I couldn't bear it if you go away! Did you believe I could live without you? I know you didn't.

I threw your clothes, your suitcases, your shoes in the garbage. I did it, with my own hands. I found your kid in my house and that was the reason why I performed the experiment. I wanted to make sure how everybody would behave. To be honest, I knew what Madame Percha and her two "husbands" had done — Peter's hair dyed a hideous shade of red spoke volumes, and it was Percha's whim that had forced Todd to surgically lengthen his tongue. I put up with this woman because of her disgusting capability of jeering at people. I believe our Bulgarian gene is most pronounced in our ability to take the piss out of those beneath us. The money they lack! And that's wonderful. What fun would I have if your former employer Mrs. Percha didn't exist?

Anna, you know you're the only one in the world I wouldn't order to do something you'd hate to do. I ask you to tell me something. What did Percha do after she saw I threw your clothes, your shoes, and your child out of my house? Of course, Anna dear, I only wished to demonstrate what would happen to you if you left me. What would the future offer you? I did it not because I wanted to force you to stay with me. I did it because I was terrified.

What will happen to me if you go away; if you close the earth behind you — you've told me that some obscure poet Dimitar Milanov wrote a poem about the impossibility to close the earth behind you, Anna. I hate Dimitar Milanov because he made an impression on you, something that I failed to do.

✳ ✳ ✳

"First, Mrs. Percha made me shine her shoes," the dark-haired woman replied. "Madam was barefoot. Her perfectly polished toenails gleamed. 'Kiss my toes!' she ordered me. 'All of them. One by one!'"

"Did you?" the man's eyes bowed to the thin woman and his body bowed as well. "I'll shine your shoes, Anna. I'll kiss your toes..."

"I stood up and tried to leave," she said.

"You didn't have a penny to bless yourself with."

"Percha summoned her two husbands."

"And?"

It was a quiet, magnificent room, beige and brown wall panels, green carpets on the floor, a picture of a lake painted by a famous Chinese artist; a splendid work of art in a sumptuous frame that had survived over the centuries. "To survive" was an expensive verb. Could a work of Chinese art be preserved if a woman of means and high repute didn't pay enough for it? In addition, Mrs. Percha had paid a poet who wrote in letters of gold the following text under the famous picture: *I've planted a young moon in the meadow behind your house.*

"What did her husbands do to you? Answer me, Anna!"

"I think you know."

"I know, but I want your version of what happened."

"Todd informed me he'd be my pimp. He said that the full program with me would cost 2,500 euros."

"Bald men have always struck me as extremely cruel, Anna," the man remarked. "You know I'll never allow them to touch you, don't you? But you had to see what your life would be without my protection and without my love."

"I believed I could summon the scent of death," the woman said quietly. "'I did summon it. I wanted to die. Percha shrieked at me, and Todd dragged my daughter into the room. Madam said she'd make me perform the whole program, which cost 2,500 euros, in front of my child."

"Go on," said the man. His voice was soft.

"My daughter had been bitten more than a dozen times. Everywhere — in the head, on the neck, on the back, on the belly. She was not crying. She stumbled forward as two boys, one with waist-length blond hair, the other dark, his shaved head glowing, burst into the room. Elizabeth was right at their heels. Mrs. Percha gave them a dazzling smile.

"Young Elizabeth," muttered the mam. "Her heart is a guillotine. I like her."

"Well, Anna, oily rag, you got sacked from your love-making job, eh? I am very glad," Elizabeth said as she tried to kick and missed. "I've always had it for your little daughter. You've got the nerve to stare at me, too. I'm glad Uncle Vasilev kicked you out. I love him for that. Get down on your knees! Now!" she yelled.

I made for the door, but Mrs. Percha shrieked, "Kneel on the floor! Now!"

I refused to obey, and the two lads, the one with the blond hair and the other with the shaved head, began to pinch me. Their fingers were quick and strong. Then the boys bit my legs. Their teeth were young and sharp. They were cruel. Blood leaked into tissues under the skin and caused the black-and-blue color. My belly and my breasts hurt. But that was a minor detail. My daughter, scruffily dressed, bitten black and blue, her face flushed, ran and shoved Elizabeth against the wall. I didn't know where she hit the big girl. Strong Elizabeth slumped to the floor and roared so piercingly the burglar alarm system went off. The athletic girl obstinately gave a series of high-pitched howls, and Ivan, the butler in his elegant suit, came to the rescue of the victim. Evidently, the man had got pretty confused, and as Mrs. Percha later put it, "the idiot was definitely barking up the wrong tree." 'Anna, are you in a lot of pain?' asked the poor bugger. Percha glared at him and gritted her teeth. Freezing in his tracks, the butler stammered out an apology. A few seconds passed and the man drowned in his own shoes. The ill-starred elegant Ivan..."

"I quite like Ivan," Phil said. "'What did they do to you?"

"I wasn't thinking of myself. Elizabeth kept on screaming as she lay on the floor, kicking her powerful legs in the air. The two lads bent over her at once, one making desperate attempts to arrange her hair, the other caressing her tear-streaked face. 'Strangle her!' thundered Percha's daughter her eyes blazing. Mrs. Percha, your business partner, was smiling."

"My business partner? I wouldn't let her lick the dust off my cupboards," the man declared. "I wouldn't let her kiss the toilet seat in my bathroom."

"The boys pounced on my daughter. This is the end, I thought as I leaped to her rescue. My girl growled, 'If anyone touches me, if anyone so much as scratches me with a fingernail, I will send for death.' Mrs. Percha straightened in her chair and her daughter ceased to wail. The two lads stared. The blond Viking, naked to the waist — he'd got a skull tattooed on his soft belly — coughed. The other with the shaved head, naked to the waist as well wheezed, a tattoo of a bigger skull glistening under his belly button. 'Death will come,' my daughter, a gnawed, splintered piece of bone, said. "Death will see the skulls on your stomachs. And death will get you!' The two boys spat on their hands and rapidly turned the tattoos into a dirty layer of black paint.

"Nonsense!" croaked Percha.

"Death will come, Percha. You know me. I wouldn't waste time with idle talk just to frighten you." My daughter spoke evenly, her dirty face scary, the bruises on it smeared with tears. A blue-red scar glistened on her chin.

The room fell quiet... The clock stole an hour from the afternoon and threw it at eternity. I watched my daughter's crumpled, fearful face and wondered how it was possible for stars, pain, and blood to flow through a girl's heart. If there were no human beings, time would have nowhere to fly; minutes and days cannot exist outside of a person's veins. My daughter was more important than time to me.

"And I? Is there a place for me in your veins?" whispered Phil who had given me his wine.

Philip Vasilev hated silence. I went on, "Unexpectedly for me, Percha ordered, 'Anna, out! Dirty rag! Get out of here!' she took a deep breath and croaked, 'Take your little freak with you!'

'You're a freak, Percha,' my daughter said. It seemed to me that the bruises and bites on her body had spoken. 'Nobody insults my mom and gets away with it. Write this down and read it after breakfast, lunch, and dinner, Percha,' my daughter's voice rose, a high-pitched squeal, her face flattened and pale. I was suddenly cold. What did her small voice do? Maybe I imagined it, but I could smell roasted almonds in the room.

'Let's go, mom!' She took a step towards me, grabbed my hand, and said looking at no one in particular, 'Elizabeth, I'll remember you. I won't forget your two snails too, the lads, Elizabeth.'"

Konstantin Kossev — Kosso was waiting for me in front of Percha's room, Kosso, the hero who had thrown me out of his car in the middle of the Balkan ridge a century ago. He had hurled abuse and a hundred stones at me.

"Now. You'll see what's in store for you, bitch!" he said. Saliva seeped from the sides of his mouth as he winked at me.

"Anna's a piece of ham on somebody else's plate," Percha said. Her words seemed to paralyze him. Perhaps it was true there were strait-jacket voices able to turn a smart-aleck into a sack of household waste. I was insensitive to mouths issuing commands.

"Philip, I think it is impossible that Percha stood on her own two feet. You have written the screenplay. You are the mastermind behind the open wounds and scabs on my daughter's body. You played your little tricks, so Todd offered to become my pimp. You're excellent at devising your moves, Philip, but life is bigger than your plans. People are weak and helpless in front of bigwigs, but there is a power that outwits them."

"A power that you and your daughter feel very comfortable with. The smell of roasted almonds… Death, eh?"

Soon October would end, but what could the month of October do if there were no hearts through which time could flow; if there were no eyes to enjoy the tango of falling leaves? The important man was silent. He stood up slowly, and his body, thin and long in an expensive suit, leaned towards the woman. She stared at the wall on which no picture hung.

"Would you like to know who dares to bring an accusation against me, Anna? No one! I did not allow that. Never have! They've made plenty of death threats against me, and it didn't feel good. Yes, many have threatened to bump me off, but an imaginary power… I won't have any of this scheme."

The woman said nothing. She was thin and wore an unflattering dress — a woman who hardly deserved much attention. The wall on which no picture hung looked far more interesting.

"Anna?"

"Yes, Philip."

The thin body in the expensive suit — everything was expensive under this roof, or it wouldn't be here — stirred. Philip Vasilev's hand cupped the woman's dark face in its pincers of fingers and knuckles. Then the man's voice calm as the rain behind the window, arranged the necessary words and issued a well-balanced statement. It sounded colder than the marble slabs on the floor.

"Anna, did you really think I've been dreaming of you? Of you — haha — of all people, since the day I realized I existed in this vile world?"

The woman, dark as a cherry that most Bulgarians called "Wolf's Eye," did not answer.

"Did you really think I was taken in by your scam? The smell of almonds roasted in death's oven. Almonds my foot!"

The woman was silent, a grey bat hunting for flying insects on a warm night.

"Do you seriously believe I have seen you in my dreams since I was an innocent boy? I hit on his idea years ago. My father had put it into practice with respect to my mother, and she, a tough, practical, and very shrewd lady, a brilliant lawyer, took it at face value. My mother did not buy fakes. She could smell fake like wet paint from a mile, and no dealer could deceive her. But dad's trick, the one about his dreams, worked. Yes, mom bought it. I wonder how you felt when I played it on you."

The dark woman spoke quietly, "It made me sad. I felt how lonely you were. Now, I'm relieved to hear that you're not. I'm not lying about the smell of roasted almonds, I often catch it. It's hard, but one gets used to it. I wonder, Philip. Why did you choose me?"

"I love being challenged, Anna. I'd like to find out if I'll have the strength to throw away something or somebody I've taken a fancy to," the man smiled. "I got emotionally attached to objects when I was a little boy. I lost my pocketknife before I turned five. I ran a fever and was sick for months. I made up my mind to increase my willpower. I threw away the object I liked the most, so I got rid of the embarrassing attachment disorder. Now, I'm throwing you away. Do you understand? If you like a girl, you become her slave. I don't want that."

The woman looked at him. Her dark eyes made one think about a small box that a child had opened, but there was no present in it.

"I believed you'd been dreaming of me ever since you realized that time flew. I believe that when one's almonds are roasted, there is only one person in the world, only one who forgets that time is running out, that the night is dark and the day is bright, that one drinks water and doesn't eat sand. That person grabs the roasted almonds to save your life. He doesn't care if the New Year has started, or it's a hot August afternoon; it is unimportant if it's morning or midnight after his one and only has gone. Some people dream of this person and are happy after they wake up. I believed you were dreaming of me. But you were speaking about your father's dreams. I'll be all right," she said. "The world is a big place. Somewhere, someone must have dreamed of me."

The woman in the dark dress started for the door. She closed it behind her and the wall, on which no picture hung, grew dark.

"Anna," said the man.

He ran to the door, opened it, but the woman was gone. The smell of roasted almonds wafted across the corridor. The universe was baking almonds in the huge oven of loneliness.

"Anna!"

It had grown dark, and the day turned into the usual gathering dusk of late October. It was going to rain.

"I've really been dreaming of you, Anna!"

✳ ✳ ✳

Fifty yards of the street had been paved, but the winter winds and the snow had eaten away at the paving blocks, and deep muddy puddles gaped at the sky. The rain had stopped, the road climbed the hill, passed by the village cemetery, but did not stop there. Behind the cemetery was the strawberry field. Just below the low pine trees, a little wooden hut stood — a molehill, boards, beams, and slats hammered together — and multicolored pieces of linoleum in place of a roof. The path that ran to it was muddy and narrow. This year, nobody had picked the fruit or taken care of the strawberry beds. The summer was hot, most berries withered and died, so the villagers planned to plant potatoes in the field. You made money growing potatoes. Strawberries? No! Who was going to keep the beds weed-free, who was to dig them four times a year and get rid of the slugs? The hut had been abandoned for a long time. This year, October was warm and smiling like a baby wrapped in a soft towel, but then suddenly the wind got angry, brought frosts and rains, and it was very cold in the wooden hut.

Two little moles sat on the floor in the hut, one brown, the other black because one of the coats was black, eaten by moths and mice, the other was a burlap coat, thick and still good, but it was so faded that one did not know whether it was brown, white, or beige. Two heads stuck out above the coat collars, one red-haired — its hair so short that the head looked like a punctuation mark — a full-stop. The other head was a volcano of thick black hair. The two kids were eating. The black-haired one had just bitten into a hamburger patty, and the red-haired molehill was chewing on a meatball.

"We won't tell them we're here," said the hamburger patty. "Keep your chin up, Shushomir. We are at the end of the world, and they can't find us."

"They won't find us, but the world doesn't end here," objected the full stop. "Look at the sky. The minute you lose sight of Bare Hill, you'll know — that's where the end of the world begins."

"You're the cleverest child in the world, Shushomir," said the girl deeply impressed. "Here's some patty for you," and the hand, thin as a spindle, wriggled out of the coat-sleeve that was shabby and badly moth-eaten indeed. Then the girl reached out and patted the shorn head. "This is for you. Come on!" she said. The boy opened his mouth and took a gigantic bite out of the patty.

"You are the bravest girl in the world," said the punctuation mark quietly as he smiled in admiration. "Mom makes delicious meatballs. This one is for you," a hand, a little thicker than a spindle, flew to the volcano of black hair. The girl opened her mouth and took a huge bite. "Now we can make a cloud trap. What do you say to that?" the boy suggested.

"How do you make a cloud trap?" the girl sounded very interested and forgot to chew the big bite of meatball in her mouth.

"I'll tell you. Listen! We'll put that empty paint can in front of the hut," the boy pointed at it and tried to swallow the lovely patty that was melting like a chocolate nugget in his mouth.

"Then what?" the girl asked burning with curiosity.

"Then..." the boy's voice dropped, but not really, it was a tiny drop, just enough to let the lazy clouds go somewhere else. The sky might clear or it might not. "Then we'll wait."

"What will we be waiting for?"

"'For the rain," replied the red-haired boy. "It will start raining soon. The cloud will turn into water, and we'll catch it in the paint can, our trap! Then we'll tell it, 'Hey, cloud, if you want us to let you go back to the sky — there you can play with other clouds, and it will be much better for you. You won't be a prisoner in this narrow can — do you know what you'll have to do?"

"What? What?" the girl asked.

"We'll say, 'Hey, cloud, please ask the sun to climb up high in the sky, so Annie and I can play in the woods!"

"Well... how could the water in the paint can tell the sun all this?" wondered the girl. "There's so much space between the sky and our hut. Even if that water shouts ve-e-ry loudly, the sun won't be able to hear it."

"Oh, the sun will hear its cloud! "The river will shout, too, because it is the cloud's elder sister," explained the boy.

"Have some more patty, Shushomir. You must be very strong. You have to be back to full strength in order to save us from the wolves."

"Okay, don't you be afraid. The cloud and the sun are neighbors like Mom and Aunt Darina. The water in our can is a cloud, and it can talk to the sun the way mom talks to your mother Darina."

"Shushomir, you are the smartest child in the world!"

Unfortunately, this hill would no longer be a strawberry field. It did not produce enough fruit, so the villagers were going to plant potatoes there. Two women were slowly climbing up the thin path to the wooden hut. The tall one wore a black padded coat, a thick black hat, and black rubber boots. She was heavy, and the potholes shook under her feet. The other woman looked like a walking toy boat, round and short, a pitcher that had gone to a well once too often.

The two women were chattering about things that didn't seem serious.

... the last days of September... what a pity that there will be no strawberries here… the plants are drying up. What can you do? You can do nothing... The river has not dried up yet… not enough water for the strawberries...

... where are these children? They took to their heels, little idiots. The weather's turning bitterly cold... it smells like rain...

... Vera, have you dried elderberry flowers? If Annie gets a cold or flu, or if she starts coughing...

...Yes, I have and I'll give you as much as you need. And you, Darina, have you dried fresh chamomile?

... No, I haven't. Neither chamomile nor thyme. I have dry quince seeds and linden blossoms...

O, that's good. Quince seeds and linden blossoms do wonders to a sick child.

The two women almost reached the wooden hut.

The potholes, though deep as saucepans, did not prevent the big black jeep from accelerating. Its powerful engine gobbled up the gaping craters in the road as if they were candy bars. The car whizzed past the tall strong woman and snagged her padded coat hem. The black jeep kept roaring and leaping until it reached the ramshackle hut. A tall man got out of the automobile. He wore a great suit the likes of which this field had not seen since the beginning of the world. His shoes had been meticulously polished. You wouldn't believe it, but they shone like the cross in St. Nicholas Church that dated from the 13th century. Now it rose in the center of Staro, not far from the town hall. This gentleman was a treasure trove of valuables. Gold bracelets added glow to his wrists, and a heavy gold chain necklace hung around his neck. He waded through the wet yellow grass and forced his way into the wooden hut. In less than a minute, he returned to the ruined strawberry beds. The perfect sleeves of his suit clutched tightly a kicking bundle wrapped in a black, moth-eaten coat.

"Let go of me, Ivan! Let go of me! You monster!

A brown burlap coat, so faded that it could neither kick nor bite, swooped down on the suit that was more expensive than St. Nicholas Church. A ginger-haired boy slammed into the stranger with terrible force, bit into the trouser leg of the designer suit, then burlap sleeves and pockets grappled with the immaculate jacket and the gold chain necklace. The red-haired punctuation mark stomped on the fashion shoes, kicked, hit, and bit them. The boy thumped and punched and slapped the stranger's chest, spat and screamed, but one expensive shoe — the right and the more horrible one — landed on his forehead. The kid, a pebble, a speck of dust, snapped like a twig and rolled down to the dry strawberry beds.

"Annie!"

"Shusho....!"

The man threw the kid and her moth-eaten coat into the jeep.

The burlap jacket rose up and flew like a plastic bag snatched by the wind. In October, the wind's eyes were green. The burlap sleeves stuck to the Jeep Wrangler's windshield. It was an original equipment glass windshield, thick and so dark you saw nothing through it. But the green eyes of the wind did see!

The boy pounded the vehicle with his fists, with his forehead and his chest.

"Annie-e-e!"

The Jeep took off and the boy in the faded burlap coat fell into a pothole, a deep and perfectly normal one for the roads in this part of the country. But the crater could not stop him. The boy jumped. He ran and wailed like a tortured dog. He writhed like a centipede trampled underfoot, but still alive and crawling along that narrow dirt road. The boy did not hear anything. He saw no stones, no road, no potholes. He was running and shouting, "Annie! Ann…ie!"

The two women had come to the end of the road and stopped in front of the wooden hut. They saw a brown ball in a coat. How could that be? The sleeves were bigger than the burlap ball.

"Ann….! Ann…ie! Ann…ie! Annie-e—i!"

It was then that the two women saw the face above the coat collar — cheeks smudged with dirt, scary and wet even though the clouds were calm. It didn't look like rain. The boy's face was flushed and terrible.

The sky was waiting for the month of October to pour some drops of rain into a small cloud trap. The sky wanted its clouds to clean the road, the fields, the wooden hut, and the river.

∗ ∗ ∗

A woman jutted out in the middle of the stony road. She waved her hands in front of a black Jeep Wrangler. Strong and big as a mountain, the woman refused to budge an inch. She stood firmly, a robust lady in black rubber boots.

"Stop the car!" she thundered.

The Jeep Wrangler ground to a halt. A white-haired man in a designer suit got out of it.

"Okay, Okay," he mumbled. "I mean no harm, Madame."

It was cold.

"Let Annie go!" the woman snarled.

A stiff wind blew. The man shook in his designer suit.

"I—I—, "he mouthed. "I'll let her go."

About the Author

Zdravka Evtimova is a Bulgarian writer born in 1959. Her short stories and novels have appeared in 31 countries in the world, including USA, UK, Canada, China, Australia, Germany, France, Japan, Italy, and Switzerland. In 2022, she won Romania's Mihai Eminescu Annual Award for Fiction.

Fomite

Writing a review on social media sites for readers will help the progress of independent publishing. To submit a review, go to the book page on any of the sites and follow the links for reviews. Books from independent presses rely on reader-to-reader communications.

For more information or to order any of our books, visit:
http://www.fomitepress.com/our-books.htm

More novels from Fomite...

Joshua Amses — *During This, Our Nadir*
Joshua Amses — *Ghats*
Joshua Amses — *Raven or Crow*
Joshua Amses — *The Moment Before an Injury*
Charles Bell — *The Married Land*
Charles Bell — *The Half Gods*
Jaysinh Birjepatel — *Nothing Beside Remains*
Jaysinh Birjepatel — *The Good Muslim of Jackson Heights*
David Borofka — *The End of Good Intnetions*
David Brizer — *The Secret Doctrine of V. H. Rand*
David Brizer — *Victor Rand*
L. M Brown — *Hinterland*
Paula Closson Buck — *Summer on the Cold War Planet*
L.enny Cavallaro — *Paganini Agitato*
Dan Chodorkoff — *Loisaida*
Dan Chodorkoff — *Sugaring Down*
David Adams Cleveland — *Time's Betrayal*
Paul Cody— *Sphyxia*
Jaimee Wriston Colbert — *Vanishing Acts*
Roger Coleman — *Skywreck Afternoons*
Stephen Downes — *The Hands of Pianists*
Marc Estrin — *Hyde*
Marc Estrin — *Kafka's Roach*
Marc Estrin — *Proceedings of the Hebrew Free Burial Society*
Marc Estrin — *Speckled Vanities*
Marc Estrin — *The Annotated Nose*
Marc Estrin — *The Penseés of Alan Krieger*
Zdravka Evtimova — *Asylum for Men and Dogs*
Zdravka Evtimova — *In the Town of Joy and Peace*
Zdravka Evtimova — *Sinfonia Bulgarica*
Zdravka Evtimova — *You Can Smile on Wednesdays*
Daniel Forbes — *Derail This Train Wreck*
Peter Fortunato — *Carnevale*
Greg Guma — *Dons of Time*

Fomite

Ramsey Hanhan – *Fugitive Dreams*
Richard Hawley — *The Three Lives of Jonathan Force*
Lamar Herrin — *Father Figure*
Michael Horner — *Damage Control*
Ron Jacobs — *All the Sinners Saints*
Ron Jacobs — *Short Order Frame Up*
Ron Jacobs — *The Co-conspirator's Tale*
Scott Archer Jones — *A Rising Tide of People Swept Away*
Scott Archer Jones — *And Throw Away the Skins*
Julie Justicz — *Conch Pearl*
Julie Justicz — *Degrees of Difficulty*
Maggie Kast — *A Free Unsullied Land*
Darrell Kastin — *Shadowboxing with Bukowski*
Coleen Kearon — *#triggerwarning*
Coleen Kearon — *Feminist on Fire*
Jan English Leary — *Thicker Than Blood*
Jan English Leary — *Town and Gown*
Diane Lefer — *Confessions of a Carnivore*
Diane Lefer — *Out of Place*
Rob Lenihan — *Born Speaking Lies*
Cynthia Newberry Martin — *The Art of Her Life*
Colin McGinnis — *Roadman*
Douglas W. Milliken — *Our Shadows' Voice*
Ilan Mochari — *Zinsky the Obscure*
Peter Nash — *In the Place Where We Thought We Stood*
Peter Nash — *Parsimony*
Peter Nash — *The Least of It*
Peter Nash — *The Perfection of Things*
George Ovitt — *Stillpoint*
George Ovitt — *Tribunal*
Gregory Papadoyiannis — *The Baby Jazz*
Pelham — *The Walking Poor*
Christopher Peterson — *Madman*
Andy Potok — *My Father's Keeper*
Frederick Ramey — *Comes A Time*
Howard Rappaport — *Arnold and Igor*
Joseph Rathgeber — *Mixedbloods*
Kathryn Roberts — *Companion Plants*
Robert Rosenberg — *Isles of the Blind*
Fred Russell — *Rafi's World*
Ron Savage — *Voyeur in Tangier*
David Schein — *The Adoption*
Charles Simpson — *Uncertain Harvest*
Lynn Sloan — *Midstream*
Lynn Sloan — *Principles of Navigation*

Fomite